T0103926

Iraq Dreams

IRAQ
A Novel
DREAMS

Gerard R. D'Alessio

iUniverse LLC
Bloomington

IRAQ DREAMS
A NOVEL

iUniverse books may be ordered through booksellers or by contacting:

iUniverse
1663 Liberty Drive
Bloomington, IN 47403
www.iuniverse.com
1-800-Authors (1-800-288-4677)

Because of the dynamic nature of the Internet, any web addresses or links contained in this book may have changed since publication and may no longer be valid. The views expressed in this work are solely those of the author and do not necessarily reflect the views of the publisher, and the publisher hereby disclaims any responsibility for them.

Any people depicted in stock imagery provided by Thinkstock are models, and such images are being used for illustrative purposes only. Certain stock imagery © Thinkstock.

ISBN: 978-1-4917-2279-4 (sc)
ISBN: 978-1-4917-2280-0 (e)

Library of Congress Control Number: 2014901371

Printed in the United States of America.

iUniverse rev. date: 03/21/2014

This book is dedicated, with deep respect and appreciation, to all members of the National Guard and the US Army Reserves who served in the Iraq and Afghanistan wars.

Other novels by Gerard R. D'Alessio:

Dr. Cappeletti's Chorus
The Giantonios: Family Matters

I wish to acknowledge the very helpful contributions made by the iUniverse editors who worked with me on this project.

I

Coralee was hunched over, writing at the kitchen table. Early morning sun slanted in through the window facing the backyard. Sighing, she picked up her coffee mug. She sipped at it and then stretched to relieve the knot of tension in her upper back. Screwing up her face, she returned to reading over the letter she'd written:

Thursday, November 18, 2004

Dear Rick,

I was writing to tell you that we moved back here to Momma's in Oklahoma City. I was halfway through the letter when I received a call from the army telling me that you had been wounded a couple of days ago by one of those IED explosions. The man, Captain Dunlavey, I think he said his name was, had been trying to reach me at home in New Jersey, but of course I was no longer there—I moved back here with the kids this past Monday, the fifteenth. Anyway, I figured it would be better if I started the letter over again. But I wanted you to know that I'd made the decision to move—to leave you—before I knew that you had been wounded.

I feel terrible about this, Rick. I don't know what kind of wound you've received. Captain Dunlavey said something about your leg. I guess he wasn't too sure himself, except to say that you were being moved to Walter Reed and that I could visit you there. I'm not so sure that's a good idea. I don't want to start things up again, and I don't want to give you any false hopes. I think it's better this way—a clean break. We've been headed in this direction for a long time. This god-awful extended separation has only made our situation clearer, that's all. Of course, the finances have created a lot more stress, and your not being available has been hard on Thomas—your not being around has been especially difficult for him. But at least here in Oklahoma, I've got my mother to help out. Not that her friend George or my brother is of any use at all.

Anyway, I'm sorry to hear that you're hurt, and I hope it's not too bad, but I won't be coming to visit, and as soon as I'm able, I'll be filing for a divorce. I hope you understand and will accept this decision and not go creating any trouble. It's bad enough as it is without your making it worse.

One more thing: I'm enclosing some papers from your accountant, Fred. Your New Jersey office is closed up (as of October 31), and all of your records and papers are still there, locked in your safe. Fred thinks you might want to sell the building, and if you do, he can help with that. Our apartment upstairs is empty, except for your things and some of the furniture. I didn't know if you'd want to rent it out or not. Your attorney, Arnold, also wrote a letter, which I'm enclosing. As you'll see, he thinks you should go ahead and file for bankruptcy. I'm not sure how the military angle fits into this, if at all. I'm sorry that your business ended up like this, but don't go blaming me. I didn't send you off to Iraq. While we're on that subject, I don't understand why the Army Reserves can't get your paycheck to us on a regular and timely basis. Things are bad enough without having to wait endlessly for your check and being forced to borrow and go into debt! Anyway, I guess that's it for now. I'll send you the papers when I file. Good luck.

Coralee finished reading what she had written and decided that there was nothing more that she wanted to add. She signed her name, deliberately avoiding using the word *love*, but which out of habit she almost wrote, and put it and the other papers into a large brown envelope addressed to Richard Garcia at Walter Reed Hospital. Then she sat back and finished her coffee.

Coralee's mother ambled into the kitchen as Coralee was sealing her letter. "Smells like you made some coffee."

"Yes, I did, Momma. You want me to pour you some?"

"I can still pour my own coffee, thank you. I ain't that decrepit yet." Millie shuffled to the counter and poured herself a mug, putting in some sugar before going to the fridge to get some milk for it. "You want some toast or something to go with that?" she asked her daughter.

"No thanks, Momma. I don't usually eat anything in the morning."

Millie looked over her glasses at her daughter and, stirring her coffee, stepped over to the table, where she gathered her chenille robe around herself and sat down.

"Looks like you've been doing some writing."

"Yeah, I wrote to Rick to tell him I'm here."

Millie pursed her lips and looked at her.

"I know," Coralee said, sighing. "It's about time I wrote. I've been avoiding it. To be honest, I think part of me was hoping he'd get killed, so I wouldn't have to write to him."

Millie sipped at her coffee.

Coralee wasn't sure if her mother had heard her, but she looked and saw her mother had her hearing aids in, so she knew that she'd been heard.

"I know. It's rotten to think that way. But it really would make everything so much simpler. I mean, it would be easier for the kids to understand."

"You mean, they wouldn't blame you for their not having their daddy around anymore."

Coralee grimaced.

"Well, you've got to do what you've got to do. I know I never ran out on your father. And Rick is a damn sight better husband and father than your daddy was."

"Yeah, well … maybe you should have left him. Maybe we all would have been better off."

"How could I leave him? The poor man was blind. He depended on me."

This was an old and familiar argument, one that went back to when Coralee was about twelve years old, when she had first exhorted Momma to leave. Bernie Stein was not only blind—he was also a lazy, dependent, demanding, whining, weak, selfish son of a bitch. Of course, her mother had never seen him that way. Momma thought he was wonderful and generous and intelligent and kind and brave. But from Coralee's perspective, her parents' entire relationship had revolved around his total dependency on Mildred. His absolute need for her was the glue that held them together and gave their lives meaning.

Coralee always thought that her mother, who was part Cherokee and part African American, loved the idea of being married to a white man, especially an intellectual Jew, and being the dominant and capable one in the relationship made it all the more sweet. Looking at her mother, Coralee was reminded that she had her mother's dark, coffee-colored complexion and attractive facial features, while she physically resembled her father in being taller and more muscular than her mother, who was softer and more fleshy.

"Yes," Coralee said softly, "Daddy certainly was dependent on you. And so is George, and so is Larry. Fact is, Momma, you just love having all the men in your life totally dependent upon you."

"Girl, what nonsense are you talking? George is eighty-five years old, and he doesn't hear nearly as good as I do. The man is stone-deaf. Of course he needs me. I didn't make him that way, but I take him the way he comes. And your poor brother has a disease. Those drugs got hold of him and won't let go. Do you think I should just abandon him? You think I should just make life easy on myself and let my man and my son die of neglect? And what's going to happen to your Rick? How do you think he's going to feel, finding out that you and the kids have left him while he's over there fighting to stay alive? You think I should do like you're doing?"

Coralee shook her head. She and Momma had been gnawing at this bone ever since she had called and asked if she could move out here from Jersey. Her mother had agreed to be helpful, but she had made it quite clear that she disapproved of the decision to separate from Rick. Coralee could imagine what Momma would have to say if she knew that Rick had been wounded. She wasn't ready to deal with that.

"No, Momma. I'm not saying that you should abandon anybody. But the truth is that it might be better for Larry if he had to accept some responsibility for himself. He's fifty-one years old, for goodness' sake. And he's still living here? He doesn't work. He doesn't pay rent. All of that makes it easier for him to spend his disability money on drugs. He's just a shiftless drug addict. You aren't helping him, Momma. He's not a little boy anymore."

"Yes, he is. He's always going to be my little boy. Same as you will always be my little girl."

"Momma, I'm going to be forty years old next year. I'm not a little girl. I'm a grown woman with two kids, and I'm taking responsibility for my life and my decisions."

"Is that what you're doing? Sitting at my kitchen table? Drinking my coffee? Here in Oklahoma City instead of at your home in New Jersey? With your husband off serving his country in Iraq?"

Coralee took a deep breath.

Millie continued, "And while you're being so responsible, you tell me how your living here with your two kids is any different from Larry living here."

"Okay, Momma. You win. Maybe you're right. Maybe I'm not being as responsible as I'd like to think I am. But at least I have plans to get on my feet. This isn't a permanent arrangement for me. Hopefully, I'll find a job soon, and we'll be able to get our own place. But for Larry, I'm afraid this is a life decision. He's been here so long he's growing roots. And if that's fine with you and it's fine with George for Larry to live out the rest of his natural life sponging off you, then what the hell. It's really none of my business."

"That's right. It's not. You've got enough business of your own to take care of without trying to run this house too."

Millie finished her coffee and got up and carried her mug to the sink, where she rinsed it out and put it on the drain board. Then, without another word, she left the kitchen.

Coralee sighed as she looked through the doorway and watched her mother disappear down the hall. Then she put the envelope in her purse to mail later, when she went out job hunting.

II

————•◆•————

E ven before he was fully awake, Rick knew this was going to be a very bad day. There was that wobbly, anxious feeling of dread, an unarticulated fear. He felt like moaning. Occasional sounds from the corridor found their way into his awareness, and he realized, with a real sense of disappointment, that the woman he had been dancing with and squeezing so deliciously close existed only in a dream. Now more fully awake, his attention went to his leg. This was going to be his first full day without it.

There wasn't any real pain; in fact, there was no real sensation of any kind, except for some soreness in his right thigh where they had done the amputation. The hard part was not going to be physical pain. He knew that. The hard part was going to be in letting go of his past life, a life that had depended a great deal on his legs—his business, his running, his way of thinking about himself. What kind of a life did he have to look forward to? There was no life for the Rick Garcia he knew. He'd have to start over and build a new life, a new identity, become a whole new person. He wasn't sure he could hack it. He wasn't sure that Coralee could hack it.

Rick tried to roll over in his bed and inadvertently pushed down on his right leg. He felt a sudden stabbing, searing, hot pain that brought tears to his eyes, and a gasp escaped from his mouth. A nurse passing his door at the time stopped and looked in.

"Are you all right?" she asked.

Rick shook his head no.

She came farther into his room. "Pain?"

Rick took a deep breath and nodded.

She bent over closer to him.

"You have this morphine pump right here, Colonel," she said quietly, pointing to the plastic button device that was pinned to his mattress. "Just press this when you feel that the pain is too much. Don't worry about overusing it. It's not a big deal." She stood up and looked at him. "Can I do anything else for you?"

Rick shook his head slightly and then managed to mutter, "No thanks. I'll be okay. Thank you."

She smiled before she turned and left the room.

He looked at the button and decided against using it. But he'd have to be careful about putting pressure on that leg. It was only then that he noticed that it was still dark and that the only light was from the corridor. Rick looked at the small travel clock on his bedside table. It was only four o'clock. He'd thought it was later. He thought about trying to fall back asleep and realized he had to pee. He looked to his left, to the bedside table, and saw the pitcher-shaped urinal. Gingerly he reached for it and put it under the covers to use. *A hell of a way to go through life,* he thought. But at least it was better than that damn catheter he'd had to use until yesterday.

When he finished relieving himself, he struggled to replace it on the table, but in stretching, he felt another sharp stab of pain in his thigh that made him drop the urinal. The loud metallic clatter rang through the room like an alarm.

The nurse hurried in and turned on the light above his bed. She saw immediately what had happened and the look of embarrassment on Rick's face.

"I'm sorry," he apologized. "I was reaching, and I got this pain ..."

"There's no need to apologize, Colonel. I understand. It happens all the time."

She picked up the urinal and left the room with it. A couple of minutes later, an aide returned with a mop to clean up the floor. She smiled when she came in and when she left. A minute later, the nurse returned with his urinal.

"I know a lot of this is going to be difficult for you, Colonel. But at least for the present, there are going to be some things that you may want some assistance for: turning, stretching, sitting up, lifting yourself, voiding and evacuation … all of these things. You understand? Don't be afraid or embarrassed to ask. That's why we're here. We're a resource for you. Learn how to use us. All right?"

Rick managed a weak smile of resignation.

"I know you're going to do fine with all of this, Colonel. Just give yourself some time. Meanwhile, if there's anything you want to do or need, use the call button. Then, once someone is here, if you want to try to do it on your own, that's fine. At least we'll be here to assist you if you need us to."

"Yeah, I understand," he said. "I'm sure I'll catch on."

"I know you will," she said.

Rick tried to read the name tag on her uniform, but he couldn't make it out. "What's your name?" he asked.

"Jennifer," she said.

"Thanks, Jennifer."

She smiled at him again and, indicating that she'd be back later, left the room.

Fully awake now, Rick reached for the bed controls and raised himself up slightly. *What a fucking week,* he thought. He recalled the explosion that had blown up his Humvee, mangling his leg and killing his driver. That had been on Monday. He recalled only a tiny portion of the flight to the hospital in Germany, and a couple of days later, the longer flight to Walter Reed Hospital. *Then yesterday, there was the surgery. That would make today Saturday.*

He thought about the surgery, about his missing leg, and realized that he was angry and that he felt guilty about being angry. On the one hand, it was true … as a member of the military reserves, he had signed a contract and had an obligation to serve when needed. That was the purpose of the military reserves, wasn't it—to be in reserve, to be available when extra forces were needed? After all, it wasn't like he didn't get any benefits from being in the reserves. Time-in got counted toward his retirement pension. There were medical benefits, pay, and free travel on military planes—when there was space. So he had agreed to go when called.

In spite of his age (he was forty-four at the time) and the length of time he had been out of active duty (fifteen years), he was vain enough to think that he still had something to contribute: skills, maturity, and leadership. Of course, he hadn't been happy about having to be away from his business for six months. He had built up a nice little engineering company and had made a decent living for his family. But it was a business that relied heavily on him. Still, there were enough contracts and projects, either in process or in the pipeline, that enough work could be maintained for six months without an excessive amount of hardship. And like he said, there was this obligation, a duty. He really had no choice.

But six months had turned into a year, and a year had turned into fifteen months, and those fifteen months had been capped by that explosion. That's what pissed him off. There was no good reason for civilians—which is what he really was—to be 40 percent of the fighting force. *Fifteen months! It was unconscionable. It was stupid. There hadn't been sufficient training. We weren't in shape. Our equipment was outmoded and subpar. My Humvee lacked armor. It wasn't fair.* He had been willing to do his share, but this was more than his share. Goddamn it. It was his life. Now his business was all but bankrupt. All of his employees had been let go. His marriage was falling apart. He hadn't seen his kids in over a year. *And I have no fucking right leg! For what? To save America from Saddam Hussein? What bullshit!*

He had been both pleased and angered as it had become increasingly clear that there were no weapons of mass destruction. He hadn't really believed that there were any, but there was a part of him that had hoped his president hadn't been lying to him.

He had wanted to believe that the administration really did know things that hadn't been made public, that the United States really had been in danger of Al Qaeda being supplied with nuclear or biological or chemical weapons. So he was relieved, on the one hand, to be reassured that Iraq had never been in a position to create that dreaded scenario. But, on the other hand, he had been infuriated to realize that he and the rest of the military personnel, his buddies, his friends, had been used—sacrificed—for some ulterior motive.

Rick knew that he didn't know enough to comment intelligently on long-term geopolitical strategies. But he did know that he didn't believe that a foreign policy based on preemptive war was consistent with American values. America didn't go around attacking other countries unnecessarily. Not the America he believed in. That's not what he wanted to be fighting for. He wasn't interested in building an "American Empire" to make the world safe for McDonald's and Coke and GAP, not to mention Halliburton and the big oil companies.

Rick felt himself becoming more agitated and realized that the level of burning in his thigh had intensified. He assumed it would be all right to push the morphine button, and almost immediately he began to feel significant relief … a thick, soft dreaminess. He closed his eyes and let himself float in it. It was almost seven o'clock when Rick next opened his eyes. A new nurse, not Jennifer, was standing to his left, and Dr. Singh was standing to his right, lifting back the covers to look at the leg.

"How does it look?" Rick asked.

"Good morning, Colonel. I'm just now taking a look. How does it feel?"

"I don't know. All right, I guess. It only hurts when I stand on it."

"Ah, very good. Humor is a very good sign. But you will be standing on this leg again. I have no doubt about it. None at all. You will see. In no time at all you will be up and about. Almost like new."

Rick thought to himself, *Easy enough for you to say*, but he said nothing out loud.

By this time, Singh had removed the bandages. There was a good deal of swelling, inflammation, and ugly discoloration. Rick saw the stitches where they had sewn the flap of skin across the stump. There was also a drain inserted in the incision leading out under the covers to a receptacle under the bed.

Singh examined the wound closely. "It is looking very good, Colonel. No sign of infection and not too much swelling. The swelling will take a few days to go down, but that is normal." He asked the nurse for new bandages and began to rewrap the stump. "Have you had to use the morphine pump yet, Colonel?"

"Just once. Earlier this morning I was stretching to put the urinal back on the table and must have pressed into the mattress."

Singh looked at him, his eyebrows raised above his round dark eyes.

"Yes?" he encouraged.

"It was a sharp pain, and it throbbed for a while afterward. So I used it then, and I guess I fell back asleep."

"Very good," he said. When he finished redoing the bandage, he turned to Rick again. "Any questions, Colonel?"

"Yeah, I guess. What comes next?"

"First, we let all of the tissues heal. We'll give that at least a week. Then, as soon as we are able, we will start some physical therapy to strengthen the muscles and tissues. We'll get you up and about using crutches and a wheelchair. Then we'll fit you with a prosthetic leg, and you will learn how to use it. Meanwhile, I suggest that as soon as you are able to get out of bed, that you join one of our amputee support groups. I think you will find that very helpful in making the adjustment."

When Dr. Singh was finished, they shook hands and the doctor left. The nurse looked at him and asked if there was anything he needed while she was there.

Rick was about to shake his head no and then realized he was thirsty. "Could I have some water?"

She took his thermos and poured him a glass. Then she got the bed table from where it had been at the foot of his bed and moved it closer to him. She put the thermos and glass and urinal on it along with a box of tissues.

"There," she said. "How's that?"

"Thank you," Rick said. "When's breakfast around here?"

"About an hour," she answered, "but I can bring you some juice now if you'd like."

"That sounds good. Thanks."

The nurse left, and Rick realized that he was feeling exhausted. He took a sip of water and then lay back on the bed and closed his eyes. He was drifting off when the nurse came back in with a container of juice. Rick thanked her and then read her name tag: Lt. S. Browning. "What's the S. for?" he asked.

"Shirley," she said.

"Thank you, Shirley." She smiled and disappeared.

During the course of the rest of the morning, Rick gathered from his conversations with Shirley that he'd be spending only the next couple of days in bed, to allow his leg to heal, before they would be getting him up and out of bed for at least some of the day. At first, he'd be spending some time in a wheelchair, but later he would learn to get around on crutches. He figured he might as well make the most of these next couple of days and rest up as much as he could. He still found it difficult to concentrate for too long, and reading anything longer than a magazine article was too tiring. Shirley explained that he was still being affected by the anesthesia in his system and wouldn't feel completely free of that for another couple of days.

The only thing on TV worth looking at was CNN, and the news from Iraq only depressed him more. Mostly he dozed, drifting lightly in and out of dreams and memories. He thought of Coralee and the kids and wondered how they would react when they found out he'd been wounded and lost a leg. Somehow, he felt a sense of shame, as if he had done something terribly wrong in allowing himself to be wounded and crippled. He wondered how Thomas would react to him. He was such an introverted kid that Rick never knew what was going on inside him.

He remembered that when he himself had been twelve, he had felt inadequate because he was such a small and skinny runt. The only thing he had going for him was that he could run fast, faster than any of the other kids. That's what had motivated him to go out for track when he got to high school. Christ, he loved running. He loved winning. He loved running through pain, beating older, bigger kids. Then finally, in his junior year, when he was sixteen, he began to grow. When he reached five feet ten, he towered over his father and mother, not to mention his younger brother. When he graduated from high school, he was almost six feet tall and the captain of the track team—and a wide receiver on the football team. Miracle of miracles, he was popular. No longer the runt. God, he had loved running.

He had gotten a scholarship to college, and he had run successfully there as well. He had kept on running, even after college, after he had gone into the army as a lieutenant, a result of his having been in the ROTC. He could think of no other aspect of himself that had been so helpful in his life. More than his brains or personality or looks, he felt indebted to his legs.

Christ, he thought, slamming his fists against the mattress. *Goddamned Christ.* Tears came to his eyes, and the overwhelming sense of loss he had been trying to suppress finally filled him up and spilled out of him. He found himself sobbing and was glad that no one else was in the room.

Later in the afternoon, an aide and an orderly wheeled a gurney into the room and slid a young man onto the bed next to his. The guy's head was all bandaged up, and he seemed totally out of it. Once they got him settled in, both the aide and the orderly left without speaking. Later, when Shirley came in, he asked her what the story was, but she just shook her head, indicating that she wasn't going to talk about it, at least not then. Rick was curious, but he had his own problems.

He was worrying about everything: his engineering business, his marriage, his kids, and especially his own future. Rick thought of his parents back in Texas. He wondered if they knew he had been wounded. What would they think? He'd have to write to them. Everyone in the family, including him, hated using the phone, resorting to it only when necessary. *Christ! So much to think about. So many unknowns.* He thought of his unit back in Iraq, wondering how the guys were making out … if they were all right. All of this was making him nuts. He decided he needed to get away from the turmoil and pushed the button again, releasing the calming drip of morphine, and almost immediately, he started to fade out.

———

Hennessy looked up at him from where he was crouching down on the ground, putting something together. "You're really getting to like that shit, aren't you?"

Rick grinned back at his sergeant. "Why not? They said it was no big deal."

"Yeah, I know. No big deal if you use it just for pain. Physical pain, that is. You're not supposed to use it just for copping out, you know."

"Copping out? What the hell would you know about that?"

"Yeah, I know. You got your leg blown off. Could be worse."

"Fuck you, Henn. I lost my goddamned leg. My business is in the shitter. My wife's pissed off. My boy is acting out. How could it be worse?"

Hennessy smiled up at him. "Could be me," he said, laughing. Then he faded away.

"Who're you talking to, son?"

"Just Hennessy, Pop. He's always busting my chops."

Rick's father folded the newspaper in his lap. "I remember your writing to me about him, about how much you respected his opinion and experience."

"Yeah. Henn's quite a guy. I don't know what I'd do without him. He's been all over. He was here back in '91 too. He's got close to twenty years' experience … really on top of everything."

Johnny Garcia reached over for his glass of iced tea. "Well then, maybe you should listen to him about this too."

"Don't worry, Dad. I'm not going to get addicted. I just need a little time to adjust to all of this."

"I know, son. It's not easy. You have a lot on your plate. But you have to be strong. You were always very strong, Rick, very determined. That's why you always came out on top. You're a real winner. I know you can do this. I know you'll beat it."

"I will, Dad. I will. Just be patient with me, okay? Christ, it's only been a day."

"I know. I know. But you've got to nip these things in the bud. Don't start out on the wrong foot."

"That's what I've been telling him, Mr. Garcia." It was Hennessy again, coming into the living room from the kitchen with a can of beer in his hand.

"What is this?" asked Rick, throwing up his hands. "You bozos ganging up on me?"

Dad laughed. "Well, if we don't do it now, when are we going to get another chance this good?"

Coralee came out of the kitchen. "Here, hon. I thought you might want some iced tea."

"Hey, thanks." He took the glass from her, but it slipped from his hand and ended up in his lap. "Oh, shit!" he said. "What an idiot I am." He felt the cold wetness spreading over his legs. Then he woke up.

At first he was disoriented, but almost immediately he realized where he was. Then, remembering his dream, he looked down to his groin … nothing. He felt himself under the covers and was relieved to find that he hadn't wet himself. He breathed an enormous sigh of relief, but realized that he had to urinate. He took the urinal from his bed table and used it. He was becoming more comfortable with it, but was looking forward to the day when he'd be able to go to the bathroom again in a normal way. Finished, he replaced the urinal on the table, relieved that he didn't have to make the stretch anymore to the bedside table next to him.

Rick sipped at his glass of water and recalled his dream. He thought about his dad, still back in Texas, only recently retired from his job as an engineer with one of the oil companies. Dad had always tried to motivate him to do the best he could. He felt appreciated and respected by his dad, but he'd always felt pushed—never allowed to rest in place. He always felt that he was expected to reach for the next level. He knew he could count on his dad's support, but he'd be expected to be successful in overcoming the challenge of his new physical reality. Mom, on the other hand, would be all chicken soup, fussing and wanting to baby him. She'd be glad for the opportunity to feed him and empty his urinal and anything else she could do. He'd have to be on guard against letting that happen, because— truth be told—right now some of that sounded pretty damn good. Coralee, on the other hand …

———

"Jesus Christ, Rick, you've got to be careful. Now look what you've done."

"What are you talking about? The glass slipped. It was wet. You should have dried it off."

"Oh, so now it's my fault you dropped your glass. For Christ's sake, Rick, can't you ever take responsibility for your own actions?" Coralee brought him a dish towel so he could dry himself off.

Rick looked to his father, as if to say, "Can you believe this?" But his father must have gone back into the kitchen. Hennessy had gone too. He looked back at Coralee.

"What are you talking about, Cora? I take responsibility for my actions all the time."

She made that funny face of hers, screwing up one corner of her mouth.

"You are a hard woman, Cora. You're always so quick to criticize me. Can't I ever do anything right in your eyes?"

"Sure you can, Rick. You do lots of things right. That doesn't mean I have to throw a parade for you every time. You're spoiled, that's all. You always expect everything to revolve around you. Rick, the star. Rick, the champion. I'm not your mother, Rick. I'm not going to put your picture up on the refrigerator every time you sign a new contract with someone or come in among the top three in some race. My goodness, a grown man and still running footraces like a ten-year-old."

"Jesus Christ, Cora, don't you ever appreciate getting a little recognition when you do something that makes you feel good?"

"If it makes you feel good, then why do you need someone else to validate you? You're not a twelve-year-old, like Thomas. He's still learning about who he is. He needs feedback to know when he's on track and when he's not. You're forty-five years old, Rick. You shouldn't need me or your mother or father to tell you that you're good enough. I don't want to be in that role, Rick. I've seen my momma play that role enough. I'm not going to do it. Two kids are enough."

"Jesus, Cora. Is it too much to expect a little sympathy, a little compassion from you? We're married fourteen fucking years. Just once I'd like to feel a little love from you—a little understanding, like my feelings mattered just a little bit to you."

"Rick, I admire your strength and your perseverance in the face of difficulty. I admire you, but I'll be damned if I will constantly proclaim that admiration from the rooftop for all the world to hear. You're a smart man, Rick. You're resourceful and determined and ambitious, and you should feel proud of what you've accomplished. You've come a long way for a Tejano, and you've overcome a lot. But that's who you are. You do what you do. You are who you are.

Don't go pretending that you're living your life for me. And don't go expecting me to be leading some fan club for you. If I didn't respect and admire who you are, I wouldn't be here."

But will you be here when you see this leg? Rick looked up and opened his eyes. Shirley was taking his pulse again.

"Looks like you were dozing off again."

Rick smiled weakly. "Yeah, I guess. I keep drifting off … dreaming."

"Good dreams, I hope," she said as she inflated the blood pressure cuff.

Rick shrugged. "I was having an argument with my wife."

Shirley made a face. "Oh? Who started it?"

"Who knows? It's an old dance we do. We fall right into it and follow the music. We both know the steps. I look to her for some kind of recognition or appreciation or something—"

"Love?"

"Yeah, love … that would be nice. Then she reacts like I'm asking for the moon. Jeez, how many women complain that the men in their lives never say a kind word to them? If this were turned around and she was the one complaining of not feeling appreciated enough, I'd be painted as the typical male chauvinist pig. But if *I* complain, I'm just being a spoiled baby."

"Is that what she says?"

"Just about." Rick was growing disgusted. "Ah, it's not worth talking about. She'll never change."

Shirley looked at him as she marked down his blood pressure and pulse. Then she stuck a new thermometer in his ear to take his temperature.

"It doesn't sound like you expect a very sympathetic response from your wife. Does she know about the amputation yet?"

"I guess not, unless someone from here has called her."

Shirley shook her head. "I think that's going to be something you're going to have to do."

Rick looked at her and then looked away.

"I'll see you later," she said as she left the room, taking his urinal with her.

Rick felt angry and upset, and he thought about hitting the button again, but he could almost see Coralee and his dad and Hennessy standing at the foot of the bed with their arms folded across their chests, staring at him. *Okay*, he thought to himself, *you win*, and he picked up the remote and turned on the TV. *There's more than one way to stop thinking*, he said to himself.

After a while, a volunteer came around delivering mail. She brought Rick a large brown envelope. He looked at the return address and saw that it was from Coralee, but the return address was Oklahoma City. At first Rick was confused, but then he assumed that Cora must have decided to visit her mother for the upcoming holiday, maybe even stay through Christmas. The envelope was thick, and he opened it eagerly, wondering what she might have sent him. It had been a long time since he'd heard from her.

Rick noticed the envelope from Fred, his accountant, and the one from Arnie, his lawyer, but first he read the letter from Coralee. His stomach dropped away, leaving a huge empty space. His whole being felt like it had collapsed. *Oh, no*, he thought. *Oh, holy Christ, no. Not this too.* He dropped the letter onto the bed and closed his eyes, shaking his head from side to side. Without thinking, but with a feeling of angry defiance, he reached for the button and pressed it hard, urging the calmness into his bloodstream. Gradually, he relaxed and let everything become obscured by a thick, warm fog.

———

"Bad news, Rick?"

"Yeah, I'd say so. Coralee is leaving me … has left me. She closed up the apartment and the office, took the kids, and went to stay with her mother in Oklahoma City."

"Why on earth would she do that?"

Rick made a face. "It's a long story, Ma. We've been having trouble for a long time. But I think if I hadn't gone to Iraq, we might have been able to work it out. This goddamned war has ruined everything."

"I must say, Rick, I never did think that Coralee gave you the credit that you deserved. She never struck me as a very loving or nurturing person when it came to you. I always thought that you deserved more."

Rick didn't really disagree with his mother, but he didn't feel entirely comfortable agreeing with her either. He knew what her agenda was. She would never have thought that anyone would have been good enough for him. He knew how special he was in her eyes, and any wife was competition. On the other hand, he had thought some of the same things himself. Granted, Coralee was great with the kids, especially ten-year-old Ella. The two of them were wonderfully close. But when it came to him, it was like pulling hens' teeth to get a compliment out of her. She wasn't quite that bad with Thomas, but she was definitely less supportive of him than she was with Ella.

He looked at his mother, her book on her lap, her hand holding her glasses pressed against her chest while she stared out the window. Her eyes seemed to be glistening, and he suspected that she was on the verge of tears.

"What's the matter, Ma?"

Virginia shook her head and put her glasses back on. "I was just thinking about the children, Tommy and Ella, and how they must miss you. I was wondering when you'd get to see them again."

"I don't know, Ma. I haven't a freaking clue as to what's going to happen next: what's going to happen with my leg, the kids, everything. My lawyer is advising me to file for bankruptcy. My accountant thinks I should sell the building in Morristown. I feel like I've lost everything, Ma. What's left? I don't have anything left. I lost my wife, my marriage, my kids, my home, my business ... and to top it all off, I've lost my leg. I feel like I've lost *me*, Ma. It's like I don't exist anymore. There is no Richard Garcia. I've been blown away, Ma. Those goddamned Iraqis took it all. There's just this big empty hole here," he said, punching his belly with his fist, "where I used to be. Now there's nothing. Just nothing."

His mother got up from her easy chair and came over to him. She put her hands on his cheeks.

"You're burning up, Colonel."

He opened his eyes. It was Sanja, the late-afternoon nurse. Shirley must have left for the day. Sanja took his temperature.

"Over a hundred and two," she said. "You're running a fever." She went into the bathroom and emerged with a wet washcloth and put it on his forehead. She left the room and then returned shortly with some medication to help reduce the fever. Then she lifted the covers and took a look at his thigh. "How does your leg feel?" she asked.

Rick turned his head toward her. "I've been using this little black button over here, so my leg isn't having too many feelings."

Sanja walked around the bed and looked at the indicator on the morphine pump. "Have you been having a great deal of pain, Colonel?"

Rick gazed up at the ceiling and then shook his head slightly. "I'm not sure, Lieutenant. I'm a little fuzzy."

Sanja turned the cloth over on his forehead.

"Here, drink some water. We don't want you to become dehydrated." She handed him his glass with the straw and helped hold it for him while he sipped it. "Just rest. I'll be back soon."

Rick closed his eyes and drifted off again.

———

"Hi, Rick. I came as soon as I heard. How're you feeling?"

"Oh, my God, Alice. What are you doing here?"

"I heard you were wounded. I came right away."

"But it's been so long. My God, how long—"

"Since 1981, when we graduated from college. Twenty-three years."

"God, Alice, you look great."

"Thanks." She made a long face. "I wish I could say the same about you, Rick."

"Yeah, well, I'm going through a tough time right now. I guess it's all taking its toll."

Alice came closer and leaned over, giving him a big kiss. He felt too weak to reach up and put his arms around her, but it felt so good to lie there and feel her full, wet lips on his. He felt his penis stirring. All the old feelings were coming back.

"Ooo," she moaned. "You feel good." She glanced down at the sheet covering his groin. "I'm glad to hear that they didn't knock that leg off," she joked.

He opened his eyes. Sanja and Dr. Singh had lifted the covers and were examining his stump. Dr. Singh heard him stir and turned to him.

"Nothing to be concerned about, Colonel; just a little infection. We'll add some stronger antibiotics to the regimen, and I'm sure that will do the trick. Right now, I'm going to give you a shot of antibiotics to get you started. All right?"

Rick nodded. He looked around the room, wondering where Alice had disappeared to. God, she had looked and felt great. Hardly changed at all since college. He barely felt the needle go into his thigh and was only vaguely aware of Sanja putting a new cool cloth on his forehead. He felt so tired. He couldn't keep his eyes open.

"You really have to watch that morphine, Colonel." It was Hennessy again, standing at the foot of his bed.

"I warned him about it earlier, Doc," he said, addressing himself to Dr. Singh.

Dr. Singh was taking another look at the wound and just glanced up at him.

"You really shouldn't be here," Singh said, shaking his finger at him. "Colonel Garcia is really too weak to be entertaining visitors."

"How's the colonel doing?"

Singh looked up at Hennessy. The doctor was shorter than Hennessy and very stout in a roly-poly way, whereas Hennessy, still dressed in fatigues and sculpted by war, was noticeably taller.

"Colonel Garcia has somehow managed to pick up an infection—a raging infection, I might say—that seems to have come out of nowhere. He's running a fever, a relatively high fever, and seems to be in and out of some delirium. But I expect that he will be much better, much stronger, tomorrow." While he had been talking to Hennessy, Singh and Sanja had been redressing the leg.

Rick turned to Sanja. "I wonder if you could give me some water, nurse."

Sanja refilled the glass and held it toward him, inserting the straw into Rick's mouth. When he finished, she put another wet cloth on his head and wet his lips.

When they left, Hennessy walked up closer.

"She's quite a looker," he said to Rick.

Rick smiled. "I lucked out, Henn. All the nurses here are drop-dead gorgeous."

"It's not right, you know, Colonel—your being here, soaking up all this attention, while we're still out there dealing with the bad guys."

"Fuck you, Henn. I didn't ask for this, you know."

"No, I guess not. Still, you knew that road was dangerous. You could have stayed off it. It's not like you got it while you were eating lunch like those poor bastards up near Mosul."

"You don't know what you're talking about, Henn. I didn't have any choice. I had to inspect that bridge firsthand. It had to be finished, pronto." Rick paused and furrowed his brow. "Whatever did happen with that bridge? I never made it up there, did I?"

"No, you didn't, Colonel. Neither did Jasper, your driver. He bought it right there. Killed instantly. You were lucky to make it out with only that mangled leg."

Hennessy pulled out a pack of cigarettes and offered one to Rick. Rick shook his head. "You know I don't smoke."

"I thought you might have changed your mind, being as you're in such a fucked-up condition."

"Thanks a lot, Henn. You're all encouragement. Just what I needed to hear to cheer me up."

"I'm not here to cheer you up, Colonel. And to get back to the bridge—no, you never did make it up there, and the world didn't come to an end, did it?"

"What are you saying, Henn?"

"What I'm saying, Colonel, is that you didn't have to drive up that road to personally inspect that bridge. You could've called up there, or waited until an armored vehicle was available, or even requested a chopper. You're a colonel, after all."

Rick was on the verge of defending his actions, but Hennessy continued, "The fact is, Colonel, you've got some kind of hero complex. You not only decided that you personally had to inspect the bridge, but you deliberately chose to take the risk—the unnecessary risk, Colonel—of going up that road unprotected."

Rick remembered. He and Jasper had left their camp. It was late morning, the sun high in the clear, cloudless sky. As they were riding, he remembered being aware of the risk, but dismissing it, believing that the odds were everything would be all right. Plus, they would be careful. They were driving along River Road, at least that's what they called it, along the river to where their engineering unit had been involved in repairing a small bridge. It was a pain-in-the-ass job dealing with the locals, who didn't understand why he wasn't hiring them to work on the bridge and why he was protecting the Chinese workers who had been hired by the construction company. He was responsible for providing security against the bad guys, who were doing whatever they could to disrupt everything.

There seemed to be plenty of people walking back and forth along the road, all of the usual sights and sounds and smells. Both he and Jasper kept their eyes peeled for anything that might look like a potential roadside bomb. Then all of a sudden ...

"Then what happened, Rick?"

It was his younger brother, Matthew, sitting in the easy chair.

"I'm not sure, Matt. A big bang. It sounded like a big firecracker going off, you know? More of a high-pitched crack. It didn't have that low, rumbly sound you think of when you think of a bomb. It wasn't a bomb, really. It must have been planted in the road, like a mine, and I guess it went off under us. The whole Humvee jumped up into the air and flipped over. I think I remember somebody saying the whole bottom was blown away. I don't remember much. Some medics were hauling me out. My leg was mangled. Jasper wasn't there. I had no idea what had happened to him. He must have been completely blown out of the vehicle. I heard later that he was dead. In fact, Hennessy was just here and said Jasper died instantly."

"Christ," said Matthew, wiping his brow. "That's got to be fucking scary, man. I don't know how you guys keep your sanity over there. It's got to be crazy."

"Yeah, bro, it is. Crazy scary ... or scary crazy. Whatever."

"You're lucky you didn't get killed."

"Yeah, I guess I'm real lucky."

"To tell you the truth, Rick, I'm surprised you weren't injured before this."

"Why do you say that?"

Matt chuckled and spread his hands apart. "Hey, Rick, you know how you are: always taking chances, always volunteering, putting yourself out front—"

"I do not."

"Come on, Rick. I'm not saying anything new. You've always been like that. Dad's always telling me, Christ, since I was in grammar school, not to be afraid of taking responsibility, to be a leader like you."

Rick thought about it. Maybe it was true. He hadn't seen it as such a pattern, something he'd always done.

Matt cleared his throat and changed the subject.

"So, Rick, what are you going to do now that you're home?"

"I don't know, Matt. I haven't had a lot of time to think about it. Haven't really wanted to think about it either," he said, laughing. "Did you hear that Coralee left me?"

"Yeah. Ma told me. We've been talking about it—Ma, Dad, me, and Bea. We're pretty pissed off at Cora for ditching you while you were over there."

Rick had an image of Matt's wife, Beatrice. He hadn't seen them in such a long time.

"Yeah, well, we'd been having problems for a long time. But maybe we could have had a chance to work them out without this war tearing everything apart."

Matt was sitting leaning forward, his elbows resting on his knees, his legs spread apart.

"So tell me," Rick said, "how are you doing—you and Bea?"

"Good, we're doing good. Work is going well, the kids are healthy, and the bills are paid. We're doing great."

Rick sighed to himself. "I wish I could say that. Life can be so simple sometimes. You've got a job, the family is healthy, the bills are paid … everything is fine. It's like heaven. But lose your job or your health, and everything falls apart and your whole life turns to shit. It's all so fucking tenuous."

Rick turned back to Matt and was about to finish answering the question about his plans for the future, but Matt had gone. *Probably into the kitchen*, he thought.

He closed his eyes to wait for him and almost immediately he felt someone from behind place her small, cool hands over his eyes. He knew right away it was Alice.

"Where did you go before? I couldn't believe that you'd stay for only a minute."

"How did you know it was me?" Alice giggled. Then she came around in front of him where he could see her.

"I know these little hands," he said, continuing to hold on to one of them. "So where did you go? I was looking for you, but didn't see you."

"Your doctor came in, so I thought it would be better if I left. I went for a cup of coffee in the cafeteria."

"Give me another kiss," he said, stretching his lips upward.

Alice smiled and leaned over, giving him a big smooch. His hands reached up to her breasts, but she laughed and backed away.

"Uh-uh," she said, grinning. "We're not going to start anything we can't finish."

"Pull the curtain around the bed," he pleaded.

"No, Rick. Are you crazy? You've got another man in that bed over there, and people come in and out all the time."

He looked at her and made a long sad face.

"Poor baby is one horny bastard." She chuckled. "But I'm afraid you're going to have to stay horny for a while longer."

"God, Alice, you have no idea how often I've thought about you … dreamed of you."

"Me too, Rick."

"I wish you would have waited for me or married me and gone with me."

"I know, sweetie. It was a painful decision for both of us. But we were going in different directions, Rick. You were going off to Houston to engineering school, and then you had your ROTC commitment to do—four years, probably overseas—and I needed to go back to the reservation to work with my people."

"I know. But ain't it a bitch? We were so good with each other." They were silent for a moment. "You know I loved you, Alice. I still do."

Alice pressed her lips together and sat down on the edge of the bed. "Rick, I'm still fond of you too. But that was twenty-three years ago. We've both changed so much since then. We're not the same people anymore. You don't know me anymore. You don't know who I am."

"You haven't changed, Ali. You still look the same."

"Thank you, Rick, but you're wrong. We've both changed ... a lot."

"Did you ever get back to the reservation?"

"Yes, I did. I taught there for many years. Married another teacher and had three fine boys."

"Still married?"

Alice laughed. "You never stop, do you? Yes, Nelson and I are still married. He retired two years ago, and we decided to move to New Mexico. That's where we are now with the boys. How about you?"

"What do you mean, how about me?"

"I said, Colonel, how are you doing? How are you feeling?"

Rick opened his eyes and saw Sanja standing at his bedside.

"You haven't eaten anything from your tray. Aren't you hungry?"

Rick looked around, wondering again where Alice might have disappeared to, and then he realized he had been dreaming again.

"I'm sorry, Sanja. I don't remember the tray coming in. Actually, I don't have much of an appetite."

"Try something, Colonel. Liquids are good for you. There are only light things here anyway: soup, Jell-O, milk, some crackers. Do what you can, all right?" She spoke as she adjusted the drip in a new IV, which was hanging from a stand next to the bed.

Rick nodded, and Sanja raised his bed and pushed his bed table with the food tray closer to him before leaving. Rick felt warm and a little light-headed. He pushed himself up in the bed and immediately felt a sharp stab in his incision. *Christ, I'd forgotten all about it.* He sunk back onto the bed and let his heartbeat slow down. He tried some deep breathing and soon drifted off again.

Rick opened his eyes. There were four or five people, apparently doctors and nurses, standing around his bed. The light was very bright, too bright, and he closed his eyes against it and tried to relax. The pain in his leg was excruciating, and he clenched his teeth, trying not to make a fuss.

"He's lost a lot of blood, and his pressure is low," said a voice behind him.

"Make sure he's getting enough plasma, and order two more units of whole blood," said a deeper, gruffer voice to his right. "And this foot is going to have to go. Get McCarthy over here as soon as he's available. Have him do it. Try to save as much of this lower leg as possible. See what you can do to piece it back together. Make sure to give him plenty of morphine and antibiotics. Looks like there's all kinds of shit in here."

"You want to send him on to Germany?" That was a female voice on his left.

"Of course." There seemed to be some irritation in the voice. "Get him out of here ASAP. He'll be going on to Reed for more surgery, I'm sure. But right now, let's stabilize him, people. And have Mac get rid of that foot."

My God, thought Rick, *they're going to cut off my foot. I can't let them do that. I've got to stop them.* But the next thing he knew he was on a plane, strapped onto a stretcher. It was cold and noisy as hell. He saw what he assumed was a nurse and some other patients on stretchers, strapped in. Then he closed his eyes and floated away again.

"Come on, son, wake up. Let's go. Time to get up."

Rick turned his head away, but felt his dad's hand on his shoulder, gently shaking him.

"Come on, Rick, it's six thirty. Time to get up. Big race today, remember?"

"What are you talking about, Dad? There's no race today."

"It's Saturday, Rick. The county meet is today. I'll drive you over to the school, but the bus will be leaving there at eight thirty."

"County meet?"

"I don't know how you could have forgotten. You're in three events."

Rick rolled his head away. "I'm sorry, Dad. I can't do it. I can't run."

"Of course you can run. Don't give me that defeatist attitude. I have every confidence that you can do it. You've got a big heart, son. I'm not saying you'll win every race—maybe not any of them—but you've got to try. You just can't avoid trying."

"You don't understand, Dad. They're going to cut off my foot. I won't be able to run anymore, ever again."

"What are you talking about? Nobody's going to cut off your foot. You must have had a bad dream. Now, come on. You get yourself ready. Mom has breakfast ready. But be quiet. Matt is still sleeping. Okay?"

Rick shook his head. *He doesn't understand. He's never going to be able to accept this.*

"It's that thickheaded macho Latino pride of his," his mother said sarcastically. "Don't worry, son. I'll talk to him. It'll be fine."

Rick didn't open his eyes, but mumbled a "Thanks, Mom" before drifting back to sleep. It felt so good to be able to sleep late and not have to get up for school. He enjoyed the special attention that came with being a popular athlete, especially after those miserable earlier years in junior high school when he'd been shunned and picked on. Granted, he wasn't the only one who had a Mexican or Indian parent. But when you're a target, everything about you is used against you. The fact that his father's family was Tejano and had inhabited the land for over four hundred years was irrelevant. His father's Indian ancestors had inhabited what later became Texas after the Spanish first attempted to colonize the area. They were Mexican Indians who married the Spanish settlers (and later on, when they married American Indians, as his grandfather had done, they were often referred to as half-breeds). His father was the first of his family to marry a Norte Americano, a Gringo. Virginia, his mom, was unmistakably Irish stock through and through, with auburn hair and fair, freckled skin.

Rick heard the murmuring first and then felt the movement and pressure on his leg. He opened his eyes. He recognized the nurse, Sanja, but not the man, who apparently was a doctor. He saw the scalpel in the doctor's hand and tried to call out. He felt paralyzed but tried with all of his strength to shout out, "No, don't cut off my foot." But only a moan escaped his lips.

The doctor told Sanja, "Give him some more sedative. I don't want him moving around during this."

Oh Christ. He's cutting off my foot. Then everything faded out.

———

"Rick, you're forty-four years old. You've been a civilian for fifteen years. Surely you can get out of this. You don't even believe in this war in the first place."

"That's not the point, Cora. I signed a contract. Sure, I only expected to go out on maneuvers a couple of times a year. And up until now, that's all it's been. They hardly ever call up reserves to actually go fight in a real war. That's for the younger guys, for the regular army. But the contract says they have a right to call me if they want to, and if they do, then I have to go. Otherwise, it's desertion. It's a very bad thing, hon. I really have to go."

"And what are we supposed to do while you're over in Iraq? What are the children and I supposed to do?"

"Look, it'll only be for six months. My crew and the office can run things for that long. There's enough work to keep them busy, and there shouldn't be much of a drop in income, if there's any at all. And I'll be getting combat pay."

"Rick, I'm not talking just about the money. What about the kids? Tommy needs a father around. How do you think this is going to affect them, wondering if their father is going to get killed or not?"

"Hon, I know it'll be tough, but you've got to be strong for them. They're going to need your strength and support."

Coralee shook her head. "Why do I keep getting the idea that you want to do this? You're like a kid going outside after school to play army. This isn't play, Rick. I don't understand you. I would think you'd be looking into ways to get out of this … plead hardship or something. You're a forty-four-year-old out-of-shape civilian. Big deal, you run around the high school track a few times every week. That's not the same as carrying a pack … what do they weigh? Seventy pounds? You're too old for this shit, Rick."

"I tell you what, Cora. You call up the president or the secretary of defense and tell him it's not fair. See where it gets you. And it's not that I want to go. Hell, I'm not looking forward to going. I know I'm not in the same shape as those young regulars. But they're just kids, Cora. Eighteen, nineteen, twenty years old. They can use somebody around with some maturity and some wisdom. I am a colonel, after all. I know some stuff. I can make a contribution. And I have an obligation. Don't be angry with me, Cora. I didn't start this war. But now that they've called me up, I've got to go. And that's it. We'll have to do the best we can. But like I said, it'll only be for six months, and then I'll be home and all this will be behind us. You'll see, hon. It'll be all right."

Coralee fixed him with her evil stare, eyebrows furrowed and lips pursed. "Well, I can see that my opinion doesn't amount to a hill of beans. But know this, Mr. Richard Garcia. You'd better not go getting yourself killed or wounded, you hear me? You'd better take goddamned good care of yourself, and don't go playing the hero."

"Cora, do you think I want anything to happen to me? Short of wrapping myself up in cellophane, I'll take very good care of myself—don't you worry. You can take that to the bank."

Rick got up out of bed and left Coralee sitting there, propped up against the pillows, her book in her lap.

"I'm going to take a shower," he said. "I'm feeling sweaty."

That was true, but he was also angry. Sure, this was going to be tough, but you'd think that she would show more concern about him, show a little sympathy about his having to go to war instead of just criticizing him for doing his duty. In the bathroom, he stripped off his pajamas and stepped into the warm shower. It was soothing and relaxing, and he enjoyed feeling clean and renewed. When he turned the water off and started to dry himself, he started to feel chilly and shivered.

"He's getting chills again. Keep up with the sponge bath. Hopefully, we can bring that fever down."

Rick opened his eyes. Jennifer was putting another cool, wet cloth on his forehead.

"Would you like something to drink, Colonel?"

Rick told her yes, and she brought the glass and straw to his lips. He took a few long swallows. The cool liquid felt good in his throat. He licked his lips and discovered they were dry.

Jennifer wet his lips and then his entire face. Then she put something on his lips to help keep them moist.

Rick noticed the man on his right, a doctor. "Did you cut off my foot?" he asked.

The doctor looked at him and at the nurse and then back to Rick. "You had surgery yesterday, Colonel. They had to amputate your right leg, about five or six inches above the knee. I'm sorry. They couldn't save your leg."

Rick looked at him questioningly. "You didn't cut off my foot?"

The young doctor looked at him, resting a hand on Rick's arm. "No, Colonel. I didn't cut off your foot. As I said, you had surgery done yesterday."

"But I saw you with a knife … a scalpel."

"Ah, yes. You did see me with a scalpel. I opened up the incision around the drain to relieve some of the pressure from the infection. The drain had become clogged, and I inserted a new one. It should help, and the infection should be subsiding over the next few hours. Right now, you're running a pretty high fever, and we're trying to get you more comfortable."

So he wasn't cutting off my foot. That's good. Rick made an effort to take another look at Jennifer's pretty face and then gave in to the urge to close his eyes again.

He looked across at Hennessy, who was writing a letter home. "First thing tomorrow morning, Henn, I need to go up to check out the bridge. Have a Humvee and driver ready about 0800, all right?"

Hennessy looked at him. "You know that we don't have any armored vehicles?"

Rick stared at him. "I know," he finally said. "Just do it."

Hennessy returned the stare and then nodded. "Yes sir," he said, taking another drag on his cigarette before returning to his letter.

Rick thought about asking him what his problem was, but he really didn't want to do that. Sometimes, he needed to assert his authority with Henn, who could get a little too big for his britches and forget who the officer in charge was. But Rick knew what Hennessy was thinking: there was no need to travel River Road; it was too dangerous. And besides, his approval on the project was only pro forma anyway. He didn't actually have any authority over the job. It was really between Baghdad and the contractor, when you came right down to it. But he didn't like that arrangement, and he wanted to have his say. If the design and construction were shoddy, he wanted to be on record somewhere as having said so—even if it didn't accomplish anything. After all, that was allegedly what he was supposed to be doing here, and if he was going to spend fifteen goddamned months away from everything at home, at least he would do his job to his own satisfaction. Without saying anything further to Hennessy, Rick turned out his light and rolled over.

Later on, he heard noises and pushed himself up on his elbow to see what was happening. It seemed that a couple of orderlies and nurses were behind the curtain, attending to the guy in the other bed. When Jennifer came into the room, he motioned her over.

"What's going on?" he asked.

"The corporal, the young man in the bed next to you, died about a half hour ago. We're going to be moving his body out of here."

"My God," Rick exclaimed. "What happened?"

Jennifer shook her head. "It's very sad, Colonel. He had come home on R&R for two weeks. Apparently, he couldn't stand the idea of returning to Iraq. He stuck a gun in his mouth and tried to commit suicide." She paused. "Instead of killing himself, he succeeded only in shooting off the front of his face and part of his frontal lobe. He's been undergoing extensive surgeries to rebuild his face: his upper palate, nose, eye socket … the whole works. But he's been very unstable, and tonight he just didn't make it. Finally got what he wanted, I guess."

Rick sank back into his bed. *Christ*, he thought, *how the hell do you live with that? Blowing your face off? Shooting away half your brain? He's probably better off dead.* But all of the activity behind the curtain started him thinking. Was suicide an option? He could never run again. He'd be a cripple for the rest of his life. His wife had left him. God knows when he'd ever get to see the kids again, or even if they'd want to see him. He'd lost his business, would have to declare bankruptcy, and would probably lose the building in Morristown. He'd lost everything he owned or valued. He was left with nothing, a total failure. Maybe the corporal had the right idea. He started to think of how he might do it.

Gradually, he became aware of a presence by his bed. He opened his eyes and looked to his right, half-expecting to see the nurse or the young doctor again, but instead, it was his young son, Thomas.

"Tommy, what are you doing here?"

"I came to see you, Dad. Mom said you were wounded."

Rick reached out his hand to him, grasped his hand, and gently pulled him in closer.

"Yeah, son. I was."

"Was it bad?"

"Yeah, Thomas. It's pretty bad. The doctors ... they had to cut off my leg."

Tommy grimaced. "Did it hurt?"

"Well, it didn't hurt when they did it. They gave me medicine, anesthesia, to make me unconscious, so I wouldn't feel anything. But it's kind of sore now."

"Do they give you more of that stuff, the ana ... so it won't hurt?"

Rick grinned, thinking of the morphine pump. "Yeah, Tommy, they do. So it's not too bad right now."

"Is this it?" he asked, pointing to Rick's stump under the sheets.

Rick nodded.

"Can I see it?" Tommy asked.

"Do you really want to?" asked Rick, surprised.

Thomas gave a slight nod.

Gingerly, Rick reached down with his right hand and lifted the sheet, uncovering the bandaged stump.

Thomas looked at it intently, but silently.

"What's this?" he asked, pointing to the drain.

Rick looked down at his stump. "That's a drain, son, so excess fluids and stuff can drain out of it. Otherwise, the whole leg would swell up real bad."

"Why is there blood on the bandage?"

Rick took a deep breath. "They just did the surgery yesterday, and sometimes there's a little bleeding around the stitches where they sew it closed. Oh, and I almost forgot, a doctor was in here earlier, and he had to open up the incision to put in a new drain. So I guess there was a little bleeding from that."

"How are you going to walk and stuff? Will you have a wooden leg like Captain Hook?"

Rick half-smiled. "No, not a wooden leg like Captain Hook. They make much better legs now than they did back when there were pirates. But yes, I will have a false leg. And I should be able to walk again, although I may have to use a cane. I don't know yet."

"Will you be able to run again?"

Rick looked away before answering. "I don't know, Thomas. I don't know. But ... I don't think so. I don't think I'll ever run again."

"I started to run at school this year."

Rick's eyes widened. "You did? Your mother never told me."

Thomas hung his head. "Well, it wasn't anything important. They started different kinds of clubs in junior high this year, and one was a track club, so I joined. We've been running races and learning about how to run properly and stuff like that."

"Wow," said Rick, grabbing Tommy's hand and squeezing it. "I'm real proud of you. So tell me, how do you like it? How are you doing?"

Thomas shrugged his shoulders. "Pretty good, I guess. It's fun. I won some of the races."

"Cool," said Rick, and he saw a smile creep across Thomas's face.

"You know, Tommy, when I was around your age, I was very much like you."

Tommy looked up at him.

"Yes, I was. I was kind of small and wiry and sort of quiet, the way you are. The other kids used to call me Runt and Chihuahua and Prairie Dog, stuff like that. The only thing I had going for me was that I could run fast. But I didn't get into track and competition until I got to high school. I didn't have the nerve. That's why I'm so proud of you, to see the courage you have. Then, in high school, that's when I started to grow. The running really helped a lot, Tommy. It got me onto the football team. It got me a scholarship to college." Rick sighed and looked away. "It's been very important in my life," he said quietly. Then, looking back to his son, he added, "I hope that it brings you a lot of pleasure in your life."

Thomas swallowed and asked, "When are you coming home, Dad?"

Rick made a sad face. "I'm not sure I know what you mean, Tommy. Your mother and I ... it doesn't look like we're going to be living together anymore. She's moved with you guys to Oklahoma City."

"Can't you come there?"

"I don't know, son. I don't know how long I'll be here in the hospital or what the future holds in store for me. I just don't know."

"Why don't you tell the kid, Colonel?"

Rick looked to the source of the voice. There was Hennessy again, at the foot of the bed.

"Go on. Why don't you tell him what you've been contemplating? That maybe you won't leave the hospital at all, except maybe foot first, like your recent roommate."

"Shut up, Hennessy. What the hell do you think you're doing, talking like that in front of my kid? You're out of line."

Tommy looked at Hennessy and then back to his father. "Who's that?" he whispered to his dad.

"That's Sergeant Hennessy. He was with me over in Iraq. Sergeant, this is my son, Thomas. He's a runner too, just like me ... like I was."

"I'm glad to meet you, Thomas," said Hennessy as he walked over to the side of the bed and stood beside him. "Like your dad said, we were together in Iraq. The colonel is a brave man and a smart man, and a very stubborn and conscientious man. You should be very proud of him. But like the rest of us," he said, turning toward Rick, "sometimes he gets foolish ideas."

Rick saw that Hennessy was confusing the boy.

"What the sergeant means, Tommy, is that I was feeling discouraged before—kind of feeling overwhelmed by it all, you know?"

"But I want you to come home, Dad. Both Ella and me ... we need you to be home. You've been away a long time. All of sixth grade and now half of seventh grade are gone. I really need you to come home, Dad. Don't you want to see me run?"

"Of course I do. I can't think of anything more important." He paused and thought a moment. "Let me find out first what's involved with my leg, what the doctors say about how long I have to stay here, and what comes next. Then I'll talk to your mother and see what we can work out so I can see you kids and be near you."

Tommy sighed and looked away.

"You're just going to have to have some patience with this, son. It's not all up to me. But I promise I'll do what I can, all right?"

Tommy reached over and gave Rick a big hug. Rick looked over Tommy's shoulder and saw Hennessy giving him a thumbs-up sign, and Rick smiled to himself, sinking back into a state of contentment, enjoying the moment of closeness with his son.

Rick woke to Jennifer coming into his room, the sounds of footsteps and voices in the hallway, and the clattering of food carts and breakfast trays. The room was bright with sunlight.

"Good morning, Colonel. How are you feeling this morning?"

Rick opened his eyes wide and took a deep breath.

"Actually, Jennifer, I feel pretty good. I know the food smells good."

"They'll be bringing yours in pretty soon." She walked around his bed, noting the readings on his morphine pump and checking the rate of drip from the IV bag. Then she took his temperature and blood pressure. "You're looking pretty chipper considering the rough night you had."

"I had a rough night?"

Jennifer gave a soft chuckle. "You had a raging fever all night. It only broke earlier this morning. I can't believe you're back to normal already."

"I remember something about a doctor being in here ..."

"Yes—Dr. Green. He replaced the drain in your incision. That's what caused your infection. But you seem to be all right now. Your leg is looking good, but Dr. Singh will be in later to look at it."

Rick noticed some activity to his left and turned his head to look, seeing his roommate from yesterday, propped up in bed and being tended to by another nurse.

"What's he doing here?" he asked, full of surprise.

Jennifer cocked her head. "What do you mean, Colonel? We brought the corporal in yesterday."

Rick looked at her and half-whispered, "But I thought he died during the night and that they removed his ... you know, his body."

"No, Colonel. Nobody died during the night. It must have been a dream or part of your delirium."

"But," Rick persisted, "didn't he attempt suicide by putting a gun in his mouth and, you know, trying to blow his brains out?"

Jennifer shook her head and smiled and came closer so that she could speak softly to him.

"Corporal Gonzales didn't attempt suicide, Colonel. He was defusing an explosive device, and it went off. It blew off both of his hands and forearms and most of his face. He's been with us for a while now, undergoing a series of surgeries. He's a remarkably brave young man. If you knew him, you'd understand that suicide would be the last thing on his mind."

Rick looked over at the young man. "Christ," he said, half to himself. "Both arms and hands and most of his face." He shook his head, trying to comprehend what that would be like.

III

Dear Coralee,

I wanted to write to you as soon as I could about my situation, but to tell you the truth, this is the first chance that I've had. As you may know, I got wounded in an explosion last week and after I was shipped out to Germany, I got airmail-expressed here to Walter Reed, where, this past Friday, I had surgery (apparently, my second). They had to amputate my right leg above the knee, what they refer to as a midfemoral amputation. The incision got infected, and I went through a pretty weird time with a fever, but I am fine now, although still a little bit in shock from the explosion and the surgeries.

I received your letter. Needless to say, I was surprised. And of course, I would have to receive it on the morning after my surgery. So you might say that Saturday was a bad day. I lost my leg, my wife and family, everything it seemed, in one awful earthquake. I felt like the earth dropped out from under me. Yes, you are right (I know what you're thinking), I was feeling sorry for myself. Absolutely! I think I had a right to. When someone loses everything and everyone he values, he has a right to feel angry and sorry for himself. And no, I am not dwelling on it. I am moving on.

Just in the past two days, since they got me out of bed and into a wheelchair (for short periods, a couple of times a day), I've seen too much of what some of these guys (and gals—there are lots of women patients here as well) have lost and have to contend with for me to go on feeling sorry for myself. For example, my roomie is a twenty-one-year-old corporal, married with a baby girl. This poor guy has lost both of his hands and forearms and had half of his face blown away as well. Compared to many of these heroes (not necessarily for what they've done, but for their courage in facing what they now know is in front of them), I came out of this damn lucky.

Still, the rehab program I will have to go through will take a long time. Maybe a year; I'm not sure. But from what I gather, there's an excellent VA hospital in Oklahoma City. I think it's in the northeast section of the city, probably pretty close to where you're living with your mother. I'll try to get transferred there. I hear they have a state-of-the-art prosthetic program and a first-rate prosthetist.

I can understand if you have some doubts about visiting me. You may be right. Seeing you might get me to thinking about us getting back together again. But I don't think so. After my initial reactions of anger and disappointment, and a feeling of having been abandoned and betrayed, I came to realize that you were right. Our relationship had a fatal flaw: my need to be acknowledged and made to feel important and loved—and your inability or refusal to express those kinds of feelings. I'm not saying that you should be like your mother and go seeking out weak or disabled men to take care of. But honestly, Cora, what the hell do you think marriage is?

Your refusal to make your partner feel loved or valued is a real weakness and something I think you should work on before you even consider getting into another relationship with any man … including me. To tell you the truth, Coralee, I admire your courage in having been the first to face the reality of our flawed relationship and to admit that it wasn't working. But now that you showed me the light, I agree with you that we should get divorced. I know now that I need more and am entitled to more. There must be a woman out there who is able to really love me for who I am—even if I am a one-legged Tejano.

Truth is, we never should have gotten married. But I'm not sorry. We have great kids, and right now, my relationship with them is the only thing I have to look forward to. Don't get me wrong. I fully intend to start over and build a new life for myself. I thought that when I'm all healed and have my new leg, I'd get an engineering job in Texas. Dad still has contacts even though he's retired. I'm sure that I'll be able to stay with my folks or my brother outside San Antonio until I get a job with one of the oil companies and am able to get a place of my own. But the kids are the reason for it all.

You were right when you said that they needed me. I want to be there for them. But for the next six to twelve months, it'll have to be based on their visiting me in the hospital. If you don't want to bring them, then maybe your loafer brother can do it. Once I move back to Texas, hopefully we can work out some arrangement on custody so that the kids can spend a sufficient amount of time with each of us.

In the meantime, tell them I'm all right and that I love them and miss them, and that I will be writing to them and hope to see them relatively soon (I really don't know when) in Oklahoma City. Have them write to me here. I want to know what's going on in their lives, what they're doing, and what's important to them. Don't shut me out of that process, please!

Meanwhile, I hope you are well and that things work

out for you. I miss you, but … hell, I'm going to miss a lot of things. Life has changed. Life moves on. We'll all be fine eventually, I'm sure.

Rick

IV

As soon as his clinic appointment was over, Rick made his way outside to the warm and sunny curbside, where Phyllis was already waiting in her car. Rick tossed his crutches onto the backseat and lowered himself awkwardly into the passenger seat, gingerly lifting his right leg into the car. The prosthesis had a slight and permanent bend at the knee, and he was still having trouble with it. Because the leg often seemed uncooperative, he usually felt like he was moving stiff-legged like a comic Frankenstein, and, as a result, he felt clumsy and self-conscious regardless of the situation.

Phyllis leaned over to kiss him, sticking her tongue into his mouth.

He felt himself immediately growing erect, as if there were a direct line from the tip of his tongue to the tip of his penis. But all he said was, "I hope you weren't waiting long."

"No, not at all," she said, putting the car into drive. "I assumed you'd be ready about eleven o'clock, like you said. But I didn't want you to have to wait at all, so I got here a few minutes early."

Rick put his arm onto the back of her seat and watched her as she drove. Phyllis was an attractive woman with light brown hair cut short, making her look cheerful and vivacious. She was slim and athletic and a kind, caring woman. Today, her day off from her nursing job, she was dressed in a jeans skirt and a T-shirt and sneakers. The short skirt rode up far on her bare thighs, and he smiled appreciatively.

"Any trouble getting away?" he asked.

Phyllis turned to him briefly and smiled before returning her attention to the driving. She shook her head.

"No, the girls are in school all day, and Harold already left for work, so we're good until about two thirty, when I need to be home for the girls."

Rick smiled in anticipation of their opportunity to spend a few hours together.

"I fixed us a picnic lunch," she said.

"You mean something else in addition to us?"

Phyllis looked at him again and then ran her tongue over her lips. "Definitely in addition."

"My goodness. All of this," he said, spreading his arms indicating the whole length of her, "and food too. This must truly be paradise."

"Paradise, yes. But, unfortunately, not eternal. We only have until two thirty."

"Then we shouldn't waste a moment."

Phyllis drove the car out of the city, and soon they were in the hilly countryside, where she pulled off the highway onto a rural road that led to a county park. During the middle of the week, when most people were in school or at work, the small park was seldom used. Phyllis drove to the end of the empty parking lot and parked the car. Carrying a blanket and a shopping bag with their picnic lunch, she led the way down a path toward a small lake. Phyllis spread the blanket in the shade in a small grassy opening surrounded by tall grasses and shrubs, where they had a partial view of the water and its resident ducks. Rick followed on his crutches, not yet able to put his full weight on his new leg. Arriving at the blanket, he dropped his crutches and relied on Phyllis for support as he lowered himself awkwardly to the ground.

Almost immediately, he reached up to cup her face in his hands and then, pulling her close, kissed her firmly on the mouth. Phyllis held on to his shoulders as he helped lower her to the blanket, where they both eagerly embraced. In a short time, Phyllis had undone his pants and pulled them off. Rick undid the strap that held the socket of the leg snug around his stump, and they pushed the disembodied leg aside. Phyllis then leaned over him, taking him in both her hands and covering his shaft with a variety of wonderful attentions.

Rick alternated between watching her making love to him and lying back, eyes closed, enjoying the stimulation, as well as the idea, of what was happening.

Rick found the notion of having an affair with one of his nurses—an attractive, young, and married woman—exciting. This was still a new experience for him: having sex with a woman other than his wife. Although Coralee had not been his first sexual partner, until this past November when she had informed him of her intention to get a divorce, he had not had anyone else since their wedding almost fifteen years ago.

After his leg was blown off in Iraq, he hadn't thought that any woman would be interested in him physically, but he had been pleasantly surprised to find out differently. Coralee had never been one to compliment him sexually, just as she had adamantly refused to compliment him for anything else. Therefore, Rick had always entertained a certain degree of doubt about his virility and sexual adequacy. He knew he was adequate. What he didn't know was whether he was more than adequate, more than mediocre. It seemed strange and somehow perverse that it was only after losing his leg and becoming a cripple that he was in a position to get feedback from more than one young attractive woman that he was indeed the stud he'd always aspired to be. Although it didn't make up for all that he had lost as a result of that explosion, it was a very happy surprise.

Now, as he watched Phyllis, he could see how she kissed and stroked his stump, almost as if it were a giant penis. It was hard to tell which swollen entity gave her more pleasure. If he could have inserted his stump into her, then there would have been no contest. He had come to understand—although he was still mystified by it—that it could be sexually exciting to a woman to be involved with him *because* he was an amputee. Maybe it gave them a leg up, so to speak, giving them more control and more power. Perhaps there was also a sense of the forbidden—doing something even less socially acceptable than having an affair—having an affair with a one-legged man, a one-legged brown-skinned Tejano.

Feeling himself approaching the point of no return and coming dangerously close to losing control of himself, Rick reached down and pulled her up so that he could kiss her. Reaching under her skirt, he pulled off her panties and then indulged himself in devouring her. Rick enjoyed the view of the world from this perspective, feeling the strong muscular firmness of her thighs and belly, and the long view upward across her belly toward her rounded breasts and smiling face … her closed eyes … her quick, soft sounds … and the convulsive thrusts of her pelvis … not to mention the soft fuzz of her pubic hair and her sweet, musky smell and taste.

Eventually, Rick rolled over and Phyllis straddled him, inserting his erection into her and sliding slowly down its length. They made love languorously until, unable to control himself any longer, he exploded into her. They lay exhausted in each other's arms, enjoying the warm air on their bodies, the country stillness, and the smells of the earth and the lake. All seemed reverentially silent except for their breathing and an occasional quack of a duck.

Rick enjoyed feeling her petite frame collapsed on him, her face resting on his shoulder, her mouth on his neck.

"That was wonderful," she said softly. "You're a wonderful lover."

"It was fantastic," he agreed. "And you're an amazing inspiration. You're a beautiful woman, Phyllis. And a beautiful person too."

In response, Phyllis turned her head slightly and kissed his neck. Rick thought about his good fortune. Since coming out to the VA hospital in Oklahoma City from Walter Reed about six weeks ago, he had had a brief fling with another woman, which, although satisfying, quickly ran its course (this after a brief romance with his physical therapist back at Walter Reed). Then, about three weeks ago, he'd asked Phyllis if she wanted to go out, and she had agreed. He knew she was married, but that hadn't stopped him from asking or her from saying yes. Phyllis had told him early on that her husband, Harold, a jealous and irritable man, was totally inept as a lover. She had tried to teach him what to do, but for some reason, he never made any changes in his straightforward and predictably mechanical approach.

"It's like trying to teach someone who has no sense of rhythm how to dance. It's hopeless," she had said.

Although Phyllis had expressed a certain degree of guilt about having affairs (this was not, she'd admitted, her first), she also felt justified: if Harold couldn't give her what she deserved, then she felt entitled to get it on her own—as long as she didn't hurt Harold or the girls.

Rick also felt a certain degree of anxiety about having an affair with a married woman. He knew what he might have felt like doing if he'd found out that someone was screwing his wife. And out here in Oklahoma, where almost everyone owned a gun, he had some concerns about what Harold might do if he found out about them.

After a while, they untangled themselves, and, as Rick reattached his leg, Phyllis removed the food and drinks from the shopping bag and laid out their lunch. Once they had finished eating, they returned to pleasuring each other until Phyllis abruptly stopped and looked at her watch.

"Damn," she said. "It's almost two o'clock. Time for me to be getting back."

Phyllis carried the blanket and shopping bag, and Rick followed her on his crutches until they reached her car, where she put everything on the ground in order to get the key to open the trunk. Then she stopped dead in her tracks.

"What's the matter?" Rick asked as he leaned against the car.

Phyllis patted her skirt, bit her lower lip, and stared off into space.

"You don't have the keys?" he asked incredulously.

Phyllis looked at him briefly, eyes wide, and then she looked inside the car. There on the front seat were her keys. "Oh, Christ," she said.

"Do you have an extra set? A magnetic box under the fender or anything?"

Phyllis shook her head. "I carry an extra set in my purse, but I locked my purse in the trunk. I was so focused on remembering everything for our picnic that I forgot about the keys. Oh, Christ, Ricky, what am I going to do? I've got to be home in half an hour, or I'll have a lot of explaining to do."

Rick lowered his head and tried to think. "You're sure all the doors are locked?"

Phyllis said yes, even as she went around the car physically trying each one. "Locking the driver's door automatically locks all of them. It wouldn't lock if I had left the keys in the ignition, but for some reason, I must have laid them down on the seat. Rick, help me." The strained, wavering sound of desperation was already in her voice.

"Calm down. Relax. We'll figure something out." He looked around the parking area. "There's no ranger station or anything like that, is there?"

"No," she said, shaking her head. "This is only a county park. Sometimes the county or state police will patrol through here, but no one is stationed here."

Rick couldn't see any other cars. There was probably no one else around for God knows how many miles.

"My guess is that there's a public phone around here somewhere, so it would be possible to call a locksmith. But that could take forever. The only other thing I can think of is to break the window."

"How the hell am I going to explain a broken window to Harold? Shit! This is what I get for screwing around. Christ, we never should have done this. God, what am I going to do?"

Rick was getting a little nervous himself. He had a vision of Harold walking toward them with a shotgun slung over his shoulder and a leather band of bullets strapped across his chest. He had never seen Harold, but he had developed an image based on Phyllis's description: medium height, prematurely balding, something of a paunch from physical inactivity … *but that looks like a pretty big shotgun he's carrying.*

Rick spoke as much to himself as to Phyllis. "Calm down. Getting panicky isn't going to help anything. Is there anyone you can call to pick up your kids?"

"I suppose I could call Joan, one of my neighbors, to take the girls in when they get home. I could tell her I got stuck in traffic or something."

"Good," he said. "Now all we need is to find a phone. You don't have a cell?"

Phyllis made a face and gestured toward the trunk.

"It's in your purse?"

"And that has all of the phone numbers. Without that I wouldn't even know what number to call. I'm not even sure of Joan's last name. We only call each other by our first names."

Rick hung his head again and thought. "If we could find a public phone, we could call 911, and maybe the local police could help us or send a locksmith."

"Rick, I don't think there's a phone anywhere around here, maybe for miles. It's over two miles back to the highway, and we didn't pass anything on the way in."

"Okay. Then suppose we find a rock or something and break the window, and then you tell Harold that you decided to go for a ride in the country. You could even tell him that you drove out here. The more truth you include, the better it is. You got out to take a walk, take a look at the ducks, have a little picnic, and locked everything in the trunk, to be safe. Then you discovered that you'd locked yourself out of the car. There was nothing else you could do except break the window to get into the car and retrieve the keys."

"Harold is going to wonder why I decided to drive out here to the country in the first place. I never do that."

"You just got the urge. Maybe somebody at work had told you

about it, how peaceful it was. You thought it would be a good way to relax and get a little sun."

Phyllis made a face and looked around. "You win," she said, sighing. "I wish there was some other way, but I can't think of anything."

"Short of a miracle—your finding a key in your pocket or the Royal Mounties showing up with a tool like auto thieves use to open the door—I can't think of anything else either."

They stood looking at each other, Rick still leaning against the car.

"So," he said, "you want to look for a rock that's big enough to break the window?"

Phyllis rolled her eyes, which were beginning to glisten with tears of frustration, and then went toward the edge of the parking lot to search for a rock. Presently she came back with one the size of a brick.

"How's this?" she asked.

"Fine," said Rick. "That's good."

She handed it to him. Rick looked around, just in case God, in the form of the state police or a car thief, showed up.

"Here goes nothing," he muttered, and he swung the rock against the window. He was unprepared for it bouncing back on him, and it flew out of his hand.

"Holy shit," he said. "That window's hard."

He picked up the rock and this time put his one hundred eighty pounds into it. Again the rock bounced back from the window, and Rick had to move out of the way to make sure he didn't hurt himself. He took a look at Phyllis. She was standing there biting her nails and looking like she'd just heard that she was about to be executed.

Rick had an image of Harold galloping toward the park on a horse, shotgun held in his right hand, the reins resting lightly in his left. He felt a sense of urgency. *Break the fucking window now, or get shot dead on the spot.* He could see the headlines: "Beautiful Blonde and Ugly Mexicano Cripple Found Shot Dead in Lovers' Tryst." Rick picked up the rock again and put everything into it. The window broke. *Fear is a great motivator,* he thought.

Using the rock, he knocked out the remaining safety glass from the window, and then he reached in and opened the door. Phyllis used their blanket to brush the glass out of the way. Rick reminded her to throw their picnic remains into the nearby garbage can. Fumbling, she retrieved her cell phone from her purse in the trunk and called Joan to ask her to take in the girls, saying only that she'd be a little late getting home.

Once on the road and heading home, they looked at each other and sighed in relief.

"Just tell him what happened … except for the you-me part. It's the truth. He may be pissed that there's the expense of fixing the window, but he'll have to believe it. It's true."

Phyllis glanced at him sideways and half-smiled. "Easy for you to say." Then she added, "I'm also going to have to take a shower. I've got the smell of you all over me."

"I'll see you tomorrow at the hospital?" he asked.

"Yeah, assuming I'm still alive. I'll let you know then how things went."

"Good. Listen, when we get into the city, leave me off anywhere it's convenient. I'll take a cab back to the hospital. I don't want to hold you up any longer than necessary."

Phyllis looked at her watch, already showing a quarter to three. "Okay," she agreed.

When she stopped at a corner where Rick could hail a cab, he leaned over and gave her a big kiss. "Thanks for the adventure," he said, laughing.

She took a big sigh. "I'm getting too old for this shit," she said.

"Wait till you get to be my age. This is the shit that keeps you young."

Phyllis reached into the back and got his crutches, and Rick maneuvered his way out of the car and closed the door. She blew him a kiss and roared off. Rick looked after her fondly, half in disbelief and half in relief. Then he looked around for a cab.

V

———•◆•———

Rick made a determined effort to replace the phone slowly into its cradle. Teeth clenched, he felt like slamming the receiver down as hard as possible or throwing it across the room. But deliberately he placed it all the way down and then slowly unclenched his fingers from around it, as if he were letting go of her throat after deciding not to strangle her. *Goddamn it!* He lay back on his pillow, recalling the glorious sex from earlier that afternoon ... and then to hear from Phyllis now that she didn't want to see him anymore. The contrast of emotions was too much. He couldn't take it all in.

The conversation replayed itself in his head: "I'm sorry, Rick, I really am. It's not what I want to do. I just can't think of another solution. I can't go through this again."

"But what happened? Tell me what happened. Did he find out? Did he hurt you?"

"Rick, it was just awful. He wouldn't stop asking questions. No, he doesn't know anything. Not really. But he suspects something. I swear he was like—I don't know what—a dog with a bone. He wouldn't let go. Why did I need to go out into the country? Was I meeting somebody out there? Did somebody attack me? Was somebody after me? He couldn't believe that I broke the window in the car. 'I can't believe you did that,' he kept saying. 'It's not like you. This doesn't make sense. You're not telling me the truth. What are you covering up? Why won't you be truthful with me? Is there somebody else? Who is it?' Rick, he wouldn't let up."

"What did you tell him? Did you tell him anything? How did it end?"

"I told him essentially what we had decided on: that I decided to drive out to the lake to relax and ended up locking myself out of the car. Rick, I don't really understand why, but he was suspicious from the get-go. Maybe things between us have been worse than I thought. I don't know. Anyway, Rick, it's been great. You've been great. Fantastic. You're a real sweetheart. Really, you are. But I can't take any more chances right now. We can't see each other anymore. Even at the hospital, let's be real cool and careful. I don't know if he's got somebody watching me or what, but I can't risk it. Listen, Rick, I have to go. I just stepped out for a minute, and I've got to get back. I'll see you tomorrow at the hospital." And she hung up.

In recalling the conversation, Rick could hear the fear shaking her voice, and he knew that it was unfair of him to complain. She was the one who was gambling with her life, after all. She was risking her marriage, her daughters, scandal. While he wasn't putting anything in jeopardy—*well, maybe getting shot by a jealous husband*, but he knew that that was probably far-fetched and unlikely. On the one hand, it was reassuring to have heard her say that she really liked him. On the other hand, maybe she was only being nice, letting him down easy. Had the sex really been as great as he thought it was? Had she been faking it all along? He wasn't sure he believed her. Coralee had never given him any indication that he was great in the sack.

And then, there was that little abortive romance with his physical therapist back at Walter Reed. When you come right down to it, she had dumped him too. Well, that wasn't entirely true. What Peggy had said was that if he had no intention of getting more serious, if all it meant to him was getting laid, then regretfully she was going to call it quits. She had actually used the word *regretfully*. There had also been another brief affair with a woman named Tina since he'd been here in Oklahoma City, but that ending had been as much from his lack of interest as it was from hers. Still, insofar as it had been something that had not worked out, he now felt like it also represented a failure of his.

Maybe he was feeling sorry for himself, wallowing in self-pity by listing all the recent rejections he had suffered, all the losses. Of course, the one real loss he had suffered was his leg. Maybe the reality was that after an initial fascination with him, women decided that they didn't want to be burdened by being with a cripple and were looking for an excuse to break things off, even if what they had experienced had been really good ... or not.

Rick felt sweaty all of a sudden, and he knew that he was experiencing anxiety, fear that everything really was all over for him, that now he really was a total failure at everything. What he wanted to do at that moment was to stop thinking about all of this, to go to sleep, to go back to the way things had been before the explosion, to before this nightmare ever began. In fact, just the opposite happened. Memories, thoughts, and feelings poured into his head, drowning him in whirlpools of confusion and fear.

In high school, his track coach had told him, "Look, Garcia, without the track, you're just another reasonably bright kid, no different really from thousands of other reasonably bright kids. But those legs of yours set you apart. Your talent for running makes you special, part of an elite. Colleges are going to be coming after you and recruiting you. You've got to take advantage of the opportunity, you understand? Strike while the iron is hot, and all that. Get it while the getting's good. *Comprende?* So I want you to train, to really practice. Maximize this talent. Don't waste it. Go for the gold. You hear me? You've got to work your ass off, Garcia. Don't let the world pass you by. Don't be a loser."

Don't be a loser. That's what his father was always saying too.

"Don't settle for second-best, Rick. Don't let them put you down because of who you are, because of our heritage. Show them what

57

you're made of, Rick. Don't be a quitter. You've got to give it all you've got. That's the only way we'll ever overcome those prejudices they have against us Mexicanos. Make them accept you, Rick. Make them acknowledge that you're a winner, as good as anybody and better than most."

And in college, his ROTC commander had said, "Garcia, with a degree in engineering from the University of Texas and an officer's commission in the army, you'll be set. Big firms and corporations don't want to hire some green kid still wet behind the ears with no practical experience. But give them somebody who's qualified and has experience managing people, handling responsibilities—an officer—then they'll give you the moon. You've got what it takes, Garcia, and the army is color-blind. It doesn't care if you're white, black, Latino, or what. Take advantage of it, Garcia, and look sharp. Stay in the service, and you can go all the way to the top, really be somebody special. You hear me, Garcia? You listen to me. I'm telling you like it is."

He had thought of staying in the service and, in fact, had done two tours, eight years. If he hadn't married Coralee, he might have still been in, but she had pressured him until he gave in and got out, opting to go into the reserves when he started up his business. That's where he'd been until they called him up in 2003 and sent him to Iraq.

Although they had kept his unit together, the army had put a number of experienced personnel with them, including his sergeant, Hennessy. Rick missed Hennessy even more than any of his other friends he'd trained with in the reserves. Hennessy felt like a brother and reminded him of Matt in some ways. There was a teasing give and take between them, busting each other, supporting each other, confiding in each other. For some unexplained reason, Rick felt their friendship to be special. Rick wondered if Henn was still alive.

Then Rick thought about Jasper, the driver who had been killed when their Humvee had exploded under them. *He was just a kid— what, nineteen, twenty?* Rick was old enough to be his father. Straight off some farm someplace in Pennsylvania. A rural kid with a shock of blond hair and blue eyes that girls would die for. A nice quiet kid. Rick felt his eyes tearing up. In all this time, five months, this was the first time he let himself feel the sorrow over the boy's death. Rick let himself go and felt himself sobbing, his nose running, catching his breath. He knew he was crying for himself as well as for Jasper. He let himself cry for them both. *It was so sad. So unnecessarily, unfairly sad.* Rick let himself cry it all out and fell asleep mourning for the young farm boy.

———

He was driving along a country road in an old convertible. It was summer. Young women were strolling along the side of the road, wearing simple cotton dresses that clung seductively to their thin shapes. He was looking them over as he slowly drove by. They were looking at him shyly and smiling. He felt encouraged. He noticed some of them whispering to each other. He wondered what they were saying. Some of them seemed to be laughing. He noticed some of them pointing at him and laughing. He began to wonder if he could trust them. He was feeling unsafe and decided to step on the gas, but there was an explosion, and he felt himself flying up into the clouds. He could see down to the ground. It was very far away, and he couldn't make out any people. He kept lifting higher and higher. He was feeling cold and began to worry about surviving the landing when he inevitably fell back down to earth. He didn't know what to expect. He was afraid that the impact would kill him. He remembered hearing that if you dream that you're falling and you actually land, you'll die. He didn't want to die. He was scared. He thought he might be dreaming and tried to wake up.

VI

——◆·◆——

L ate in the afternoon, when all of the clinics were over for the
day, Rick and a few of the other amputees often went to a bar
a block away from the hospital. Usually, they'd wait for each other
in the lobby of the hospital, and then, in their wheelchairs or on
their crutches, they'd form a caravan and hop and roll their way
over to the Recovery Room, taking a perverse pleasure in forcing
traffic to wait for them as they meandered across the street. It was
immensely satisfying to have the upper hand over the "normals."
They called themselves the Brigade from Hell and referred to each
other as Brigadier.

Going to the Recovery Room was a long-established tradition,
passed on to newcomers as old-timers got discharged and went
home or on to another treatment facility. A table in the corner was
unofficially reserved for the Brigade, and women or other friends and
family members generally weren't invited to join them until after
six o'clock. The first hour or so was set aside for them to unwind.
Rick had been invited to join the Brigade when he arrived at the
hospital, and on most days he looked forward to the socializing, the
bantering, and the booze.

Sometimes it turned into a gripe session. Somebody always had
something to complain about. All of them were angry or bitter and
still mired in the process of grieving for their lost limbs, as well as

for any other losses they may have suffered. As a group, they didn't take any guff from anybody, and the other regulars at the bar had long ago learned not to provoke them. Their anger was always near the surface, and their heavy drinking allowed it to quickly emerge into view, like toxins from a septic system oozing up from overly saturated earth. But often, the group turned seriously therapeutic as one or another exposed himself and laid himself bare to the group, asking for feedback or advice. They trusted each other and could confront each other knowing that no real offense would be taken, that any challenge was meant to be helpful, a wake-up call.

All of the men were younger than Rick. He was the old man of the group at forty-six, and he also outranked them, although having been made a colonel while in the reserves made him less proud of his rank, as if he'd acquired it at a discount. A few of the men were still in their early twenties, and to them, Rick was something of a father figure. It was a mixed group—Mexicano, like him, whites, and African Americans. They got along well together. On this day, there were only four of them.

"So how's it going, Colonel? You seem a little down today." That was Fernandez, a second-generation Mexican American from west Texas. Like Rick, he had lost a leg above the knee. But in addition, he had suffered a mess of internal wounds and was having a lot of difficulty with his gastrointestinal system: diarrhea, malabsorption syndrome, constipation, cramps, acute pain, etc.

Rick made a face, "It shows, huh?"

"Sure, amigo. Of course it shows. Anything you want to talk about?"

"Nah, Pedro. I'm just feeling sorry for myself. I thought I had something going, but it looks like it's in the crapper."

"Well, what else is new? That's life. Sooner or later, everything ends up in the crapper."

"Ain't that the truth?" That was Osgood. Dwayne Robert Osgood was a twenty-two-year-old from Kansas City. Du-Bob, as they called him, had lost his right foot and right forearm along with his right ear and the hearing that went with it. "Ain't it something though, the way God makes everything turn to shit? I mean everything. Ain't nothing that stays the way it's supposed to. You take my pecker, for instance. When I wake up in the morning, I think it'll stand at attention forever, but it don't."

"Thanks, Du-Bob, but you can keep your hard-on, if you don't mind." Preston Jackson, Press, was a captain, the second-oldest in the group at thirty-five, and one of the few blacks. Press had been a career military man and had been looking toward his retirement pension when, like Rick, his Humvee had been attacked. A rocket-propelled grenade had pierced its thin shell and exploded inside, smashing Press's back and leaving him a paraplegic. Press's wife and kids had moved to Oklahoma City to be with him, and once or twice a week Doreen joined them at the Recovery Room.

"Du-Bob's right, though," Rick offered. "Everything does come to an end and die and decay and return to the earth."

"From dust to dust," Du-Bob agreed. "Ain't nothing lasts forever."

"Still," Press lamented, "that doesn't make it any easier to accept. A loss is a loss, and it's still shit no matter how inevitable it is. You look at us here, every one of us. We've all lost … a hell of a lot more than we were ready to. And ain't none of us is happy about it. No matter what kind of face we try to put on it, this ain't a fucking gift we've been given. No way."

Rick thought he heard one of the regulars at the bar mutter something about crying the blues.

"Any of you assholes over there got anything to contribute to our discussion, you just speak right up. Don't be shy. We don't want to miss any of your smart-ass pearls of wisdom."

Nobody at the bar said anything. A couple of guys gave them a look and then turned away.

Rick continued to stare over toward the bar and said, loud enough for them to hear, "Fucking pussies," before turning back to the table.

"Let it go, Rick," said Press. "It ain't worth getting upset about."

"I know," Rick replied, sighing. "I'm just not myself. Everything seems so ... futile, pointless. Sure, those assholes have to deal with loss too. I'm not saying that we're the only ones. But, Christ, look at us. Our whole freaking lives are turned upside down and inside out. Nothing's the same as it was. Everything's changed." He poured himself another glass of beer from the pitcher and slumped back into his chair.

There was a long silence before Fernandez piped up, "Didn't somebody say this was supposed to be happy hour? Christ, what a bunch we are today. Doesn't anybody have anything positive to talk about?" Pedro looked around the group.

"Don't look at me," said Du-Bob. "I'm still wondering where my boner went to." Everybody chuckled, and the tension eased a bit.

Rick looked over at Press Jackson. "Press, your wife coming in today?"

"Yeah, I expect she'll be here later and have a beer with us. Then I guess she'll take me home for a visit with the kids before she drops me back at the hospital."

All of them were staying in the wing of the hospital dedicated to rehab medicine, where there were medical staff to help them with their special needs. They could come and go pretty much as they pleased, except for a ten o'clock curfew.

"How about you?" Press asked. "Your wife bringing the kids in again anytime soon?"

"Not that I know of, Press. I've been here six weeks now, and she only brought them over twice. I understand that she doesn't want to see me ... you know, with the divorce and all. I know it's awkward between us. But, Christ, she could drop the kids off or have her no-good, shiftless brother bring them down. It's not like she's that fucking far away."

"How far is it?" asked Du-Bob. "I mean, if it's not too far, we could form a train and wheel ourselves over. Hell, Press and I have motorized chairs. We'll be the engines and pull you all along."

Du-Bob thought this was really funny and giggled as he imagined the scene.

"That's all your wife would need," said Pedro, "to see the fucking Brigade roll up in front of her house in our little mini-Humvees."

Rick cracked a smile. "She always said that I wanted a parade. I can picture her standing on her mother's front porch with her hands on her hips and saying, 'Well, Mr. Richard Garcia, looks like you finally got that parade you've been wanting.'"

"Well, how far is it?" asked Du-Bob.

"Too far. Much too far." Then he thought for a while. "But, you know, Du-Bob, you gave me an idea. There's nothing stopping me from getting a cab to take me over there."

Press leaned forward. "That's true, Rick, you could do that. But think it through first. I know you want to see your kids, but make sure that this would be helpful rather than make things worse."

"Hell, Press, I've got a right to see my kids."

"That's not the point, Rick. The point is, will showing up on her doorstep piss her off and make things worse, or will it really help? I don't know, but you've got to think about it."

"Have you called her?" asked Fernandez. Pedro was himself divorced and had no children—at least none he knew about.

Rick lowered his head in thought. "That's a good question, Pedro. I called her a couple of times the first week I was here. It's very strained between us. I've been reluctant to call since."

"Well," said Pedro, "you know how that counselor in our group meetings is always emphasizing good communication—good listening as well as expressing ourselves clearly." Pedro turned to Press and asked, "What does he call it?"

"Declaring ourselves, making our needs known."

Pedro looked at Rick, and Rick caught his message.

"Right, fellas. You're fucking right again. I have not been declaring myself. I'll give the bitch a call tomorrow."

"Ooh," said Du-Bob, "that sounds like a constructive attitude."

Rick tried to reach over and give him a playful punch on the arm. "Fuck you, Dwayne. Just wait until you get married and have a woman in your life to contend with."

"I've already got my mother, Colonel. That's bad enough. I don't need no more, thank you very much."

Everybody in Millie's house was in the living room watching TV when the phone rang. Ella quickly jumped up and ran into the kitchen to answer it. When she spent some time there in conversation, everyone except George expressed some curiosity about who it was.

Then Ella called loudly from the kitchen, "Ma, it's Daddy and he wants to talk to you."

Coralee's worried hunch proved to be correct. It had been a few weeks since Rick had called, and she had mixed feelings about it. She was glad not having had to deal with the tension between them. But she felt some guilt at the lack of contact between Rick and the children, and, although she rationalized that Rick had a responsibility to maintain his relationship with them, she also thought that perhaps she should have done more to encourage him in that regard. Ella looked up, smiling, as she handed the phone to her mother.

"Rick?"

"Yeah, hi. How are you doing?"

"We're doing pretty well," she said somewhat guardedly, reluctant to go into any details and open her life to him. She wanted to keep that door closed.

"Good. I'm glad to hear that." There was a brief but awkward silence.

"Listen," he said, "I was wondering how you would feel if I came by sometime ... I thought I could take a cab over and spend some time with the kids."

Coralee sucked in her breath, but remained silent.

"I just figured," he continued, "that it seems it's difficult for you to arrange for me to see the kids over here. I just thought ..."

Coralee felt pressured to say something, to answer him one way or the other, but she didn't want to. She didn't want to have to deal with this.

"I don't know. I'm not sure, Rick. When were you thinking of?" She was hoping that he might mention a time when she'd be at work or, almost as good, a time when her mother might not be home. She knew that Rick's visiting the house would give her mother a truckload of ammunition for her almost daily attempts to get Coralee to give up the idea of divorce and to attempt a reconciliation.

"Well, originally, I guess, I was thinking of this evening, but I know that's pretty short notice. I guess almost any afternoon after four thirty would be good. During the week, that is. Weekends I'm pretty much open. We don't have any regular clinics on the weekends. What do you think?"

Coralee shifted her stance and scratched her ear, and then she became conscious of the fact that Rick couldn't see that she was trying to think. "I tell you what, Rick. Suppose I bring the kids by the hospital for a visit. Maybe this Saturday?"

"Coralee, that would be terrific. Wonderful. What time?"

Coralee hesitated. She was angry that she was being forced to make the decision. At the same time, she knew that if he had suggested a time, she would have resented his assumption that everything should go the way he wanted. She smiled to herself and, in a moment of generosity, suggested late morning, imagining that it could lead into lunch and that the kids would get a kick out of eating in the hospital cafeteria.

"That would be great, Cora. Really. I really appreciate this. You have no idea." His voice grew a little raspy. "I'll be waiting down in the main lobby for you." Then he added, "You're coming too, right?"

Coralee had assumed that she would be there and, in her mind's eye, pictured herself having a good heart-to-heart with him, clarifying some things between them.

"Yes, Rick, I'll be there. There are some things I suppose we should talk about."

"Yeah," he said, "I guess so. That'll be good. I mean, it'll be good to see you and good to talk about this."

"Yes. Well, then, we'll see you Saturday morning about eleven in the lobby."

There was a slight pause, and then Rick said softly, "Thanks, hon," and replaced the handset on the phone.

When Coralee returned to the living room, all eyes, except for George's, turned to her. Her mother quickly turned back to the TV, but she had a big smile on her face. Coralee had a vision of her mother's cheeks bursting like a child's birthday balloon. Coralee thought that the kids seemed more wary, as if they were unsure if it was safe to reveal their feelings. She felt a twinge of guilt at that and made an effort to force herself to smile naturally when she spoke to their upturned faces.

"It's all right to be happy. We're going to visit your father on Saturday. We can have lunch there in the cafeteria."

"Cool," said Thomas, and he and Ella gave each other a high five.

George turned to Mildred and asked what was going on, and she told him, speaking loudly into his ear, "Coralee and the children are going to visit Rick in the hospital on Saturday."

George looked at the kids and then at Coralee, smiled, and then returned to watching the TV with its subtitles for the hearing impaired.

Coralee saw that the children were sneaking smiles at each other, and she felt glad for them. She tried to get her mind back on the program, but she kept imagining how her conversation with Rick might go and felt her whole body growing tense in anticipation.

"I have an idea," she said, getting up from her seat on the sofa. "Why don't I go out and buy us some ice cream?"

"Can I come?" shouted Ella.

"Sure you can, angel," she said.

"Get something with chocolate in it," suggested Mildred.

"Of course," Coralee agreed.

"Don't get coffee," Thomas pleaded, "or pistachio."

"Don't worry. I know what you like."

"Where's Cora going to?" asked George.

"To buy you some ice cream," Millie yelled in his ear. "She's so happy, she's just got to have some chocolate ice cream to celebrate."

"Go on, Momma. You keep it up, and Ella and I will eat it all up ourselves."

But she smiled to herself as she and Ella went out the back door to get in the car. *Such a mixture of feelings,* she thought. *I'm nervous and angry and scared and happy all at the same time.* She shook her head in confusion as she got into the car after Ella and turned the key in the ignition.

Rick wheeled himself over to where Press and Pedro were, and when the next commercial came on, he answered their questioning looks with a smile.

"She's bringing them over Saturday morning."

"Way to go, man," said Pedro.

Press smiled. "You'd better do some serious practicing with that leg of yours between now and then. You don't want your kids to find out you're a cripple."

"Fuck you, Press."

"Hey, I think this calls for a celebration," Pedro said quietly.

Rick looked at him curiously. "You got something stashed away?"

Pedro put a finger to his lips and leaned in closer. "I've got a bottle of vodka hidden in my room. Next commercial, I'll go get it. You guys get some soda, and I'll pour some into the cans."

Rick shook his head in disbelief, but also smiled in admiration at Pedro's ingenuity. He really could use a drink right now. Having alcohol—or, God forbid, drugs—in the hospital was one thing the staff was dead set against. It was a major violation of rules and could result in a discharge from the program; although they suspected there had to be serious and repeated violations for that to really happen. Still, there was some sense of excitement at breaking the rules and secretly getting away with something. At the next commercial, Rick got the cold cans of soda while Pedro went back to his room. Press had caught Dwayne's eyes and nodded to him, so by the time Pedro returned, Du-Bob had joined them. They sat, gathered toward the back of the room. There wasn't much need for talking. They watched the movie and sipped at their drinks, enjoying the feeling of sharing something, being comrades. It felt good.

VII

———◦•◦———

Rick was sitting in the lobby when he saw Thomas and Ella get out of Coralee's car and, holding hands, walk toward the entrance. He had come down early and had been waiting nervously for half an hour, but he breathed a sigh of relief at seeing his kids. Rick struggled to his feet, and supporting himself with his crutches, started toward the entrance so that they would see him as soon as they got inside.

Ella saw him and ran to him. She reached up to be hugged and almost made him lose his balance. Thomas took his time walking over and kept his hands in his pockets. But he smiled and said, "Hi, Dad. How are you feeling?"

Rick reached out his hand and laid it on the side of Thomas's cheek.

"I'm doing fine, Tomaso, fine. Hey, you guys are a sight for sore eyes. I was afraid you might not be coming. Goddamn, you look good."

Thomas smiled and hung his head. Ella, gesturing toward his crutches, asked if they should sit down.

"Isn't your mother coming in?" asked Rick.

"Uh, she said to tell you that she was going to go pick up a couple of things and give us some time together and that she would join us in a little while." Thomas stammered slightly in delivering this long speech and seemingly examined the ceiling of the tall lobby with great interest as he spoke.

Rick noticed and thought back to when Thomas had been two years old. What a sweet boy he'd been. At one family Christmas dinner, before Coralee gave birth to Ella, Thomas had charmed the entire family at his mother's long dining room table with his engaging attempts at being funny and getting everybody to laugh. Now he seemed shy and uncomfortable with himself. He reminded Rick of himself at that age.

"There's a little courtyard back here off the lobby. I thought we might sit out there. Mom will be able to see us, or we'll see her when she comes in. Okay?"

Ella nodded vigorously, while Thomas, his hands still in his pockets, looked around to see where Rick meant. Rick led the way out to the tables and chairs in the courtyard. Ella held the door for them and then ran ahead and picked out a table.

Rick lowered himself gingerly onto a chair and laid his crutches to the side. "So," he began uncertainly, "what's happening in your lives?"

Thomas looked away, but Ella jumped right in. "Uncle Larry got arrested again last week. And Grandma said that he didn't do nothin' that bad, but that he broke his parole. And Ma said it would be good for him if they sent him away, that maybe he'd be able to straighten out and learn a job or something."

Rick had been wondering what was happening with his deadbeat brother-in-law and was interested to hear this news. "It sounds like Grandma is a little upset, but Mom hopes it will turn into good news."

"Uh-huh," she mumbled.

"How about you, sweetie? What do you think about Uncle Larry being put in jail again?"

She shrugged her shoulders and did her little pout thing. "Well, he was only in jail for one day, and then he got out on bail or something like that. I dunno. I'll miss him, I guess, if he has to go to prison. He's kind of fun to be around. He's always making jokes and teasing us. But sometimes he's in a bad mood, and he don't want to play or nothing. Then he can be all kinds of crabby and mean."

"How about you, champ? This business with Uncle Larry make you feel bad?"

Thomas shook his head and started to look away again.

"Hey, Thomas," Rick said. "Come here." He held out his arm, and Thomas came around from the other side of the table. "Come here, son." Rick put his arm around him and pulled him close, hugging him tightly. "I hate to see you like this. You seem so unhappy. Are you?" He looked at Thomas and saw that his eyes were glistening.

"You know, when I was back in Walter Reed, the hospital in Washington, I had such a vivid dream about you. I felt like you were right there with me, and I felt so good hearing your voice."

Thomas looked at him. "What did I say?"

"Was I there too?" chimed in Ella.

"Yes, you were there too," Rick lied, "but you ran off to play. Thomas told me he had joined a track team at school." Then, turning back to his son, still holding him, he continued, "And I was so proud of you, and I told you how I had started running track and how alike I thought we were. And I felt so close to you. And you asked me to come to Oklahoma, and I said I would. And look. Goddamn it, I did."

Thomas smiled.

"Are you glad I'm here?" Rick asked.

Thomas took his hands out of his pockets and returned the hug, putting his arms around his dad's shoulders.

"I'm glad you're here," added Ella, and she joined in for a group hug.

"And so am I," said Rick, putting his other arm around her. "I'm real glad that we can be together. I missed you both so, so much. So tell me," Rick said after composing himself, "are you running?"

Thomas shook his head and smiled. "No, they don't have anything like that here for seventh grade. But next year, in eighth grade, they do. Also, for eighth grade this year they started up a fencing club, and I thought that would be cool."

Rick raised his eyebrows. "Fencing? Wow, that does sound cool. That would be fantastic. I can just see you. Like Zorro, huh?"

Thomas smiled again. "Yeah, kind of like that. They have different kinds of swords, you know? Saber, foil. It looks like fun. I've watched them practice sometimes."

"That would be wonderful," said Rick. "And how about you, senorita? What are you getting into these days?"

Ella made a face, wrinkling her nose. "Nothing much, Dad. There aren't too many kids around where Grandma lives, so there's no one really to play with. And Ma doesn't want me going off the block, so I can't go visit my friends from school."

"So what do you do with your time then?"

"Homework. Sometimes me and Grandma and George play cards. I'm getting real good at pinochle. Or Ma and I and sometimes," she gave Thomas a punch on his arm, "my brother ... we do jigsaw puzzles."

Rick smiled. "Sounds a little bor-ing," he said.

Ella nodded. "You said it. Bor-ing."

An awkward silence ensued, during which Rick tried to think of the questions that he should ask to engage them and make them feel comfortable with him again. He wanted to ask them about living at their grandmother's, but he thought it would be intrusive and might make them feel put in the middle between him and Coralee.

"Do you guys miss New Jersey?" he finally asked.

Ella countered with, "Tommy has a girlfriend."

"I do not," he immediately blurted out.

"Well," said Rick, "I would kind of hope that you did, Thomas. A girlfriend can be kind of neat."

"He does too, Daddy. Her name is Marcia." This time Thomas didn't deny it.

"Well, good for Thomas. It's nice to have a girlfriend. How about you, Ella? Do you have a particular boy that you like?"

Ella made a face and shook her head. "No way."

"Well," Rick said, "you have changed then. I remember when you came home from your first day in kindergarten, and the first thing you announced as soon as you were through the front door was that you were going to marry Joel Greenberg when you grew up."

Thomas laughed out loud. "Joel Greenberg. That nerd?"

Ella tried to reach around Rick to swat at him. Then Rick saw Coralee entering the lobby and told Ella to go meet her and bring her out to their table.

As Coralee and Ella approached the table, Rick indicated that Coralee should have a seat and join them. He looked at her.

"You look good," he said.

She smiled and thanked him. "How you kids doing? Getting hungry yet?"

Ella and Thomas both shrugged and looked at each other.

Turning to Rick, she said, "I thought we might have lunch in the cafeteria. It would be a treat for them."

"Sure," he said. "That would be fine."

Coralee smiled briefly and turned her attention to the children. "Having a good visit?"

"I told Daddy about Uncle Larry getting arrested," Ella declared.

Coralee rolled her eyes and glanced at Rick.

"Hey, don't sweat it," he reassured her. "I don't expect you to be able to control your brother's behavior."

"It's embarrassing," she said. "Fifty-one years old, and he's still acting like a shiftless hoodlum adolescent. And it's embarrassing to have a mother who puts up with it and turns a blind eye to it all. For her, he can do no wrong."

"Kids seem all right with it."

"Sure they are. He's one of them. Just another kid to play with, and when he's naughty he gets a time-out." Then she looked at them. "If I ever—you hear me—if I ever catch you behaving like your uncle Larry, believe me, I will make your life a bloody hell."

Both children averted their gaze and shrank into themselves under her withering glare.

"The kids are good, Cora. You've done a great job with them, and they're both too smart to ever do any drugs or anything like that. Right?" he asked, turning to them.

Thomas volunteered, "There's some kids in my school … I'm pretty sure that they do drugs and stuff. They think they're cool, but everybody just thinks they're stupid. Nobody wants to be like them."

Rick gave him a squeeze. "Well," he said, "if you guys are hungry or want anything to drink, we can go into the cafeteria. They've got soft ice cream for dessert."

"I'm hungry," said Ella. "I want a hot dog. Do they have hot dogs?"

"I think so," said Rick, "and fries. Let's go see."

They got up and walked slowly so that Rick on his crutches, swinging his artificial leg, could keep up. Coralee walked ahead, leaving the kids to accompany Rick and open the doors for him. After they finished lunch, Coralee suggested that the kids get some dessert and take it outside while she and their father discussed some things privately. Excited, they hurried away to get ice cream.

"So," she started, "how are you doing?"

"Truth is they're having a lot of trouble getting this leg to fit just right. There's a lot of chafing and rubbing that's giving me trouble. Half the time it's in the shop and I don't have a chance to use it and build up my leg strength."

Coralee made a sympathetic face.

"How about you? It can't be a lot of fun for you over there at your mother's."

"I had no idea that I'd be there this long, almost seven months now. I got a job at the Holiday Inn almost as soon as we got here, but you won't believe what they pay down here. I don't know how people do it: pay rent, food, car expenses, health insurance, clothes. It's like slave labor. I've been saving up, but I still can't afford to be on my own. The truth is, I'm damn lucky to have Momma to stay with, even if she does her damnedest to drive me crazy."

"You see the lawyer yet?"

"One of the things I'm saving up for." She looked away.

"You wouldn't, by any chance, be having any second thoughts about this, would you?"

Coralee looked at him. "This is what I was afraid of," she said.

Rick returned her look. "Coralee. We've both been through a lot. We're both in a hard place. We don't need to make it harder."

She turned away again. They were silent for a minute.

"I think about it all the time, Rick. With Momma on me constantly to reconcile, how could I not think about it? But you were right, in that letter you wrote. I'm not good wife material. It's not just that I don't have patience with you, with your need to be recognized and be taken care of. I get downright furious with it. I see it every day, Rick, being with my mother, seeing her with George and with Larry. I just ..." She threw up her hands in frustration. "I have no tolerance for that at all, except with the kids. I'm a very angry woman, Rick. I like you. I like men. I'm horny as hell. I don't really want to be alone. Right now it would be great to have some help. But I'm not a loving person. I don't know if I'm capable of loving, of feeling it or showing it. I'm sorry, Rick. I wish I could give you what you want. But I can't. I don't know if I have anything to give anybody ... or if I even want to."

"Well," Rick said after a while, and then he sighed and looked out toward the courtyard where the kids were. "We don't have to do anything yet. Everything will keep as it is."

They managed not to look at each other for a while.

"By the way, I decided not to file for bankruptcy or to sell the building in Morristown. I'm renting it out, both the office and the apartment. Right now, all of the income is going to pay off our debts. I figured, with property appreciating, the longer we hold on to it, the better it'll be. It's a good piece of property. If we sell it now, we won't really have that much left over. So it's better that we pay off the debts slowly and let it continue to grow. And if either of us decides to ..."

Coralee looked at him and sighed deeply.

"Well, I'm just saying, with it being there, it gives us more options. Who knows?"

"Yeah," she murmured. "Who knows?"

"Listen, Coralee ..."

She looked across the table at him.

"I was wondering," Rick hesitated, "if we can work out some regular kind of visitation thing, you know? Either the kids coming down here, or my coming by and seeing the kids there ... or something. I'm sure it would be better for them too, knowing that there's some predictability in my seeing them."

She looked out at the courtyard at them and smiled.

"You're right," she said. "This is good ... Saturday morning and lunch."

"It works for me," he said.

"I can drop them off, and you can have a nice visit. If you're planning something for them and want more time, we can arrange that."

"That's good, Cora. I appreciate that."

She smiled briefly. "I know that you need each other. I know." Then she looked at him intently, and her eyes filled up. "They love you very much, Rick. You've been a good father, and they've missed you. Ella worries about you a great deal. Right now she wants to be a nurse when she grows up. Tommy ... he keeps so much to himself. But he was very excited about coming today. He kept changing the shirt he was going to wear." She smiled and nodded for emphasis. "I'm glad that you asked," she said.

VIII

<hr/>

D ear Colonel Garcia,

I sure was real glad to receive your letter and hear that you arrived back home in the States in one piece. Well, two pieces, I guess. Still, that's a lot better than many. As you see, I am still here. Your reserve unit returned to the States right after Christmas. All together, I think there were about 12 percent casualties. You have my sympathies. I know many of those reservists were your friends. Some of them became mine too. For me, I try not to focus on having lost them. Rather, I try to focus on being grateful for having had the opportunity to serve with them and get to know them. It works for me. Well, some of the time.

Now I am babysitting a company of the National Guard from Illinois. Aside from that, everything is the same—one step forward and two steps back. Your bridge got finished back in December and is still like brand-new, except the road at either end is being constantly cratered from car bombs and land mines, and so it doesn't get used all that much by vehicles anymore, mostly just local pedestrians and bicycles.

I was sorry that I didn't get to say good-bye or anything. They ship you guys out pretty fast nowadays. That's one thing that has really improved in this man's army. Of course, I'm sorry to hear about your leg. Tough break (no pun intended). Still, you're alive and safe and at least have a shot at getting back on your feet (ha-ha). I'll probably be here for the duration. This is the life I chose. What can I tell you? I found a home here in the army. Although, sometimes I wonder at it myself. Still, no family is perfect, as we discussed many times.

I wish you the best, Colonel. Give your kids a hug from me, seeing as I don't have any of my own. Tell them they should be proud of the contribution you made over here. It was an honor serving under you. Besides, you were a good friend, and I miss your company. Be well. Keep us in your thoughts.

Sgt. Michael Hennessy

Rick finished reading the letter. It was short, but it called up so many images: the dirty, sandy layer of dust on everything; the clear sky and high clouds; the sun; the fear; the tension; and the explosion. He could hear Henn's voice and see that cynical, mischievous glint in his eyes. He felt a little pang of guilt that he was home and Henn was still over there, but in the next instant, he was angry that he was here in the hospital and that the rest of his unit was home in Jersey and free to resume their old lives—or at least, he remembered, some of them were. He wheeled over to his bedside table and, opening the bottom drawer, took out a plastic water bottle that he'd filled with vodka. After looking around, he poured some in his soda can and then returned the bottle to the cabinet. Then he took a swig. He had been doing this more often lately.

"Henn, why the hell do you smoke those things? You got a death wish or something? Someday, they're going to kill you."

Henn smiled that broad challenging smile of his. "We're sitting here in the middle of a fucking war, and you're concerned about me smoking cigarettes?"

Rick laughed at himself, at his tendency to be a controlling and protective daddy. "Sorry," he said. "That's something my mother would do."

Hennessy raised his eyebrows.

"I know," Rick said defensively. "It's crazy, isn't it? I rely so much on your experience out here, and yet I still feel responsible for you. As if it's up to me to keep you healthy and alive."

"Well, Colonel, I appreciate the sentiment, but I thought that was my job: keeping everybody alive."

"Your mother do that to you too?"

Henn turned to look back up at the ceiling of their tent, his arms behind his head. "What my mother gave me, what I got from her, was an instinct for staying alive."

Rick looked at him, expecting more, but that was all Hennessy had to say.

Rick leaned back in his chair, lifting the can to his lips and absentmindedly taking a gulp. He thought about his mother and pictured her back at their home, outside of San Antonio. Someone from his family called every few days, but mostly it was she. They had come up one weekend in Matt's van. Thomas and Ella had been delighted to see them. Someone had suggested a picnic, and he brought them out to the park where he'd gone with Phyllis. Just thinking of her got him aroused. He had been surprised by how many people were there on the weekend, but they had no trouble finding a picnic table—two of them, actually. Matt and Dad had carried one and put it next to the other. It felt good to have the whole family together. He could still hear them laughing, having a good time. At one point, he had looked over and noticed his mother's eyes. He sneaked a look at his father, and his father was looking at him.

Then his father had said, "Hey, Ginny, you want another soda pop?"

She had started a little and then smiled and said, "Okay." And then she looked at him and gave him a tired smile.

He had felt guilty at being the cause of such sadness. He drank again from the can.

Phyllis had come up to his table in the cafeteria a few days ago. She stood there holding her tray, as if she weren't sure if it was all right to sit down.

"Hey," he said. "Sit down. Come on."

She put her tray down, and sat down and looked around before smiling at him.

"How are you, Rick?"

"I'm coming along. My leg is getting stronger, and I'm resigned to the fact that I'm not going to get a newer model, at least not for quite a while." He laughed. "Maybe never, unless I decide to shell out fifty grand of my own money for it."

He didn't have to explain. He knew she understood how it worked. These new models were like Ferrari sports cars: filled with computer chips, handcrafted, and custom made for the wearer. Not like the off-the-shelf model he had with its stiff, permanently bent knee, which was constantly being altered to fit him as well as possible.

"How about you? How are you and Wild Man doing?"

"I'm getting a divorce from Harold."

Rick's eyes bugged out. "So," he said thoughtfully, "a divorce?"

She shrugged, as if to say, "Can you believe it? That I finally did it?"

"Congratulations," he said. "How did he take the news?"

Phyllis looked down at her coffee and muffin. "You know, Rick, I don't think he believes me." She took a sip and broke off a piece of her muffin and nibbled at it in small bites.

Rick watched her and started to grow hard, which made him grin.

81

Phyllis saw him and apparently misunderstood. "No, I'm serious. I'm sure he knows I intend to divorce him. He knows I want out. He has to know that. How could he not know that? But he looks at me with that sly, insulting grin, that superior I-know-something-that-you-don't-know-bitch grin on his face. I don't know what's going on in his mind. I don't trust him, Rick. That's the only reason I've been keeping a distance from you. You know that, don't you? I don't know what he's capable of. But I saw a lawyer, and things are in the works."

He deliberately did not respond to her question. He wasn't sure he knew how to respond to it. "Have you left yet?"

She shook her head.

"At first, I hoped that he'd move out. The girls' school is practically around the corner. I'd hate to have to move and make them change schools." She leaned back and reached for her coffee. "I guess that's what I'm going to have to do, though. He definitely is not going anywhere." She sipped. "What scares me is that he doesn't believe I'm going anywhere either."

Rick took another forkful of his dessert. After a few moments, he sat back, still chewing his pie.

"Phyllis, why are you telling me this?"

She glanced at him and then looked away, and after taking a deep breath she turned back to him. "I don't know. I wanted to talk to you. I missed you. I guess I was hoping you'd want to know what's been happening." She averted her eyes and drank some more of her coffee; then she looked up over the rim of her cup as he leaned forward.

"Phyllis, I don't know what to say. I've missed you too. Part of me understood that you were frightened and maybe feeling some regret that we'd gotten together. Mostly, when I think of our last time together, I think of how beautiful it was. And then I laugh at how funny it seemed, even though I realize it could have ended disastrously. But I was also very hurt. To see you in the halls and around the hospital these last few weeks or so and not even have you look at me or smile or anything … I don't know if I really understand that. I look back and I question everything. I don't know what to believe anymore. You know what I mean? I don't know what's true and what's not. So now I'm wondering, what is it you want? What are you hoping for?"

Phyllis gave a little shrug and kept her eyes averted.

Rick continued, "I'm assuming that you don't really intend to start seeing anybody until this divorce thing is all over and Mr. Prickly Balls is out of your life." He paused and waited.

"Phyllis, am I right?"

She looked up at him and after a moment said, "I guess so. I guess I hadn't really thought it through. I saw you here, and I wanted to talk to you, wanted you to know what I was doing. I hoped you would care."

He sat back and finished his coffee.

"I do care," he said. "I hope it works out for you. I'd love to see you happy, and there's no doubt that once you're free of that prick, you'll at least have a shot at being happier. If I'm still here then, who knows? Lately, I haven't been much of an optimist, so I'm not building any castles in the air."

She smiled weakly and reached her hand across the table. He raised his eyebrows.

"You're sure you feel safe enough to do that?" he asked.

She flinched.

He smiled sheepishly and leaned forward and put his hand on hers. "I'm sorry. I can be a prick sometimes too."

Rick raised the can to his lips and drained it; then he turned his chair away from the window and wheeled himself out into the hall and down to their dayroom. *Too much time alone. Not a good thing sometimes.*

When he got to the dayroom, he saw Pedro sitting by the window, reading. He wheeled himself over.

Pedro looked up from his book. "Hey, compadre, what's up?"

"Nothing, much, Pedro. Just wondering if you want to get an early start over at Brigade headquarters."

Pedro grimaced. "You know what I've discovered? My stomach just won't take that shit anymore. I've tried everything so I could still enjoy a shot or a beer, you know?" He lowered his voice. "But the good news is ... I've discovered weed."

Rick raised his eyebrows.

"No shit. Weed settles my stomach better than all the other pills they push on me here."

Rick looked puzzled. "Where the hell do you smoke it? You sure as hell don't smoke it here."

Fernandez smiled. "Tell you what ... you want to go for a walk?"

"My fucking leg is in the shop again getting the damn socket refitted. It keeps sliding around. But give me a minute, and I'll get my crutches."

Pedro put his book down. "You do that while I get my hat."

A few minutes later they were downstairs and out on the street. Pedro's prosthetic leg was essentially the same as Rick's, only slightly shorter. Pedro had advanced to walking with a cane. They went a couple of blocks west of the hospital where there was a small city park. Like an elderly couple, they slowly followed the level asphalt bike path as it snaked its way through the trees and shrubbery that formed the perimeter around an empty baseball field, until they found an unoccupied bench in the shade. They lowered themselves onto the bench and sighed in relief.

"Whew," Pedro said. "This is hard time, isn't it?" Pedro took out a box of Marlboros and offered one to Rick, who looked at the proffered "cigarette" with curiosity.

"Don't tell me you ain't never done this shit before."

Rick looked sheepish. "Only once or twice, back in college. For me, it wasn't that different from drinking and wasn't worth the hassle."

"Yeah, I dig it. I felt more or less the same way. But now ..." he paused as he lit up, "now it's the best thing since tortillas."

It took Rick a few inhales for his throat to get used to the superheated air. For a few minutes, they smoked in silence, focusing their attention on the process and on their changing sensations.

After a while, Pedro stretched out his legs. "That's better, man." He nodded and let out a deep sigh. "What do you think?"

Rick pondered for a moment, looked sideways at Fernandez, and smiled.

"It's real nice, Pedro. Thanks. I think I'm starting to mellow out." Then, after a moment, he added, "I needed this: getting out, chilling out, getting buzzed." Rick saw Pedro looking at him quizzically and continued, "Uh, it's just that everything feels shitty, you know? This whole business with my divorce. It's not so much that I miss being with Coralee. I mean, I still like her and she's a good person and all that, but she was never what you'd call a red-hot lover, you know? More often than not, she'd find a way to put me down."

He inhaled another toke. "I mean, she's a good mother to the kids, but she just wasn't very good with me. She never really made me feel important to her, like I really had made it with her, even though we were married. But I was always in there trying. Yes, sir. Big dumb-ass Rick. Never give up. Keep on trying. See where it gets you." He took another long inhale, holding the roach by the very ends of his fingers before he took one final hit and dropped it under his shoe.

"Still, I miss being with a woman, you know? You know what I mean, Pedro. You're divorced. You've been there."

Pedro shrugged. "Tell you the truth, Rick, I'm not sure I do. My experience with women has never been all that positive. Aside from the sex, to tell you the truth, I'm kind of glad not to have a woman in my life. I find it peaceful."

Rick laughed. He couldn't stop giggling. It was contagious, and pretty soon, Pedro was chuckling too. Finally, Rick caught his breath.

"Yeah, I know what you mean. It is peaceful. And maybe you're right. Maybe it is mostly about sex. But for me, it's something more than that, I think. For me, being with a woman … you know, in a real relationship … it adds a purpose to my life. It's like a core that everything else adheres to, like the relationship has something to do with the essential definition of who I am." He looked at Pedro. "Does any of this make sense?"

"I think you're stoned, man."

Rick laughed again. "Maybe I am." He sighed heavily. "Do you know I had a thing starting up with one of the nurses here at the hospital?"

"From down where the clinics are? Petite? Light blondish hair?"

Rick looked at him. "Yeah, but don't say anything to anybody, okay?"

Pedro squeezed his lips together.

"Anyway, she said she was afraid her husband was going to find out, so she broke it off. Maybe it did some good. She's decided to get a divorce. But where the hell does that leave me? Who knows how long it'll be before I can get back to some kind of work? I've been away from my profession for two years. It'd be like completely starting over. Then, I've got two kids, and she's got two kids. How the hell am I supposed to carry my weight? Goddamn it, I can't even carry myself. I'm doing a shitty job with my own kids as it is, hardly seeing them. For Christ's sake, I haven't put either of those kids to bed in two years, never mind helped with their homework or anything. Pedro, sometimes I feel like I don't even know who they are. And Lord knows, they haven't the faintest idea of what's going on in my head." He paused and leaned back. "I don't know," he said.

"Well," started Pedro, "I don't have any kids, but I had a wife who cheated on me."

Rick looked at him.

"Yeah. I had a good job with Amtrak. But I'd be gone two, three days at a time, and then home for a while; you know, like an airline pilot. So while I'd be away, the cat would play. I could tell something was going on by the way people were treating me, you know? Somebody talks to you, and their voice is full of question marks, like they're waiting for you to tell them something or ask them something. Guess the secret word or something. Finally, one of my cousins told me how she was going out dancing to all these clubs, sometimes not coming home at all.

"At first, I was pissed. Shit, I've got a mother like that. I've got a sister like that. I sure as hell don't need a wife like that. Then I thought about it. Who am I to expect anything different? *I'm* like that! While I've been away, I've done my share of catting around too. Not only that, but it seems like everybody I know is doing it or having it done to them. So, finally, I said fuck it. Who needs this shit? I confronted her and told her I knew and it was okay. Only we should get divorced so we can fuck around all we want without worrying about it."

"So you don't miss being married?"

"Hell, no." Pedro paused for a few moments. "What I miss," he started, "is the feeling I had that I knew what the rest of my life was going to be like. I might have been wrong," he said, laughing, "but that don't matter. I had a job, a place to live. I just assumed that my life was a train and it was on track and I knew the destinations ahead. I had the schedule. There were no decisions to make. I could just sit back and enjoy the ride." He paused and sighed, looking up at the trees.

"Now I don't know jack shit. I don't know if I can get my old job back or if I'll ever be able to work again. It's not this leg so much as it's my goddamned gut. Rick, I'm not a complainer, but I'm in almost constant pain. And if it ain't cramps, it's the fucking diarrhea. So what's in store for me? Living alone in an apartment someplace? Being on disability and watching TV and staying stoned all day long? I tell you, Rick, I ain't gonna to settle for that. If that's all there is, I'll just wrap it up right now. There's got to be more than that."

"We're a couple of world champion losers out here, aren't we?"

"This war fucked us up bad, Colonel. No fucking way we should have been over there in the first place."

Rick stared at his stump. "Pedro, I'd never argue with you on that point. But like they keep telling us, we have to accept that this is where we're at and deal with it as well as we can. Neither one of us knows what the future holds. Part of the problem is that we don't know what's possible, so how can we choose? I keep going back and forth between feeling determined to make a future for myself and saying the hell with it and just sitting back and drinking myself to death. Sometimes, I feel like it doesn't make much of a difference."

Pedro took out another "Marlboro" and lit up, and they shared it between them silently until, after a while, when the sun had lowered a little in the sky and it had started to cool off, they made their way back to the hospital.

The Brigade had been sitting at their table for well over an hour and were approaching the point of calling it a day and heading back to the hospital to get something to eat when someone said that a good-looking black woman was heading their way.

Out of curiosity they turned, and Rick said, "Well, I'll be damned."

Coralee came straight toward their table and with an air of determined urgency said, "Rick, we have to talk."

"What's happened? Is it the kids?"

"Please," she said, looking around the table at the others. "Can we talk in private?"

Rick looked at her and, with a sigh of annoyance, reached for his crutches. He pushed himself up from the table onto his feet, adjusted the crutches under his arms, and started for the front door, with Coralee right behind him. The others looked at each other and made an awkward attempt to continue with their conversation as if nothing unusual had happened. Outside, Rick moved a little ways from the entrance and then turned to Coralee.

"So what's happened?"

She took a deep breath. "Larry's been shot," she said.

Rick sobered up instantaneously. "Go on," he said.

"He had the kids in the car. My mother had given him money to do some food shopping, and he took the kids with him. They asked to go, and Momma let them."

Rick held his breath.

"They were almost home, coming up the boulevard, and apparently another car came alongside and somebody shot into the car. Larry was hit, and the car went out of control and turned over."

As she described what had happened, Coralee kept her eyes focused on a spot in the middle of his chest. She looked up briefly, and her eyes were filled to overflowing. Rick felt his good knee grow weak and wobbly, and he leaned back against the building for support. His throat was closing up, and he couldn't speak. He could only wait for Coralee to finish telling him what had happened.

"Ella was sitting up front. She was shot twice, in the arm and in the leg. She had a seat belt on. Tommy was in the backseat. There's no seat belt back there in Larry's car. He has a concussion and some broken ribs and a shoulder injury. They're both in Children's Hospital. I've been there all afternoon. I tried calling you at the hospital, but they said you'd gone out. I didn't know what else to do. I just left them now to come look for you."

Having held herself together long enough to convey the news, she fell onto Rick's chest and began to sob uncontrollably. Rick put his arms around her and held her. Images of the scene flashed through his head: Ella, his Ella, getting shot, twice … blood spurting from her thin little arm and her leg … blood from Larry probably exploding all over the kids and splattering the whole inside of the car … the car flipping over … the horrible crunching, tinkling sounds of metal and glass … Thomas being flung like a rag doll, banging off every surface of the inside of the car. Rick leaned against the wall, paralyzed by the images. Finally, he returned his attention to this woman, his wife, their mother, leaning against him, her own chest heaving spasmodically against his.

Rick forced himself to make his mouth work, to speak.

"They're okay? They're going to make it?"

He felt her nodding her head up and down against him.

"What about Larry?" he asked.

Coralee shook her head and then raised herself away from him to speak.

"He's still in a coma, but he's in bad shape. He got shot in the face and the neck three or four times. He's lost a lot of blood. I don't know. It doesn't look good. Momma and George are with him over at St. Anthony's Hospital."

"Can I see them, the kids?"

"That's why I came here—to get you."

"Do you know who did it?"

"No," she said. "I can only imagine that it was somebody Larry was mixed up with. Probably something to do with drugs. I can't think of anything else. It's hard to believe that it's some kind of random violence, some punks looking for somebody to shoot."

"Let me tell the guys so they know where I am ... so they'll know in the hospital where I am." He felt like he couldn't talk straight, couldn't think straight. He lifted her off his chest, and she straightened up, letting him go back into the bar. He was back out in a couple of minutes, and she held lightly on to his arm.

"I've got my car in the hospital parking lot. You want me to get it and come back for you?"

"No," he said. "It's not that far. I'll go with you."

They didn't speak the rest of the way. Rick followed along as if in a dream. His head was foggy. He allowed himself to be led, unthinking, not really wanting to think, until finally, as if by magic, he was in the waiting area of Children's Hospital, where Coralee led him to a sofa so he could sit down and stretch out his leg.

Coralee was talking to him. "Both of the kids are in intensive care. I'll let them know at the desk that I'm back and that you're here, and I'll find out if we can see them, all right? I'll be right back."

Rick nodded mechanically. He was dimly aware of his lack of responsiveness. He didn't know if he was drunk or in shock, or what. He only knew that he had trouble getting his brain in gear. He kept visualizing Larry's car tumbling in slow motion, the kids' faces pressed against the windows while they yelled silently to him for help. Then it was no longer Larry's car, but his own Humvee slowly lifting off the ground, somersaulting. A leg, his leg, flying out a window. He both saw and felt himself in the Humvee. There was a loud explosion and then a pulsating static sound that kept breaking up, fading from deafening loudness to silence. He nearly jumped out of his skin when Coralee shook him by the shoulder.

"Rick, are you all right?" She had her face close to his and was looking at him intently.

"Yeah. Sure. I'm fine."

"We can go in to see the kids, but we have to be quiet. They're sleeping."

Rick indicated that he understood, and he got his crutches and lifted himself up. They made their way past the nurses' desk, and he followed Coralee down the corridor to the room Ella shared with three other children, all of whom seemed to be either sleeping or unconscious. Another set of parents sat by one of the beds.

Coralee went to Ella's bed and looked at her sleeping daughter. IVs dripped into her body. She looked pale. Her lower lip hung slack in what appeared to be a deep and peaceful sleep. Her left upper arm was heavily bandaged. Various monitors were hooked up to her.

Rick felt himself breathe for the first time since Coralee had walked up to their table in the Recovery Room. He could see that Ella was alive. She was going to be all right. She would recover. He knew it. He took a deep breath and let it out. He felt the tears come to his eyes. It was all right to let go now. Automatically, he shifted his weight off a crutch and put an arm around his wife. He felt her lean into him, and he squeezed her close. Rick told himself that Ella was going to be all right.

"What about Thomas? Can we see him?"

Coralee looked up at him and managed a brief smile. She led the way down the hall to another room, which Thomas also shared with three other children. By comparison, Thomas looked much worse. In addition to being attached to IVs and monitors, his head was bandaged, his face was purple with bruises, his shoulder was in a cast, and tentlike structures were under his blanket to keep anything from aggravating injuries to his legs and torso. Oxygen tubes ran into his nose. Rick looked at her questioningly, his eyes full of fear and anxiety.

"He's got bruises all over his body, Rick. When I left to go find you, the results of the X-rays and other tests hadn't come back yet. Maybe we can find out at the desk."

Rick couldn't take his eyes off Thomas. While he had felt so relieved and optimistic, joyous almost, to find Ella so much better than he had feared, he didn't feel the same way about Thomas. Rick understood that there might be many serious internal injuries that were invisible to him now. He looked at the cast on Thomas's shoulder and wrist. Certainly he was not going to be doing any fencing this year. Rick had no way of knowing if Thomas was going to survive, never mind completely recover.

He turned to Coralee. "Let's go see if we can find out."

At the nurses' station, a nurse said that she would get the doctor on duty to come and explain things to them, and that they should wait in the lounge. About fifteen minutes later, a tired-looking man came toward them and introduced himself as Dr. Patel. He explained that there was every indication Ella's injuries were pretty much limited to what they had seen. The bone in Ella's upper left arm had been grazed and slightly splintered, and the muscles in both her arm and left thigh had been damaged by the bullets' trajectories. Still, she should be completely recovered within a couple of months. Aside from some bruises to her torso from the seat belt, she was doing pretty well. The seat belt had saved her from more serious injuries and possibly death. Surgery had already been done to repair the damage done by the bullet wounds. The arm bone should mend completely within six weeks, and the little girl should have no lasting physical complications from the incident.

Thomas was another story. He had suffered a severe concussion, four broken ribs, a punctured pancreas, and a punctured lung, as well as a dislocated shoulder, a broken collarbone, a broken wrist, and a broken ankle. He should be able to recover from all of these injuries, but the extent of any brain injury was as yet undetermined.

And additional complications—spinal problems, for instance—might still show up.

Both Rick and Coralee asked the doctor more questions and then thanked him. They sat down in the deserted lounge, and Dr. Patel disappeared back into the depths of the hospital.

Rick sighed heavily. "I feel like I need to kill somebody for this."

Coralee looked at him and opened her mouth to say something. Rick saw the look on her face.

He continued, "Not you. I'm not blaming you. Larry, maybe. Larry, sure as hell, has some responsibility for this. But no, I'm thinking of the shooters. I really don't care if somebody had a beef with Larry. I really don't give a shit. But, Christ, they see kids in the car, and they still go ahead with this? What kind of fucking maniac would do something like this?"

Coralee sat slumped in her seat. "You're right. Still, I can't help but feel some responsibility too. I knew that Larry was mixed up in shit. I should have been able to see that, sooner or later, he was going to bring trouble home with him. And if the kids and I were there, there was going to be some chance that it would fall on us. Now I feel like I've got to get out of there, but I wonder if it's too late."

"If your brother dies, then there shouldn't be any more trouble."

"Yeah, but what if he doesn't die? Is somebody going to come back to get him? Is everybody there at risk … my mother, me, the kids, even old George?"

Coralee grabbed Rick's hand, and her voice cracked. "What if Thomas doesn't make it? I don't know what I'll do if he doesn't make it."

Rick returned the pressure from her hand. "If Thomas doesn't come through this, there is no way I'm going to let this rest. One way or another, I'll find out who did this."

Coralee frowned. "Rick, you let the police handle this. Don't go doing something stupid. I don't need to go losing you too."

Rick looked at her, surprised.

She said, "You know what I mean. We need to hang together on this, for support. The kids are going to need both of us, right?"

He agreed. Rick was picturing his son, all bandaged up, and in his mind he was back in his hospital room in Walter Reed, his stump bandaged up and that young soldier in the bed next to him, his face and arms blown to pieces. He felt himself being drawn tighter and tighter, with a humming sound in his head that kept climbing higher and higher in pitch.

Then Coralee said, "Look, they're both sleeping soundly. They're going to be all right for the rest of the night. Why don't we leave and come back in the morning. I'm dead on my feet." Rick agreed.

Coralee dropped him off at the entrance to the VA hospital and told him that she would pick him up in the morning. They'd go together to Children's Hospital to see the kids.

He didn't even bother to wave as she drove away. When Rick got to his floor, some of the guys were still in the dayroom watching TV. He gave them a cursory nod and headed to his room, where the first thing he did was reach for his bottle. Then, after removing his pants and his leg, and putting on a pair of sweatpants, he sat in his chair and looked out on the night and drank and thought.

IX

Rick was in the cafeteria eating breakfast. He usually came down early for breakfast because of his difficulty in sleeping, but last night had been particularly difficult. It was becoming obvious to him that the vodka was losing its effectiveness in blocking out his dreams of Iraq. He had to decide whether to continue increasing the amount he drank, try something else, or just endure the nightmares and go without sleep. Last night he couldn't stop thinking about the kids and his relationship with Coralee. It seemed only natural that they would come together on this, support each other, and be a stable, reassuring source of strength for Ella and Thomas. But what had she meant when she'd said that she didn't want to lose him? Was she having second thoughts? Was he? He had eaten his breakfast almost without awareness and was drinking his coffee when he realized that Phyllis was pulling out a chair and sitting down across from him.

"Good morning," she said.

"Hi," he said as he lowered his cup to the table.

"You're down here earlier than usual."

"Yeah," he said. "Couldn't sleep."

"That happen a lot?"

"What are you, my fucking doctor now?"

"Hey, relax. I just asked a simple question."

Rick gave an embarrassed shrug. "Yeah, I know," he mumbled.

Phyllis looked at him as she transferred her cereal and coffee from the tray to the table.

"My kids were hurt last night," he offered.

She waited for him to continue.

"Coralee came over last night to tell me and brought me to see them. They're in Children's Hospital. She's coming by later on to pick me up and take me over there again this morning."

Phyllis looked down at her food for a moment.

Rick continued, "Her good-for-nothing drug-addict brother had the kids in the car with him, and somebody pulled up alongside and tried to take him out. Shot into the car. Fucking car turned over. My little girl, Ella—she's ten—got shot twice. Luckily only in the arm and the leg. She could have been killed, for Christ's sake. But it looks like she's going to come out of it all right, at least physically. Thomas … he's twelve … he's … he's in worse shape. He has a severe concussion and a lot of internal injuries and some broken bones. He's really messed up. I don't know how he's going to come out of this."

Phyllis sat in her chair with her hand up to her mouth.

"Oh, my God. Oh, Rick, how terrible. I can't believe … that this happened to you, to your kids …" She pushed her plate away from her. "Oh, Rick."

He sighed and finished his coffee. Rick waited for her to digest the information.

"Children's Hospital is a good hospital. I know people who work there. What service are they in? Do you know?"

"Intensive care, I think. They're each in a room with three other kids."

"They tend to do that a lot more with kids, so they don't feel so isolated. Do you know who their doctors are?"

Rick shook his head. "I guess I'll find out today."

"Maybe I can give you some feedback about them if you can let me know."

"Sure."

"Rick, I'm so sorry to hear this. I can imagine what you and your wife must be going through. I picture my own two little girls … I know how I'm constantly afraid that Harold might do something to them. Rick, please let me know if there's anything I can do."

He managed a weak grin, which seemed more like a grimace for all the pain that it conveyed.

"Shit," she said. "I've got to get to work. Let me know what happens. All right? Promise?"

"Yeah, I will. Thanks."

She blew him a kiss and then left.

Rick decided to wait in the lobby for Coralee to pick him up. A little after seven o'clock, he saw her car pull up in front of the main entrance, and he got up from his chair and went out. When he was in the car, he asked her about Larry, if she had heard anything from her mother. Mildred and George had spent most of the night at St. Anthony's Hospital. Larry was still in a coma and still in critical condition. The police were investigating, but as far as she knew, no one had seen anything and no witnesses had come forward. Chances were that no one would ever pay for this.

Rick digested all of this information. In truth, it was what he'd expected. This would not be a high-priority case in any big city, and without witnesses, it would be very hard to pin on anybody. Neither Mildred nor Coralee knew anything about Larry's criminal contacts or activities, so it would be an impossible task to track down possible suspects. And that wasn't even taking into account that it could have been random—some young punks needing to try out a new toy to see if it really worked, to see if they could really shoot someone. Really kill a person. It seemed hopeless. All he could do was hope that they all came out of this alive.

At the hospital, the nurse at the desk asked them to wait for the doctor before going in to visit the kids. They had barely sat down when a doctor Coralee recognized from the day before approached them.

"Good morning, Mrs. Garcia. Mr. Garcia?" he asked, and Rick nodded.

"I'm Dr. Connor. I'm afraid I have some troublesome news."

They waited.

"During the night, Tommy's blood pressure dropped precipitously, indicating the possibility of internal bleeding. We rushed him up to the OR. He's still there. It looks like a blood vessel burst. My guess is that it had been weakened by the initial injuries, and then, as his blood pressure increased back to normal, it ruptured. I can only tell you that they're doing all they can and there's every reason to be hopeful. But he has lost a lot of blood, and he was unstable to begin with."

Rick didn't know how to respond. He let himself sink back down onto the chair. Thomas was going to die? Is that what the doctor was saying?

"Is he going to die? Is that what you're saying?"

Dr. Connor skipped a beat before answering. "No. Not at all. That's not what I'm saying, Mr. Garcia. No. What I'm telling you is that your son is in critical condition, but that there's every reason, every reason," he repeated, "to be hopeful. Dr. Petrie, one of our best surgeons, is up there with him. Rest assured. I expect that the surgery will be over soon. As soon as we know anything more definitive, we'll let you know. I assume," he continued, looking at Coralee, "that you'll be in 245 visiting your daughter?"

Coralee nodded.

"So as soon as we hear anything, we'll come and notify you." He waited a moment and then turned and left them there.

Coralee sat down slowly next to Rick. They looked at each other and simultaneously reached for each other's hand.

"What do you think?" she asked.

"I think it's not good," he said. "I think he fed us a big dose of bullshit. I think they're preparing us. I think they screwed up somehow, and our boy, our son, is going to pay the price."

"Rick, we need to let your family know what's happening."

"Yeah," he agreed. "I thought of calling them last night when I got back to my room, but I decided to wait until today to see what happened." He took a deep breath. "It's probably better if I call them now rather than wait. If it's going to be bad news, then they're going to want to be here."

"They could stay with me, if they want. They can use the kids' rooms, or Larry's."

Rick thought a moment and then thanked her. "I'll go find a phone and call them."

"I'll be in with Ella," she said, biting her lip.

"Okay," he managed, and he pushed himself wearily onto his feet, tucked the crutches under his arms, and went to find a phone.

"Hi, Mom. It's me, Rick."

"Rick, what's wrong? Are you all right?" she asked.

He could tell from her voice that his parents were still in bed, taking advantage of the empty house and the flexible definition of time in their retirement.

"I'm fine, Mom. It's not me. Something has happened to the kids. They're both in the hospital."

"The hospital? What happened?"

He told her the story. He told her chronologically so that he led up to the present. It went slowly as he paused between sentences so his mother could feed everything, spoonful by spoonful, to his father, who was lying beside her.

"So, right now, Coralee is in with Ella, and we're waiting to hear from the doctors how Thomas is doing." He heard the matter-of-fact tone in his voice, keeping his emotions out of it, not wanting to expose his mother to the depths and extent of his rage and anguish, his sense of impotence. Rather, he tried to convey that the situation might turn more serious but that they were "hopeful" and "hanging in there."

His father got on the phone. "Rick, is there anything you want us to do?"

"No, not really, Dad. Coralee and I thought that you should know. Maybe you and Mom might want to come up and be here … just in case, you know?"

His father said, "Of course we're coming up. We'll be there this afternoon."

"Coralee said you could stay at her house if you and Mom want. You could use the kids' rooms or Larry's."

There was a pause. "That was nice of her. We'll see." Then, after another pause, "How are the two of you getting along?"

"We're fine, Dad. It's hard to say. This is just too unbelievable. I don't know how we're reacting to it. Maybe we're not even reacting to it yet. It seems unreal, like it's happening to somebody else and I'm just watching it, like on TV. We're only going through the motions here. It's another bad dream I wish I could wake up from."

"Do they have any idea who did the shooting?"

"I don't think so. I don't think they've got a clue. I'm not optimistic about their ever finding out anything."

"Don't bet on it, son. They'll find the bastards. You hang in there, Rick. Your mother and I will be up there this afternoon. I'll call Matt and let them know."

Rick thanked him, gave him the details about the hospital and Coralee's address, and then hung up. He wanted a drink. He wanted a cigarette, weed, a morphine pump … something, anything that would make it all feel different. He went to the men's room and emptied himself of the morning's coffee and washed his hands and face before going back out and finding his wife, the mother of his children.

That night Rick lay in his bed and thought over the day. Thomas had survived his ordeal in the OR and eventually had been brought back to his room. The poor kid, despite transfusions of blood, looked pale and washed-out; his drugged body appeared drained, limp, and lifeless except for the reassuring rhythmic—albeit shallow—rising of his chest, with the blips on his monitor indicating that he was alive. Still, he was now in critical care, and no one was feeling overly confident. Once they'd arrived, Rick's parents put on a brave face, but he didn't think that his mother and Coralee let go of each other all day.

The good news was that Ella was beginning to come around. Her natural energies were overcoming the effects of her anesthesia and the shock to her system. She was up to watching TV and asking for ice cream, and asking about what had happened. Maybe it was a good thing that she didn't remember most of the details, retaining only a hazy recollection of the car crashing and a hot, stinging sensation, and then pretty much a blur until she woke up in her room. Nobody wanted her to remember any more than that.

The police had been around asking the predictable questions, but when they saw the situation and how little Ella remembered, they didn't push it and left after going through the motions. Just in case anybody thought of anything, they handed out their cards. One might think they were opening up a new business or something. Meanwhile, Mildred and George were standing guard over Larry's bed at St. Anthony's Hospital, along with a cop just in case he came out of his coma. Rick hoped the son of a bitch died without ever waking up. The world would be a better place without him.

Matt and his wife, Bea, would try to come up within the next few days. Rick was looking forward to being with his brother again. He missed him even more than he did his parents, with whom he found himself experiencing a strange and uncomfortable tension. He felt on guard and found himself holding back. He thought about it and realized that he was afraid of being swallowed up by his mother, as if she could surround and smother him with a gigantic breast, suffocating him as she force-fed him. He thought of calves in a pen being forcibly nourished into expensive veal.

And Dad … he just never stopped with his expectations and his suggestions of what to do and how to do it better. Christ, how different to sit back with Matt and have a beer, watch the clouds, eat. Just hang out and relax. Christ, I need to relax.

He thought of jerking off to relieve some of his tension, but sex was the last thing he had any interest in. It seemed that he'd hardly thought about sex since Phyllis dumped him. He thought of having a drink, but he was all out, which was probably just as well. That was another reason he wanted to maintain some distance from his parents. He was afraid they would smell it on his breath or in some other way notice that he wasn't completely sober.

A note was waiting for him when he returned to his room indicating that continued absence from his clinic assignments could result in discharge from the program. He'd have to haggle with them to get some time off to visit the kids, although he understood that the staff was pissed at him for not showing up. Truth was, he didn't know how much longer he'd be here anyway. He anticipated that sooner rather than later, they would tell him that they had done all they could and that it was time for him to face the future and stand on his own two feet. The problem was, he didn't know what he was going to do. He had no idea what kind of future he wanted: Stay in Oklahoma City and live off of his disability? Live with Coralee and the kids? Live at Mildred's? Go back to Texas and live with his parents or his brother? Get a job? Engineering? What? And what about Phyllis? Was she going to be available soon? Was she even interested? And that also would probably hinge on his having some kind of job. *All these fucking questions. I wish I could simply fall asleep … without dreaming.*

X

In the morning, Rick telephoned Coralee and told her he'd take a cab to Children's Hospital, but that first he had to touch base with the staff and discuss his treatment program. She told him that Larry had died during the night and that her mother was devastated. Rick realized Coralee would have to make the funeral arrangements for the brother she despised. He told her he was sorry that she had been put in that position and he'd do what he could to help her. Then he went down to the cafeteria, this time with the hope of seeing Phyllis. He wasn't sure what he was looking for, but knew he wanted to be clearer as to whether she was interested in pursuing anything with him, even though he wasn't sure if he wanted to be with her or with Coralee, or if he wanted to be alone. But he never saw her come in, and finally he left to see the physician in charge of his treatment program.

Rick explained to him what was going on in his life and his need to be with his kids while they were recovering from their injuries. In return, he found out what he had expected to hear: he was near the end of his rehabilitation program anyway. From now on, it would be up to him to work on developing his strength and mobility, and the only reason for him to come in would be for periodic checkups or for repairs or adjustments on the prosthesis. They discussed it and set a termination date for the end of the following week. This would give them some time to help him improve his ability to walk with the cane. A medical discharge from the army would soon follow. That was it then. Rick felt a sinking sensation in his belly. *Sink or swim. Sink or swim.* That was something his father would say—maybe how his father had taught him how to swim.

After he left the doctor's office, Rick hobbled around the corridors looking for Phyllis, but then he heard from one of the other nurses that she had the day off. He was about to get a container of coffee from the cafeteria and hail a cab when he realized that he'd have too much trouble carrying the coffee and using the crutches at the same time. He shook his head in disgust and went outside to find a taxi.

When Rick got out of the elevator onto the critical care floor, he went right to Thomas's room, where he found Coralee and his parents. Thomas was still a pale ghost of himself and still unconscious. All they could do was watch him breathe and monitor the blips chasing each other across the screen. Once Rick was satisfied that Thomas's condition hadn't changed, he decided to visit Ella in her room on the floor above. Coralee said that she'd go with him, and his parents agreed they would go visit Ella when he came back. This way, someone would always be with each of the kids.

In the hall, waiting for the elevator, he was surprised to find Coralee standing next to him holding on to his arm. Rick didn't say anything. His first reaction was to wonder what that little gesture said about her. Then he wondered about himself. How did he feel about it? When the elevator came, she let go to let him swing himself aboard. On the elevator, she stood in front of him, and he had a chance to observe her. She was a good-looking forty-year-old woman, more sturdy than trim, but still with a nice shape to her. He noticed her behind, one of his favorite parts of Coralee's anatomy. She had nice hips. The door opened, and they stepped out onto Ella's floor.

In her room, now a semiprivate shared with another little girl and her parents, they found Ella more spirited. She was full of questions about Thomas and her uncle Larry. Coralee told her that Larry had died the night before, and it was pitiful to see Ella dissolve into tears and confusion.

"But why?" she asked over and over again. Rick wished that he could give her an answer that would satisfy her, that would help her to comprehend the sudden finality of death, the forever absence of a presence that she associated with fun and laughter. Although neither Rick nor Coralee shared Ella's sense of loss, they tried to give her the support and understanding they knew she needed. For all of his faults, Larry had been a good-natured companion to the kids, and Rick understood why they would miss him.

After she had recovered and was again calmly watching TV and talking, she asked if the men who had shot at them would return again to shoot her and Thomas. At first, Rick thought that she was referring to what she had been told about the car crash, but then he realized that she hadn't been told anything about the shooting. He picked up on this before Coralee did.

"What do you mean, honey?" he asked. "Do you remember something about the shooting?"

"Uh-huh," she said matter-of-factly, nodding her head while dividing her attention between him and the TV.

Rick and Coralee exchanged quick glances, and he continued, "Oh, I didn't realize that you remembered any of that. Just what do you remember?"

"Well ..." Ella began, "just that we were riding home from the Safeway and were on Martin Luther King Boulevard, going back to Grammy's house, coming down the hill near the park. You know where that is, right, Ma?"

Coralee looked at her wide-eyed.

"Uncle Larry had the radio on and was making up funny rap lyrics about how we were going to have some really sweet ice cream that was chocolate, and we were going to eat gallons of it from Grammy's big soup pot, or something like that." She giggled while relating the happy silliness of the memory.

"Anyway, I was looking at him and laughing, and a car pulled up alongside, and the man reached out of his window ... and I was watching him ... and he pulled up a gun, a pistol, and pointed it at Uncle Larry. Uncle Larry didn't see the man because he was half-looking straight ahead and half-looking at me. And then the man shot. And then Uncle Larry yelled ... and the car started to turn ... and I thought I was gonna die. That's all I remember until I woke up here in the hospital. Didn't you know that? About the shooting?"

Rick smiled. "No, sweetheart. We didn't know that about the shooting. We knew, of course, that there had been shooting, but none of the details. We didn't realize that you remembered any of this."

Ella made a curious face, screwing up her face like her mother often did. "Yeah," she acknowledged, "I don't think I remembered anything yesterday. But then all of a sudden, it was all there. Just like a movie. And I could see all of it."

Coralee reached over to pet her baby's hair. "It doesn't seem like the memory is all that scary for you."

Ella laughed, "It was scary then, Ma. When the car started to turn and spin and flip upside down. It was like in slow motion. I was sooo scared. I thought I was gonna die. Really! But now I'm not dead, and I have two bullet wounds—almost just like you, Dad," she said, turning to him. "We're both heroes, right?"

Rick choked up. "Right," he finally managed to say. "You're a hero, that's for sure. You know, honey bun, the police don't know these details about the shooting either, so you're going to have to tell them what you remember."

Ella nodded enthusiastically. It was obvious to Rick that she was enjoying her new status. He and Coralee looked at each other, and he sensed that she might be having some of the same concerns that he had: if Larry's murderers realized that Ella was a witness to what had happened, then maybe she—and everyone else in the house—would be in danger.

A little bit later, Rick dug out the card that the detectives had handed him and went to the nurses' station to make the phone call. A half hour later, one of the detectives, Ellis Cook, stepped into the room. Rick and Coralee remained in the room, but kept silent and let the detective ask the questions he needed to ask. Ella told him the same story. He asked her if she could describe the man she saw do the shooting, and, to Rick and Coralee's amazement, she told him that she could and that she knew him.

"What?" Rick couldn't hold back his astonishment.

Ella looked at him with innocent surprise. "Sure, Daddy. I saw him a few times with Uncle Larry. I think his name is Tony. I don't know his last name."

"Can you tell me anything else about this Tony?" Cook asked.

Ella hesitated and then answered, "A couple of times he came over to the house in the afternoon to see Uncle Larry. He was in a different car then, a white one. When he shot Uncle Larry, he was in a dark-colored car, an SUV."

"Go on, Ella. You're doing fine. What else do you remember about Tony?"

"Well, Uncle Larry would go out to the car, and they'd talk for a while. They'd shake hands, like you know how they do. He seemed to be friends with Uncle Larry, but I never talked to him. Then once, when we were at the park, Thomas and me and Uncle Larry, this Tony came up and sat and talked with Uncle Larry for a while. They'd laugh sometimes. Like I said, they seemed to be friends."

Detective Cook put his notebook away and reached over to shake Ella's good hand. "Miss Garcia, you have done a remarkable job. I'm going to send a police artist over here so you can describe this Tony, and we'll draw a picture of him and find out who he is, all right? Then we're going to go and arrest this dude and make him pay for what he's done. And I want you to understand, Ella, that we wouldn't be able to do any of this if it weren't for you."

Ella beamed while Rick and Coralee looked on proudly. When the detective left, Rick suggested that they give his parents a chance to visit with Ella, so they left and went back downstairs to Thomas's room.

When they were alone in Thomas's room, their son still sleeping his drugged sleep, Coralee turned to Rick.

"So what do you think?" she asked.

"I think that if the word gets out that the police are looking for this Tony character, things could get a little dicey. I'm concerned about the kids' safety, and yours too, and even your mother's and George's. Somebody could throw a firebomb in that house of hers, and anybody in it would be toast. Even here in the hospital, anybody could walk into these rooms. What do you think?"

"It's easy to say that we're overreacting and that it's not likely to happen. But I don't care. This is the only family I've got. I think we should ask for police protection. Or maybe ..." She stopped. "I don't know, Rick. We'll have Thomas here even if Ella is discharged. Then there's the funeral for Larry. I can't take Momma away until that's done."

She stopped and looked at him. "Can you come over? Can you stay with us? You're a man, a soldier."

Rick wasn't quite sure what that implied. *Am I supposed to sit on the front steps cradling a semiautomatic weapon? What am I supposed to do? Karate-kick some punk into submission with my plastic leg? Club them with my crutches?* Still, he sensed that there was some logic in Coralee's request. Maybe his mere presence would serve as some sort of deterrent. And if he could get a gun, he would certainly know how to use it.

He thought about what the implications might be for them as a couple. Was he making a commitment? Was she? Was he going to be sleeping with her? Were they going to end up having sex again? Is that what he wanted?

He looked at Coralee and asked her, "You sure that's what you want—for me to be living with you at your mother's?"

The look on her face was noncommittal.

"Look," he said, "I'm as concerned as you are, and I want to do everything I can to help protect you and the kids. Maybe my being there will help. Maybe I can get a gun and really be of some use. But I'm also confused about what this might mean for us."

He kept watching her, but Coralee continued to give him the same ambiguous look without any words to clarify where she stood.

"I need to know, Cora. Does this mean that you're having second thoughts? Do you want us to give this another go? Or not? I'm not a fucking yo-yo, you know. I can't read you. I feel like I'm getting mixed signals from you."

He stopped. He was determined to say no more. He wanted her to express herself, one way or another. Suddenly he felt a little clearer within himself. He wasn't even going to think about the possibility of reconciliation unless he knew that was what she wanted. Otherwise, he reasoned, he was just setting himself up for another disappointment, another betrayal.

Coralee stared at her sleeping son with an IV and oxygen tubes and catheters running into and out of him. "When I look at him, I think of his broken bones, his scars, the fact that he might die and no longer be in my life. And the emptiness in my belly grows to the size of the universe. And what I want more than anything else is to feel some assurance that I won't experience his loss. Not now." Coralee said this almost as if speaking to herself.

"I'm not sure what to tell you, Rick. Everything seems so different now than it did last year when I left. I guess I took some things for granted: like the kids would always be there, like I could always take care of myself. Now ..." She shrugged and looked around the room. "I don't know anything. I don't know if my son is going to die. I don't know if some asshole friend of my brother is going to try to kill us all. I don't know if my son is going to be permanently injured in some way that will require me to take care of him the rest of his life." She paused and swallowed. "Somehow, that doesn't seem so bad to me right now. I'd take that. I'd take it and feel mighty grateful, you know?

"And you … I took you for granted too. I did. I took your strengths for granted and only focused on what I saw as your shortcomings, your limitations." She reached over and put her hand on his. "I know. I admit it. I could see only weakness in men, their dependence on women. I saw your need for me as a weakness in you and something that would destroy me, swallow me." She paused and looked again at Thomas and then back at Rick.

"It's not just that I think I've changed, Rick. I know I have. I see your strengths, how you've dealt with your leg, the loss of your business, everything, and I admire you. But, also, I feel my own need for you. I want you back, Rick. I want us to try again. I'm ready now. I really am."

Rick was stunned. He had never expected to hear these words from her lips. Never. He felt himself returning the pressure in her hand. He saw her eyes glistening in the soft light of the room. He felt as though he was on the edge of a precipice.

"All right," he finally managed to say. "Let's give it a try. Let's see what happens."

"You don't sound too sure."

Rick took a deep breath. "You're right," he admitted. "I'm not too sure. I'm not sure how much I can let myself feel, how much I can let myself trust again. I mean, I'd like to, I think, but I'm not sure I can. Last year, this whole past year, it's been very … hurtful," he finally said. "I still feel raw."

Coralee didn't say anything; she only gripped his hand harder before letting go and getting a tissue from her purse. Rick leaned back on his chair and looked at Coralee and his son. *Christ,* he thought, *could I use a drink now.*

Later in the afternoon, Ellis Cook returned with a young Hispanic woman he introduced as the police artist, and the two of them helped Ella come up with a portrait of the man Ella called Tony. While Ella was working with the artist, Rick took the opportunity to approach the detective and inquire about purchasing a gun. He explained that he was a colonel in the reserves and recently wounded in Iraq and that he was concerned about the safety of his kids and everyone else in the family. Cook said that he understood and that he agreed with Rick's reasoning. He gave Rick the name of a retired colleague who had a handgun to sell. Because the man was not a dealer, Rick would not have to lose time with a background check and could take possession of the gun immediately. Rick called the seller and made arrangements to meet him. He then told his parents and Coralee that he had to run an errand and that he'd see them in about an hour, and left them with the kids. Less than an hour later, he was back at the hospital with a 9 mm tucked into a holster in the small of his back. While he had been gone, he had missed the big event. Thomas had woken up.

While his parents were upstairs with Ella, he and Coralee practically crawled into Thomas's bed with him. They couldn't get close enough to him. Thomas was still quite weak, but all of his vital signs were stronger and more stable, and they felt more hopeful that he was going to make it. He complained that his head, his ribs, and his whole body hurt, but he seemed to have his wits about him and didn't show any major loss of memory. At the time of the shooting, he had been playing with his Game Boy in the backseat and hadn't been paying attention. He remembered only what he assumed was a blowout of somebody's tire and then that the car went out of control and he was tossed about. That was all he remembered. He assumed that the blowout had been to one of their tires.

He was shocked when Rick and Coralee told him what had happened. They led up slowly to the fact of his uncle's death. Thomas asked about Ella and was quite relieved to hear that she was doing as well as she was.

When it was dinnertime, they decided to take a break and to give the kids one. The four adults went out to dinner: Coralee, Rick, and his parents. When they were seated around a table at a Mexican restaurant and had ordered, Rick gave the news to his parents.

"I want you to know that Coralee and I have decided to give it another try."

His mother and father stole a quick glance at each other.

Before they could collect themselves, Rick continued. "We know we have some problems to deal with, but this shooting has changed everything. We need to give it a shot. All this … it's just too hard to deal with alone. And the kids … it'll be a big help to them if we're together."

Rick's father placed his hand on Rick's shoulder. "Of course. This is between the two of you. Whatever you think is best. We only want you to be happy, that's all. You let us know if there's anything Virginia and I can do to be helpful." Then he turned to Coralee. "Your mother will be going through a difficult time. Let us know if there's anything we can do to help out, you know, with the funeral and all."

Coralee nodded her thanks.

On the way back to the hospital, Rick's dad walked with Rick, slowing his pace to match his son's. "So," he said, "what are your plans?"

It was a simple enough question, one that Rick had asked himself without coming up with an answer. "Well," he said after a long silence, "to be truthful with you, I'm not sure. It looks like in a couple of weeks I'll be discharged from the program here."

"No kidding? That's great."

"Yeah, I've gotten about all I can get out of the treatment program for now, except they want me to do more work with the cane and get off the crutches. Then I'll be officially discharged from the army, and I'll start getting disability instead of the current active-duty pay they've kept me on. Between that and Coralee's job at the hotel …"

He let it trail off. He didn't know how it would be. He had no idea whether they would have enough money. He had no idea about the medical insurance—how that would work, whether the kids would be covered. At that moment he felt a surge of panic. He had been so tightly focused on the kids that he hadn't given a moment's thought to the hospital bills. He suddenly realized that he was looking at a bill of tens of thousands of dollars. He had no idea where that money would come from or whether they were covered by any medical insurance or not. Unexpectedly he felt hot and sweaty and light-headed. He looked at his father and resumed the conversation.

"We'll have to live with it a little and see what happens. At one point, a few months ago, I thought I'd be coming down to Texas. I thought you might be able to help me get an engineering job."

"I remember your mentioning that. You just give me the word, whenever you're ready, and I'll call some people and see what we can dig up."

"I appreciate that, Dad. Only thing is, lately I've been thinking that I've been away from the field so long now—this August it'll be two years since I've read any journals or anything. I feel like I'm out of date, over the hill."

"Don't talk like that, son. What about the work you did in Iraq? The roads and the bridges?"

Rick blew it off. "That was bullshit stuff, Dad. There were no specs. We did whatever we wanted. Who was going to question us? We did the best we could under the circumstances, and, to tell the truth, we did a pretty goddamned good job. But it's not the same as doing construction over here. They're always coming out with new techniques, new materials, new technologies, new requirements. It's constantly changing. Well, you know, Dad. You were there until you retired. You know what I'm talking about."

"Sure I do. And there's truth in what you say. But I think you may be exaggerating. I can understand your having some anxiety about going back to work, having a job, working for somebody else. It's been a long time since you worked for anybody else. But you can do it. I know you can. If you want to, that is."

"Well, we'll see how it goes with my leg ... how well I do with a cane, what happens with the money, where we're going to live ... Jesus, everything. Everything is up in the air. How the fuck am I supposed to decide anything? I don't know anything."

He turned to his father and stopped, forcing his father to stop also. Rick looked ahead to his mother and Coralee, half a block ahead. "I need to tell you that Coralee and I are concerned about safety."

John Garcia's eyes widened, and he stepped in closer to his son.

Rick continued, needlessly lowering his voice. "We're afraid that if this Tony character gets wind that Ella fingered him, it's possible he could target her or the house or the family. Who knows? That's one reason I'm moving back." He paused. "I bought a gun this afternoon, just in case."

John Garcia digested this news. "Yeah, I've been having some vague feeling of concern about the kids' safety, but I hadn't put it into words. And this decision of yours to buy a gun … it sounds right to me. In fact, I'm embarrassed that I haven't brought my own handgun with me. Maybe I should go out and buy another one so as not to be a useless old man when my son and his family might be endangered. In fact, now that I think of it, that's exactly what I'm going to do tomorrow."

"Dad, I don't know that you need to be doing that. Listen, I'm going to have to check back in at my hospital for tonight and then tell them tomorrow morning about the emergency and the fact that I'll be moving out—"

"You're going to move in with Coralee?"

"Yeah, that's the whole point, so I can be there in case there's any trouble. Both Coralee and I will feel better if I'm there to do whatever I can."

"Of course," his father said.

"Anyway, since I won't be there tonight, I was thinking … I could give you the gun I bought today. Just in case, you know?"

John took hold of Rick's muscular upper arm. "Of course, son. I'd be happy to do that."

"Good. When we get to the hospital, we'll go into the men's room and I'll give it to you then."

His father nodded. "Sure," he said.

Virginia and Coralee stood outside the main entrance talking, waiting for their men to catch up. Once inside, the two men visited the men's room off the lobby, and then all of them went upstairs to be with Thomas and Ella. Ella was her usual talkative self and made it quite clear that she was eager to come home. In fact, there seemed to be a good chance she could be discharged the next day. Thomas, still groggy from his injuries and medications and painkillers, was listless and subdued, and they sat quietly with him as he watched TV and slipped into periods of light sleep. Rick recalled his own early days in Walter Reed and wished there was some way he could infuse his son with health and hope.

When the visiting hours were over and parents and grandparents had said good night to both kids, they walked to the parking lot where Coralee had parked her car. That was when Rick told Coralee that he would have to spend the night at the hospital, but that he would make all the arrangements the next day to move over to her mother's house. Rick decided—for a reason he was not sure of—not to say anything about the handgun he'd purchased and had given to his father. He'd let his father handle that in whatever way he decided.

"Okay," she said and briefly gripped his hand.

When Coralee opened her front door, she saw her mother cradled in George's arms, sitting on the sofa, the muted TV displaying its captions across the bottom of the screen.

"Oh, sugar, I am so glad that you're home," Mildred said as soon as she saw her daughter.

"How're you doing, Momma?"

Mildred's eyes were red from crying, and she looked depleted. "Not so good," she answered. "The man from the funeral home came over this afternoon, but I just can't deal with the funeral arrangements right now. I'm going to need you to go to the funeral home with me tomorrow and help me make some decisions about Larry's burial."

"Of course, Momma. I expected to be doing that for you."

Mildred eventually noticed John and Virginia and invited them to sit down. "How are the kids doing?" she asked.

"Ella is perking up and may come home tomorrow. And Thomas is improving. He's still all …" Coralee's eyes started to fill up.

"But he's getting better?" Mildred asked, looking at John and Virginia.

"Oh, yes," said John. "He's definitely stronger and more alert today than he was yesterday. I think he's going to be all right."

"And little Ella might come home tomorrow, you say?"

Virginia put her hand on Mildred's. "Yes, she's full of sparkle and is looking forward to being home."

Mildred turned to her daughter. "Your boss from the hotel called this morning and said to tell you that if you don't come in tomorrow morning, don't bother at all."

"What?" Coralee screamed. "Johnson threatened to fire me?"

"I don't remember his name," Mildred said, "but I remember he said he was your boss and either you come in on time, or he'll mail you your paycheck. He sounded all business."

"Oh, shit! I told him my kids were in the hospital and I needed a few days. I thought he'd give me more than this."

"Coralee," Virginia interjected, "if you want, I can go with your mother to the funeral home tomorrow, and John can go to the hospital. He and Rick will be with the kids, and you can go after work."

Coralee and her mother looked at each other.

"Thank you, Virginia," said Mildred. "I truly would appreciate your help. It just seems to be so much right now."

Once he was back on the rehab ward, Rick entered the large dayroom, dimly lit now while most of the residents were watching TV. Rick spotted Pedro and Dwayne sitting together and went to join them. Pedro suggested they retreat to the back of the room where they could talk.

"Nothing good is on anyway. We might as well listen to your bullshit," said Pedro in his slow drawl.

"Either of you guys got anything to drink?"

Pedro shook his head. It took Dwayne a moment to catch what Rick meant.

"Oh," he said, as if awakening. "No, I don't have anything either. Why? You got bad news?"

Rick let out a heavy sigh. "Shit, Du-Bob, I'm not sure I even know what bad news is anymore."

"How're your kids doing?" Pedro asked.

"Not bad, considering," he said. "Ella is coming along real swell. In fact, she might be coming home tomorrow. And Thomas … he's definitely stronger, and all of his signs are more stable. But he's a weak little puppy and can hardly keep his eyes open."

"How's Coralee holding up?" asked Dwayne.

"She's holding it together. She and my mother are like two bookends propping each other up."

Rick was a little embarrassed to tell them that Coralee had asked him to come back and that he'd agreed. But he realized that he'd have to tell them that he was moving out the next day and settling in at Coralee's mother's place, along with his own parents.

"Fact is, she's asked me to come back."

The two men looked at him, and Pedro raised his eyebrows. "And you said …?"

"I said I'd give it a try. We both think it makes sense under the circumstances."

"What circumstances?" Dwayne asked.

Rick smiled to himself, realizing that they weren't aware of all that had transpired today.

"Ella remembered who shot into the car and killed my brother-in-law. She gave the police artist a description. They're checking it out. Some guy named Tony, she thinks."

"So," said Pedro, "there's a good chance they'll catch the son of a bitch."

"Yeah. At least we hope so. But both Coralee and I are concerned that if this guy, Tony, gets wind that the cops are looking for him and that Ella is a witness, then, who knows what might happen? We figured it'd be better if I was there with her. You know, a man around the house."

Both Dwayne and Pedro remained silent.

"I bought a gun."

"Good," Pedro said. "Not much you can do with a cane or a crutch."

Rick laughed. "That's what I said."

"What kind you get?" asked Dwayne.

"A nine millimeter," Rick said. "A Glock."

"Nice," said Du-Bob. "That's a sweet piece."

"So what are you doing here?" Pedro asked.

"I knew there'd be all hell to pay if I didn't check in tonight. I'll tell them in the morning and move out tomorrow. Besides, Ella only gave them the description late this afternoon, so probably things are safe tonight. And I gave my dad the gun for tonight, and he's over at the house with them."

"And tomorrow, your little girl may go home?"

"Exactly. So it should all work out."

"Shit," said Du-Bob. "If it was earlier, we could go to HQ and celebrate a little."

"My thoughts exactly," said Rick.

Later that night, Rick lay sleepless in his bed, his stump sore and aching from the day's activity. He found himself thinking about Iraq: Hennessy, the other men under his command, the heat, the stress, the frustration. Suddenly he was riding in the Humvee on a dusty and bumpy road. People along the roadway avoided eye contact with him. He looked across to Jasper behind the wheel, blond fuzz on his cheeks and upper lip. Jasper turned to him, his eyes so blue, somehow Rick thought of the Texas sky when he saw them. Then suddenly there was an explosion in his leg. Pain erupted inside him, and his body consisted of floating fragments swirling in the bright emptiness of the sky like flakes of burned paper. He felt himself rising, in pieces, higher and higher, and then he began fearing falling back to earth again. He awoke in a sweat.

The next morning, Rick sat down with the ward supervisor and told her that he needed to move to his wife's residence. He couldn't get over all the complications it seemed to cause, but he had been right to anticipate that his moving out would cause a problem. As it was, he was lucky to be allowed to remain in the program for the next two weeks as had been agreed to previously. Finally, he was permitted to go for his clinic treatment program, after which he caught a cab to Children's Hospital to meet up with the rest of the family. When Rick went to Thomas's room, he was surprised to find that only his dad was there. John told him that Coralee had to go to work at the hotel or lose her job and that Virginia had accompanied Mildred and George to the funeral home to help make arrangements for Larry's burial.

"I checked in upstairs on our little girl," John said to his son. "The nurse said that they wanted to discharge her today, so I guess they're going to have to talk to you."

Rick was filled with mixed feelings: happy that Ella would be coming home but anxious about the safety issue and scared to death to have to confront the financial questions. He looked at his little boy, still pale and listless in his bed. Thomas managed a weak smile and acknowledged that he felt sore all over and slightly nauseous and light-headed. All he felt like doing was sleeping.

"I guess that's what your body wants you to do then, so go for it. It's all right. Grandpa will stay here with you while I go upstairs to check on Ella, okay?"

Thomas acknowledged him with a weak grasping of his father's hand and let his eyelids close. Rick and his father exchanged glances. Then Rick swung on his crutches and headed upstairs.

Rick approached the charge nurse at the nurses' station as if he were attacking a machine-gun emplacement: ready to kill or be killed. But he was immediately disarmed by her brief smile.

"So are you going to be taking our little princess away from us today?" she asked nonchalantly.

Rick managed a weak, "Well, I guess so, if I don't have to sell my wife and son to get her."

"Such a charmer. She'd be worth it, I'm sure. But I don't think that'll be necessary. All we'll need is your signature on these forms."

Rick couldn't believe it. He wouldn't have admitted it to a soul, but he was glad he had the crutches to lean on. He was so weak with relief. He'd had visions of having to pay tens of thousands, maybe hundreds of thousands of dollars, and he had absolutely no idea how to do it. But, as the nurse explained to him, his children were victims of a crime, and whatever wasn't paid by the insurance policies that he and Ella had would be taken care of by the Crime Victims' Fund.

"So we won't need to keep your daughter as a hostage until you pay up. Just take her home and enjoy her."

Rick explained that he wouldn't be able to take her home until his wife arrived after work, but maybe Ella could join him and his father downstairs, where they were visiting Thomas, and that was what was arranged.

XI

Rick stayed downstairs when everyone else decided to go to bed. He was weary and fatigued, and his leg hurt, but he wasn't ready yet to face getting into bed with Coralee. She had given him what he'd thought of at the time as a wistful smile, and then she'd let her fingers drift lightly across his shoulder as she went up the stairs to her small bedroom. He had joked that he wasn't sure if there'd be room for both of them and his leg. Coralee had said that she didn't think it was funny. Ella had been so excited to be home that emotionally she had worn everybody out, even though she was still restricted by a sling for her arm and a massive bandage on her thigh.

His dad looked exhausted by the full day of visiting, as did his mother, who quietly expressed her frustration at Mildred's near complete incapacitation—which Virginia attributed to Millie's loss of her son and her anxiety about her grandchildren. The day at the funeral home had been exhausting, but eventually arrangements had been made for a small funeral service in two days.

George was like a sack of cement that had to be lugged everywhere they went. Aside from being a warm body for Mildred to lean against, Rick couldn't see that the old man provided Mildred with anything. But Rick supposed a shoulder to lean on is sometimes exactly what's needed.

When he was sure everyone was in bed, he turned out the lights but remained sitting in the living room, looking through the front windows at the quiet street outside. He retrieved the Glock from its holster and examined it, letting himself become familiar with it. It was the first opportunity he'd had since his father had returned the gun to him earlier in the day. He liked the heft and feel of it. Dwayne had been right—it was a sweet piece. He took practice aim at the TV, a lamp, and a picture. He fantasized Tony climbing through a window and blasted the motherfucker. He pictured his kids in that tumbling car, shattered glass and blood spraying in all directions, heard the sounds of their screaming, of Larry screaming, of Thomas's head and body smacking into the windows and roof, and he was filled with a sickening rage. He would love to have the opportunity to shoot that bastard, look him in the eye and shoot it out, point-blank. Shoot it the fuck out!

Earlier in the afternoon, Ellis Cook had stopped by. The detective made a big show of thanking Ella and then talking to Thomas, to see if he could remember anything more about Tony. Afterward, in the hall, he confided to Rick that Tony was, in fact, Anthony James Lewis, a local player in the drug trade. Larry, who recently had been coerced into becoming an informer for one of the detectives on the drug enforcement squad, had started supplying them with information about Lewis. Apparently, someone had tipped Tony to the fact, and that was what the shooting had been about—payback. Ellis had brought a copy of Lewis's rap sheet, and his picture was amazingly like the drawing the artist had made from Ella's description.

Cook encouraged Rick to keep a heads-up for Mr. Lewis, just in case. "Although it's likely that our boy has skipped town."

Rick was taking Cook's advice and keeping an eye out, but he agreed that Tony had probably gone into hiding and would be looking to stay out of sight.

Rick pulled out a pint of vodka he had picked up during the day and took a couple of swallows. He felt all jumbled inside: confused, scared, and totally directionless. He felt like he was faking everything, like he was expected to know what he was doing when he hadn't a clue.

Ella had been deliriously happy to find out that he was going to be living with them. "Everything's going to be all right now," she said, beaming. "Daddy's home!"

Yeah, right. Daddy's home. Minus one leg. A pistol in one hand and a bottle in the other. Scared to even go up to bed with his wife. His wife. Rick took another swallow. How long was this arrangement going to last? For as long as she thought she needed him? How long was that going to be if he couldn't get a job? What would she need him for? Protection? How long was that going to last? Once Tony was caught or disappeared or whatever, once they no longer felt threatened, then what? What good was he? He knew that for now everybody was cutting him some slack, but that wouldn't last forever. At the clinic, they were pressuring him to let go of the crutches and start using the cane all the time. They assured him he could do it, but he wasn't so sure. He had a horrible fear of falling and looking like a clown. His stump hurt, and the muscles in his thigh felt weak. He had tried talking them into waiting until his thigh felt stronger, but they were insistent. In fact, they had decided, tomorrow, no more crutches! *I can't even stand up by myself, and I'm supposed to be the man of the house? Am I the only one who sees a joke in this?*

And his dad … he'd be pushing for Rick to go to work. In fact, both of his parents had been making the case for Rick and Coralee to move back down to Texas and be near them, where they could be more helpful with the kids, lining up a job, everything. His mom put on a brave and competent face, but he saw the concern in her eyes every time she looked at him. He wanted to be able to reassure them, all of them, that he was all right. *I'm all right, folks. Just relax, okay? Give me a fucking minute to catch my breath, that's all. All right? I'll get a job. I'll earn a living. I'll protect my wife and kids. I won't be a failure, a loser, a stereotypical Mexicano peasant. Just back off, all right? Just back off. Relax. Everything will be all right. Just give me a minute, okay?*

He was breathing harder. He took another swallow from the bottle and breathed deeply. He aimed the gun at various objects in the room—the chairs, the sofa—making little explosive sounds with his mouth.

He thought of Thomas. The poor kid. He was so weak, and his whole body hurt him. His vital signs were stable, but they weren't getting any better, and more tests were planned for the next day. The kids had been glad to see each other. That had been such a sweet, happy moment when they first saw each other.

"Am I going to die?" Thomas had asked. Everyone had been quick to reassure him, but secretly, Rick didn't know the answer. He was afraid that the real answer would have been, "I don't know. Maybe." Of course, no one was going to say that. Did Thomas know that, that no one dared be honest with him? Did that make him more scared? More scared but more unable to talk about it, because they had let him know that it was not to be talked about?

Thomas had said, "I'm glad that we're a family again." Rick almost cried. *A family again? Is that what we were?* Just like before he went to Iraq? Was he going to once again be the breadwinning, absent dad—preoccupied with work, with trying to win some grudging show of affection or recognition from Coralee? Was he going to be the hero-dad, the model who showed his son how to overcome adversity and emerge a winner? Wasn't that what Thomas expected? Needed?

Rick took another swallow and then screwed the cap back on the bottle and replaced the Glock in its holster. He slid the bottle into his jacket pocket and closed his eyes and put his head back on the chair and fell asleep.

The next morning, John and Virginia left the house to visit Thomas. Coralee drove to her job at the hotel, and on the way was going to drop Rick off at the hospital for his clinic treatment.

In the car, Coralee looked at Rick. "So what happened last night?"

"What do you mean?"

"I thought you'd be coming up to bed. You slept downstairs the whole night."

"I just fell asleep, that's all. I had planned on coming up."

She arched her eyebrow. "Really?"

Rick saw that she had a slight smile on her face. "Really," he said. "I really planned on coming up. I just fell asleep. I guess I was more tired than I realized."

"Rick, I'm comfortable with your leg, you know? You don't need to be concerned about that, about how I'll react."

Rick gazed out the window. He was tempted to say, "Yeah, I know. It's not a problem." But he wasn't really sure. Even more than that, he was concerned about how he'd respond, if he'd be able to get it up with her, or if all the other bullshit—the anger about feeling betrayed, the fear of being dumped again—would get in the way.

"I know. Or I think I know, that you feel all right with that. But I guess I'm feeling some doubt about how we're both going to react to being back with each other. A lot has happened."

This time Coralee was silent for a few minutes while she focused on her driving. At last, she said, "You may be right. It might not be perfect at first. But we can work through it. We'll work it out. I'm sure of it."

"Well," Rick said, laughing, "that makes one of us, anyway."

Inside the hospital, Rick headed for the cafeteria. As he left the register, he heard his name being called and, looking around, saw Phyllis waving to him. He made his way over to her, carefully balancing his tray. Phyllis cleared a spot at the table for his tray and waited for him to settle himself.

"You're still looking a little shaky balancing that tray while you're on your crutches."

"Yeah," he admitted. "This definitely is not my forte. I don't do gimpy very well, I'm afraid."

"Some people take longer, that's all."

"Yeah. Well, I suppose I could be trying harder too. In fact, today is probably my last day on crutches. They say I've been avoiding using the cane long enough."

"To tell the truth, I was wondering about that."

"So," Rick said, sipping his coffee, "what's happening with you?"

"A lot's happened since I spoke to you last," she said. "Harold's secretary called me to tip me off that Harold was trying to wangle a transfer overseas and that he planned to move out and take the kids with him. I guess he figured that if he was in another country, I'd never be able to get the kids back. I called my lawyer, and we got a court order preventing him from doing that. My lawyer made sure that Harold's employer knew the score. So that plan is squashed. And given that his evil intent was there for all to see—he had even been looking to sell our condo without my knowing and was looking into a place in London where he hoped to be transferred—we got a court order putting him out of the condo and preventing him from being alone with the girls. Plus, we're forcing him to pay support until we get an actual financial agreement signed."

Rick grinned in admiration. "Wow! Sounds like your lawyer is really on the ball."

"He's what they call a 'shark.' He's more ruthless than Harold, and smarter. As usual, Harold has been trying to save a few bucks and hasn't even hired an attorney yet. He thinks he can do all this on his own, the asshole."

"So Harold is out?"

"He's not only out of the house, but his boss is really pissed at him and he may lose his job. I'd love to see the bastard just disappear. Even the girls are glad that he's gone. The three of us can actually relax around the house now."

Rick smiled at the picture that conjured up in his mind. "I'm really happy for you, Phyllis. I really am."

"How about you?" she asked.

Rick took another sip of coffee and scratched his head.

"Well," he began, "Ella's home and coming along great. Thomas is still in Children's Hospital and pretty much the same. Poor kid is in a lot of pain and kind of languishing. I think he's afraid he's going to die."

He looked down at his plate and the half a muffin that sat there waiting for him. "I think I'm afraid he's going to die."

Phyllis smiled sadly at him. He managed a flicker of a smile, and looking into her eyes briefly, noticed their large almond shape, the long lashes, and the thin line of eyeliner along the bottom.

"And," he continued, "Coralee asked me to move back in. Last night was my first night back."

Phyllis pursed her lips and arched her eyebrows.

He smiled and shook his head. "I spent the whole night downstairs in a living room chair."

"You?"

"Yeah. Can you believe it?"

Phyllis looked at him intently and frowned. "How did Coralee take it? Did she go along with that?"

"No," he said. "She called me on it this morning. Said we could work it through."

"And …?"

"I don't really know." He finished his muffin and then his coffee. "I'm not sure I know what I want. I mean, it seems like something that I *should* do, you know? Ella is thrilled that I'm back home, and even Thomas managed to say something about us being a family again. And right now, there's this safety issue—"

"What safety issue?"

Rick told her of his concern that Tony Lewis might come after Ella. "It's probably not even a realistic threat. But for now, I feel like I'm doing what I should be doing. Being there."

"Protecting the women and children?"

"Yeah," he said seriously. "Something like that."

"They're lucky to have you."

He looked at her, her face, her eyes. "Still," he added, "I'm not sure that's where I really want to be."

"Where do you think that is? Where do you really want to be?"

He smiled. "In the tall grass on a sunny day, with ducks quacking in the background."

"Is that all?"

"Nooo," he said, drawing it out. "I thought the rest would be self-evident."

"It was," she said, laughing. "I just wanted to be sure." For a few moments, they sat smiling at each other, his hand holding hers. "We could do that," she said softly.

Rick leaned back in his chair. "I want to," he said, "but—"

"I know. You're back with Coralee and the kids and ..."

"Riding shotgun. And visiting my son."

"Excuses?"

Rick looked down, checking his empty coffee cup.

"I don't think so," he said finally. "I think I'd really like to give us a try. I feel good with you. I think of you a lot. But—"

"You're back with—"

"It's not just that," he interrupted. "It's me. I'm seriously fucked up. I don't know who I am anymore. What am I good for? What can I do? How am I going to spend my life? I don't feel like ..." Rick raised his hands in exasperation. "Phyllis, I don't know if I can hold up my end, you know?

"My mother-in-law has a boyfriend. George must be a hundred twenty years old. He's stone-deaf, arthritic, doesn't do shit. Just sits around the house looking at TV. I think Mildred gets off on taking care of him. The only thing he contributes is that he's there to put his arm around her and give her a hug. Phyllis, I need to be more than that," he said, fighting off tears. "And I don't know if I can."

Phyllis looked at him and then lowered her eyes to their hands clasped on the Formica tabletop. Finally, she looked up.

"Rick," she said, "you're still grieving for your leg, for who you were with it. That's understandable, but it's been a long time now. Your leg isn't coming back."

He gave a nervous laugh.

"Maybe someday, you'll get a better prosthesis, but otherwise, this is it. This is your reality. You've lost a leg. That's tough, but you haven't lost your brains. You haven't lost your mind, or your eyes or your heart. You're still you. Only you without a leg, that's all. If you ask me, you do just fine with what you've got."

He glanced up at her and saw her smiling.

"What you say makes sense. I know. I can even picture myself saying the same things to somebody else. But everything seems so different, so totally different. I feel like a fish out of water, like I woke up and I'm in China or someplace and haven't the faintest idea of how to speak the language."

"Well, maybe you have changed in some special way. Maybe you are different. But you still have everything else you ever had, all your knowledge, memories, talents. All that wasn't stored in your kneecap, you know. Rick, you've still got whatever you had. If you don't feel like you used to, maybe you need to feel differently about yourself, about your life. If the old you has been shattered, then maybe you need to put the pieces back together differently from what they were before."

Rick thought about that. Up to that moment, he'd been feeling hopeless, but that image sounded hopeful. He imagined himself picking up pieces of a picture he'd had of himself, like a jigsaw puzzle, and putting them back together differently, creating a new self. He scratched his head. *Yeah,* he thought, *a new Rick, a new beginning.*

"I like the thought," he said.

Phyllis leaned back, smiling at him.

"I guess I get to decide how I want to do that. It's an interesting problem. Who do I want to be when I'm all grown up?" He laughed. "I thought I was done with that one."

"You did it once, but that doesn't mean you're stuck with the old answer. It's your life, Rick. You just have to figure out what it is that you really want."

"You know, that seems like such an obvious statement, such an obvious fact of life. Of course this is my life. Who else's life would it be? But the sad truth is … I don't think I ever felt like it was mine. I think I always felt like it belonged to somebody else and I wasn't free to choose what I did with it."

He paused and looked at her. "I'm not sure what I'm going to end up doing with this. It feels clarifying, and at the same time, I think I'm more confused than ever. Christ, I am fucked up."

Phyllis laughed. "I'd be happy to fuck you up even more—if you decide that's what you want. You still have my number?"

He nodded.

"Then feel free to call me." She gathered her things together. "I've got to get to work."

He looked at his watch. "Yeah, me too. I've got the clinic. A date with a cane."

She blew him a kiss, but he reached over and pulled her to him, kissing her on the mouth.

"Thanks," he said. "You're a damned good nurse, you know."

"I like you too," she said, and she hurried off.

At the hotel, Coralee let her boss know that her brother's funeral would be the following day and that she would have to take the day off. He said of course and offered his condolences, but she surmised from the fact that he didn't look at her, that he was deeply annoyed. As she attended to her work, Coralee was grateful that her mother-in-law could be at the hospital with Tommy while Rick was getting his rehab treatment, and that her father-in-law was at home with her mother, George, and Ella. She pictured Ella actually taking care of the older adults, and she smiled, amused at the irony and enjoying the feeling of pride she felt for her precocious little girl, so strong and self-assured. In many ways, she saw her little Ella as being more competent than Tommy, even though he was older. She didn't like to admit it, but she did see him as somewhat weak and timid. She hoped that he would survive this ordeal and emerge stronger for it.

Her thoughts turned to Rick. When she had come down the

stairs and had seen him in the chair, she thought he looked like hell. Then she had glimpsed the bottle in the inside pocket of his opened jacket. Her first impulse had been to wake him up and confront him, but she had thought better of it. She didn't want to enable his drinking, if in fact he was abusing it, but she didn't want to fall back into the role of a disapproving mother figure either. She'd keep her eyes open for any sign of his really having a problem. Maybe now that he was living with her and away from his buddies at the hospital, there would be less pressure on him to drink. It wasn't that she was a teetotaler, but she wasn't going to live with an alcoholic either—not after all the problems her brother had caused with his drugs and drinking. She'd wait and see.

Throughout the day, Coralee's mind kept turning to the situation at home. She was glad that John was there in case there was any threat from Larry's murderer, Tony Lewis. She wasn't sure that John was really up to any kind of direct physical challenge, but until the funeral was over and she could find a way to get Ella to a safer place, she didn't think she had much of a choice. She called every couple of hours to reassure herself that everything was okay.

Her fear and insecurity led her to think about her decision to invite Rick back into her life. It wasn't so much that she was having second thoughts about that; she still thought it was the right and logical thing to do. But she wasn't sure how much she really wanted to have sex with him again. She had spent months putting that kind of image out of her mind. True, she was horny herself and was often half-mesmerized by one sexual fantasy or another, usually triggered by whatever book she was reading or TV program she was watching. But in spite of real efforts, she was never able to consciously sustain a fantasy about having sex with Rick. Other thoughts kept getting in the way: she imagined long, ugly, red scars on the amputated stump of his leg. She remembered raging feelings of anger and frustration at the little-boy way he had of coming to her to ask for approval and recognition for something he'd done.

And those feelings of anger kept her from being able to picture herself responding freely to him or performing oral sex. She knew that he enjoyed her sucking him, but now she felt as if it would be something that she'd have to do to prove to him that she loved him and wanted him to stay, rather than something she desired to do. The rising resentment made her clench her jaw. The difficulties in this arrangement were only beginning to make themselves known to her. *Well, we'll just have to explore it and do the best we can and see what happens.*

Most of the time, John stationed himself in Mildred's modest living room, where he had a view through the front windows across the stoop and meager dried-out yard to the street. He knew that he could get close to the curtains and spy up and down the street without being observed from outside. Every once in a while, he went into the kitchen and checked to make sure the back door was locked and that no one was prowling around out in the backyard. He had discussed with George and Millie, and with Ella herself, what to do if he yelled a warning to them.

They took these security precautions seriously, but at the same time, they were fairly confident that nothing would actually happen. Still, John was conscientious about his responsibility and periodically fingered Rick's holstered gun, which he now wore on his hip. Part of him was scared that he would be no match for the younger and more dangerous Lewis. He was sixty-nine years old, after all. On the other hand, his mind's eye was focused on the scenario of catching the bastard trying to break in through the door and emptying the 9 mm into him at point-blank range. That thought brought a smile to his face, and his fingers automatically drifted over the handle of the pistol.

When Coralee called, he answered the phone and breezily told her that everything was fine and under control. Millie was doing some finger painting in the kitchen with Ella or making cookies, and George was dozing in front of the TV. Nothing was going on. It was just a lazy summer day. Relax and get back to work. He'd see her later on.

Then he'd think about what was going on with her and his son. He had been really pissed at Coralee for abandoning Rick while he was overseas, and even more enraged when he learned that she had gone ahead and pursued the separation even after learning he'd been wounded. He and Virginia had been appalled, but Virginia had counseled that perhaps it was for the best; Rick deserved a better wife anyway, someone who loved him more deeply than Cora did. Part of him agreed. He wished that Rick could feel loved the way he felt loved by Virginia—the way she always made him feel special. No matter what was going on in their lives, he always knew that she was there for him. He thought that his son Matt had that with his wife, Bea. He hoped that Rick could find that too. Maybe he would.

He knew that Rick was less than thrilled with the idea of reconciliation and guessed that the main reason Rick had moved into the house was because of Ella. He understood that. He'd probably have done the same thing himself. No man who believed his kids to be in danger could turn his back on the situation and dismiss it. No son of his could do that. His chest swelled a little with the feeling of pride that he felt for his son, his willingness and capacity for self-sacrifice. That brought to mind a picture of Rick on crutches and of the missing leg, and a feeling of sadness washed over him. *Goddamned war! Goddamned Iraqis! Goddamned Bush!* He thought of his son's discouragement. *I'll have to be more encouraging,* he thought, *more supportive. Maybe start calling around now to test the job market. Maybe if he has something solid to look into, he'll be more optimistic.*

John recalled an earlier time in his own professional career when he had felt discouraged with his lack of progress because of stupid prejudice against Hispanics, especially Tejanos. The fact that his family had been here for well over five hundred years, before there had been a Texas, before there had been a Mexico, meant nothing. When Anglos saw him, they saw a stupid and lazy Mexican peasant. He recalled his own despondency at having difficulty in finding an engineering position, worrying about being able to support his wife and children and wondering how on earth he'd ever be able to afford to send them to college. He'd thought of drowning himself in a bottle, or robbing a store, or even killing himself. But stupid, desperate thoughts go through one's head, nonsense, like wind blowing tumbleweeds across the desert. Empty-headed nonsense. He had been able to ignore such thoughts. He had persisted, and things had worked out. Virginia's support and belief in him was a big help and a major source of his strength. He prayed the same would happen with Rick.

Three hours after he arrived for his treatment appointment in the rehab clinic, Rick emerged fatigued and harboring murderous thoughts toward his physical therapist. The sadist had really pushed him to the limits and beyond. Still, he admitted to himself that he had been able to accomplish more than he had thought he could. He was using the cane and carrying his crutches. He'd have to bring them home, back to the house, and drop them off before going on to Children's Hospital to see Thomas. He caught a cab out front and took the short ride back to Mildred's, where he was looking forward to visiting with his father and with Ella and having a bite of lunch before heading out again. In the cab, he massaged his right thigh and his right arm. *What a freaking workout,* he thought, and then he smiled to himself. The truth was, it felt good to push himself physically. He knew that inevitably he'd get stronger and that eventually his balance would improve. Actually, he felt a little embarrassed at having avoided using the cane for so long.

As Rick climbed awkwardly out of the taxi, he saw his father peering from the front window. After paying the cabbie, he walked toward the house carrying his crutches, and smiled at his father watching from the front window. *He'd be damned if he'd come out and give me a hand,* he thought, chuckling at his dad's rigid standards.

"Hey, Dad, anything new?"

"*Nada,*" John said, shaking his head. "Nothing's going to happen here. That scumbag is long gone. Believe me."

"You're probably right," Rick agreed, laying his crutches down behind the sofa where they'd be out of the way. He'd agreed that he would use them only when he wasn't wearing his leg. "How's Ella?"

"She's fine. It'd take more than a couple of bullets to slow her down. She's been out in the kitchen all morning wearing poor Millie down to the bone. They're making cookies, finger painting, jabbering away."

Rick made an attempt to get George's attention. His eyes seemed closed, and it was hard to tell if he was asleep or not.

"Hey, George," he yelled. George started and looked up, smiling when he saw Rick's face in front of him. "How are you?" Rick shouted.

"Oh, fine, fine," said George. "You want to sit here?"

"No, George, I'm fine. I'm just home for a little while, to see Ella and have a bite to eat."

"Oh, is lunch being served?" he asked, starting to rise.

"No, George. Sit down. Millie will call you for lunch."

George nodded and turned his attention to the silent TV. Rick and his dad looked at each other and grinned. Ella had heard him and came hobbling into the room from the kitchen. The wound in her leg was obviously slowing her down, but her mood was bright and cheery. She reached up to put her arms around Rick's neck. He had to bend over for her.

"Pick me up," she pleaded.

"Pick you up? A big girl like you? I'm not strong enough to pick you up. You'd better get your grandpa to do that."

"You're strong," she persisted with a pretend pout.

"Not strong enough yet, sweetheart. But I could use some help, if you would let me lean on you a little."

"Okay," she said happily. "Can I use your cane?"

"You sure can, as long as I can lean on you."

They trudged off into the kitchen, where Mildred was cleaning up and making space at the table.

"Hi, Millie," he said. "How are you holding up?" He hobbled around the table and leaned over to kiss her on the cheek.

She shrugged her shoulders. "Best as can be expected, I guess. It's hard. I hope you don't ever have to lose a child."

Rick stopped in his tracks.

"Oh, I'm so sorry. I didn't mean …"

"No," he said. "You're right. It's a terrible thing. Hopefully, Thomas will pull through. It's a shame what happened to Larry. Nobody deserves to die that way."

"You want some lunch?" she asked, changing the subject. "Ella made some cookies for you, but I expect you want something more substantial."

"Whatever you've got, Millie. Don't put yourself out. I'm not fussy."

"I could make you peanut butter and jelly," Ella chimed in. She was practicing walking around the kitchen using his cane, and he watched her admiringly.

"Sure, I'd like that," he said. Then, motioning toward the cane, he continued, "You know, you've got that down pretty good. Only thing is, my cane is a little big for you. A shorter cane for you would be more comfortable."

"Maybe George can saw it down for me," she suggested.

"Not my cane, he's not. I tell you what, though. I'll see if I can get one for you. How's that?"

She nodded. "I think that's a brilliant idea." Then she added, "I could make you grilled cheese too. Grandma showed me how."

"Actually, sweetheart, peanut butter and jelly sounds good." Then he looked at Mildred. "How's the prospects for getting a cup of coffee?"

"I'll put a fresh pot on," Mildred said. Then she shuffled into the living room, where Rick heard her shouting at George, asking him if he wanted lunch, and then in more normal tones, inquiring of John if he wanted anything to eat.

Later that afternoon, Rick limped into his son's hospital room and found both Thomas and his mother, Virginia, napping with the TV sound turned way down. Rick looked at his mother and realized how tired she was and how demanding this week had been for her. He eased himself into the other chair in the room and reflected on what his parents had offered of themselves. His sixty-nine-year-old father was at Mildred's, actually prepared to get in a gun battle with some psychopathic murderer. And his mother, at sixty-eight, had done whatever had been required of her: hospital duty, holding Mildred's hand at the funeral parlor, even living in the same house with Coralee. He knew how resentful his mother was of what Coralee had done and how difficult it was for her to suppress it and put it out of her mind.

He knew, as he had always known, that his mother would do anything, make any sacrifice, for him. On the one hand, that had been a little suffocating as he'd gotten older. But on the other hand, it felt wonderfully comforting to know that someone was always there for you no matter what. Was there something wrong with him for wanting that feeling from his wife? Wasn't that the way it was supposed to be? He hoped that both he and Coralee gave Thomas and Ella that feeling of security, of unqualified love. But the truth was, he didn't really believe that he would ever be able to get it from Coralee.

And here was Thomas, twelve years old, who was looking forward so much to starting eighth grade and taking up fencing. Now, with his broken collarbone and broken wrist, that was very doubtful. But that was the least of their worries. The big question was, would he recover from all of his internal injuries? Would he make it out of the hospital alive? Rick felt the sudden urge for a drink, but was fearful of being observed. His son and mother might open their eyes at precisely the wrong moment. He decided to go into the bathroom at the corner of the room. When he came out, both his mother and Thomas had woken up.

"Hi, Dad," his son said somewhat wearily.
"Hey, champ. How are you feeling today?" He went to the bed

and kissed his son and then his mother. "How you holding up, Mom? You looked exhausted when I came in."

"Oh, I'm fine. Just catching up on my beauty rest," she said, smiling.

"So how's our Zorro?" Rick asked, once again turning his attention to Thomas.

"Actually, Dad, I think I'm getting a little better. Everything doesn't hurt quite as much. At least I think so. Sometimes I'm not sure if I hurt less or I just forgot how much it did hurt."

"Yeah, I know what you mean. But chances are you're not imagining it and you really are getting better. The healing can take a long time, Tomaso. I'm still noticing improvements in myself. In fact, today I started using the cane, full time, and I don't think I could've done that a week ago."

"That's wonderful, Rick," his mother said, beaming. "That's wonderful progress. You should be quite proud of yourself."

Rick smiled, half to himself, and then said, "Thanks, Mom. Actually, I am feeling proud of myself. Although I think I might have put it off for much longer if my therapists hadn't been as insistent as they were."

"Oh, knowing you, I'm sure they didn't have to push all that hard. You're a go-getter. You always pushed yourself."

"So what are the doctors saying?" He threw the question out there for either of them to answer.

His mother flashed him an almost imperceptible look and after a momentary hesitation said cheerfully, "Dr. Nadia said that the X-rays showed that the bones are healing very well."

Dr. Nadia was the pretty young resident from somewhere in central Asia—Uzbekistan or someplace—with whom they had most of their contact. Nadia was her first name, but no one could pronounce her last name, so they referred to her as Dr. Nadia. Rick was quite taken with her Asiatic features and her accent.

Rick kept the smile on his face, but caught his mother's eye.

"Great!" he said, more to Thomas than to his mother. "Listen,

Mom, you really look beat. Why don't you get some lunch and go home and take a nap. I'll be here all afternoon."

"You sure? You'll be all right?"

"Of course we'll be all right. We'll knock down a couple of beers and go chasing the nurses." Thomas blushed a little, as if his dad had come a little too close to his actual fantasies.

"Well, all right then. I guess I am a little bushed." She leaned over her grandson and kissed him on the cheek. "I'll be back this evening with Grandpa. Anything special you want?"

Thomas surveyed his growing stack of comic books and shook his head.

"I'll just say good-bye to Grandma out in the hall, and then I'll be right back in. All right, champ?"

Thomas said okay and turned to watch the TV screen.

In the hall, Rick looked questioningly at his mother. "So?"

"She said that his kidneys aren't healing as quickly as they would like, so he's going to be staying here longer, and they want to do more tests of his pancreas. They think his abdominal pain may be related to that. It's possible they may have to surgically insert a drain. But meanwhile, he's still not to get any food by mouth."

That was a major disappointment. Even though Thomas's appetite was practically nonexistent, they were all eager to see him begin to take regular food as a tangible sign of his improvement. And Nadia's concern about Thomas's kidneys and pancreas was definitely upsetting. Even though inserting a drain was not a major undertaking, subjecting the boy to any kind of additional surgery seemed like cruel and unusual punishment.

"When will they be doing the tests?"

"Early this morning she said they'd be doing it soon, but here it is, after lunchtime already. Who knows when they'll get around to it?"

"I'll check it out," said Rick. "Thanks, Mom. You go on home now. Get some rest."

"I will, honey. I'm looking forward to lying down and taking a nice nap."

"Good. That's the best thing." Rick kissed his mother on the cheek, noting the softness of her fair, creased skin and the tired sadness in her eyes. After seeing her to the elevator, Rick hobbled over to the nurses' station, where he inquired about the tests.

"Your son's blood was taken this morning ... let's see ... 9:54 a.m. As soon as the lab has the results, they'll let the doctor know. It should be this afternoon sometime."

Rick thanked her and figured his mother must have either stepped out or dozed off when the technician had come in to get Tommy's blood. He headed back to his son's room.

"So, Dad, what else did Grandma have to say?"

Rick plopped himself down into the chair and was aware of how grateful his leg felt to be relieved of the burden of bearing his weight.

Rick smiled at Thomas. "You're an astute dude for a guy who's only twelve."

"C'mon, Dad. I could tell she was upset this morning when Dr. Nadia finished talking to her out in the hall."

"Okay," said Rick with some resignation. "Looks like you're handling this in a pretty mature fashion, so I guess you have a right to know."

He paused, and Thomas waited.

"Well," said Rick, clearing his throat, "I gather that the doctors think some of the pain you've been experiencing inside your torso— your chest and belly—might be related to your kidneys or your pancreas. They may decide to put a small drain into you to let some stuff come out and make you feel better. If they do, it'll be a minor procedure, but it'll be one more thing you have to endure. Grandma and I ... we're just upset that they might have to do anything more to you, that's all. And I guess it might mean that it'll be that much longer before you get anything real to eat."

Thomas averted his eyes, looking down at his hands, at the IV tubes running into them. He had an oxygen gizmo in his nostrils, a catheter running out of his penis, and now there was the possibility of a drainage tube being placed into his gut. Rick reached out his hand

and placed it on top of his son's and waited. After a few moments, Thomas asked, without lifting up his face, if he was going to live.

Rick said, "Look at me, son."

Thomas lifted his face to his father's, his eyes glistening.

"You're a sick young man. Your body has been through a lot. You broke a bunch of bones. And everything inside, all of your inner organs—your kidneys, your pancreas, everything—got all tossed around and bruised. You understand? Your whole body, even your head, has taken quite a beating. It's like you were in a fight with a 1998 Buick and you lost. Listen to me, Tomaso, you will never in your whole life ever experience anything that is worse than this. This is as bad, as painful, and as scary as life can get. You're maxed out. It's a damn shame that you have to face all this at your age. Christ, I didn't have to face it until last year. But you're going to pull through this. Just be patient. It is painful. And it is scary. It's scary for all of us, for your Mom and me and Grandpa and Grandma. We're all scared for you. But you'll come through this.

"And afterward, after this is all behind you, you'll be able to look back and know that you survived this ... that at the ripe old age of twelve, you took everything that life could dish out. And, sure, you got knocked on your ass, but you got up again. And, Thomas, the knowledge that you survived the worst that can ever happen—'cause nothing is ever going to be worse than this—is going to make you strong and confident. You'll see."

Rick believed everything he'd said. He'd said it passionately, wanting desperately for Thomas to believe it too, to know it within himself.

Then Thomas looked at him and asked, "Is that what happened to you, Dad? Do you feel stronger now after having almost been killed and having your leg blown off?"

Rick was taken aback. He waited a few moments and then said, "I'll be totally honest with you ... I haven't the faintest idea. I haven't thought about it." He paused again. "Give me a few minutes to think about it."

It was a fair question. The kid surprised him. Did he feel stronger, more confident in himself after having lost his leg? Did he keep in mind that he had faced the worst that life had to throw at him and had survived it, had come out standing? If he was honest, the answer was no.

But I'm still a work in progress. I'm still healing. I'm still mourning my loss. It is true that I do feel like nothing could be worse than what I've been through, but I haven't realized that nothing else will ever be worse than this. This is as bad as it gets. This is as down as I get. If I can make it through this, I can make it through anything.

He looked over at Thomas. "I'm not sure how to answer your question. What I've said to you is true. I just hadn't realized that it's true for me too. I guess we're both in the same boat. We're both still healing and still scared. And I've got to realize, for myself, just as you have to realize for yourself, that we will get through our misfortunes with the help of the people who love us, and that when we're all healed and it's all over, we will be stronger than before. Different maybe, but stronger." He looked at his son. "Does that make sense to you?"

"Yeah, I guess so."

"Just trust me, amigo. We're both going to come through this. We're going to be all right."

Then, after a few minutes of silence, Rick said again, out loud, half to Thomas and half to himself, "Maybe you won't ever fence again, and maybe I won't ever run again. But we're going to be all right." Rick squeezed Thomas' arm for emphasis and watched his son to see if he had taken in what he'd just said. Thomas returned his look. Then he nodded his head and, sticking out his chin just a little, returned to watching the TV.

XII

————•◆•————

Coralee hurried into Thomas's room, a little out of breath, with a couple of his favorite comic books. She kissed her husband and son in turn and sat herself down on the edge of the bed. "How are you feeling, handsome?"

Thomas shrugged his shoulders and then winced. "Still tender, I guess."

"And how's my man?" she asked, turning her smile on Rick.

"We're hanging in," he said wearily. Sitting with Thomas, watching a steady stream of cartoons on TV was mind-numbing. He had tried reading but couldn't concentrate. At least with Coralee here, the volume would go down a bit. He had tried playing some games with Thomas, but the boy was too uncomfortable to be able to focus for any length of time.

"Listen, I'm going to go make a pit stop."

He grabbed his cane and then took a walk down the hall to stretch his muscles. He felt cramped up from hours of sitting in the chair. He decided to take his time and let Coralee enjoy some time alone with her son. When he got back, she was telling Thomas about a funny incident at work.

Rick took his seat in the chair and found himself dispassionately watching the interaction between his wife and his son. They were totally focused on each other, his son thin and pale, his dark eyes looking larger than ever. Thomas was small-boned, and, looking at him now, Rick doubted that the boy would ever experience the explosive growth spurt that he'd had. He thought of his own grandparents, his father's parents, and their small, wiry frames. Thomas would be a throwback to them, he thought, whereas Ella looked like she would take after her mother's family—larger-boned, sturdy, and muscular. Coralee, he saw, was a handsome woman with good features, but overall, she gave an impression of strength and determination rather than a more feminine fragility. He thought "woman" rather than "girl," strong rather than sexy, competent rather than loving. Good qualities for a mother.

After a while, Coralee turned to him, smiling. "I thought that when we leave here, maybe we could go someplace for something to eat rather than heading straight home. How does that sound?"

Rick's first thought was that this was a pleasant surprise. It was unusual for Coralee to suggest going out to eat. "Yeah," he said. "Sure, that sounds like a good idea."

"There's a good Mexican place not far from here. Would that be all right?"

"Are you kidding? How would it not be all right? Of course."

"Good," she said happily, and then she turned back to continue her interaction with Thomas.

A short while later, Dr. Nadia entered the room. While she was checking out Thomas's condition, Rick asked her about the results of the blood tests from earlier that morning. At first, she was hesitant to discuss them in front of Thomas, but Rick made a point of reassuring her that it was all right.

"He's a big boy. He knows what's going on."

Coralee looked at Rick and Dr. Nadia, not knowing anything about the testing.

"The results of the tests we are doing are showing that the kidneys are badly bruised. They are not healing as quickly as we would like, but some people take a little longer to heal. We are hoping that that is the case with Thomas." Then she flashed the boy one of her beautiful smiles.

Rick thought to himself that he wasn't sure if his son appreciated how beautiful and sexy this doctor was, but he was ready to jump her bones himself.

Dr. Nadia continued in her charming accent, "We were concerned that Thomas may have an abscess on his pancreas, an infection that we would have to drain. But," she seemed a little hesitant, "the results are not conclusive yet. So far, it looks like it might be all right without draining, and we are monitoring it closely to see if there are changes, one way or the other. So the bottom line is that everything is moving ahead, only very slowly, and we are watching carefully. There's no need to do even minor surgery if it's not necessary. Right?" she asked.

Everybody was in agreement. Rick glanced at Thomas and saw his look of relief at not having to have a drain inserted. Not yet, anyway.

An hour later, he and Coralee entered the small Mexican restaurant and seated themselves at a booth.

"I could use a glass of wine," said Coralee, perusing her menu. "How about you? You want something to drink?"

"Sure. I never pass up an opportunity to have a Mexican *cerveza*."

They ordered their drinks and dinner. Coralee's wine and Rick's beer were brought to their table, and they sat sipping their drinks.

"How was work?" he asked.

"My boss is annoyed that I'm taking off tomorrow for Larry's funeral, but other than that, it was the same. I'd be out of there in a minute if there were work to be found. I'm barely making more than minimum wage, for God's sake. In New Jersey, I'd be making twenty thousand more a year. I don't know why anybody down here bothers getting an education. It certainly doesn't seem to help that much."

"What'll you do if he fires you?"

Coralee shook her head and took a sip of her wine. "I don't even want to think about it." After a slight pause, she continued, "To tell you the truth, I was thinking of the possibility of our returning to New Jersey." She gave him a questioning look.

"What?"

"Well, we still have the building, right?"

"Yeah," he said, as if being shaken out of a daze. "Yeah, we still own the building. But—"

"What? I could get a job back in the insurance field easily enough, and you have contacts in engineering. I'm sure you could get something going again. I know the kids would be glad to return to their friends and schools—not to mention that the schools are better in New Jersey."

Rick took a gulp of his beer, draining the glass, and looked around for the waitress to ask for a refill. "Seems like you've been giving this a lot of thought."

Coralee laughed. "I have a lot of time to think on my so-called job as a bookkeeper." She noticed he was playing with his glass and looking around. "You look like you're uncomfortable with it, though. I thought you would be pleased."

He shook his head slightly. "I don't know what I am. I'm surprised, that's all. I hadn't been thinking along those lines."

"What lines have you been thinking along?"

He shrugged and, managing to get the attention of the waitress, held up his glass.

"Or maybe you weren't thinking about our future at all."

"What do you mean?"

Coralee heaved a big sigh. "I guess what I really mean, Rick, is …" She pointed her chin toward his empty glass.

"What?"

"This morning, when I came downstairs, I noticed a bottle of booze in your jacket pocket."

Rick rolled his eyes and slumped back onto his seat.

After some silence, she asked, "Well?"

"Well, what? So you saw a bottle, a half pint, by the way, eight ounces of vodka. What the hell is that supposed to mean?"

"That's what I want to know. You tell me what it means."

"It means simply that I decided to buy some vodka. That doesn't make me a criminal."

"Where is it?"

"Where's what? The bottle?"

Coralee stared at him.

"It's gone. I finished it."

"And you bought it yesterday?"

"Yeah," said Rick, his voice growing more belligerent. "What the hell is this, Cora? I feel like I'm getting the third degree."

"Rick," she said quietly, "I'm only trying to find out what's going on with you. You bought a bottle of vodka yesterday. Eight ounces, you said. And you finished it. You drank eight ounces in one day. Rick, that's a lot of alcohol. I'm not saying you're a criminal, but it concerns me. We're going to be burying my brother tomorrow. I've seen what alcohol and drugs can do."

"For Christ's sake, Cora, I'm not doing drugs. Don't compare me with—"

"I'm not accusing you of doing drugs," she said more loudly and firmly, her teeth clenched. "I'm not accusing you of anything. I'm simply stating the truth. You drank the equivalent of eight drinks in one day. You drank alone, as far as I know. That sounds secretive. That concerns me, that's all."

They fell silent as the waitress brought their dinners and Rick's second beer.

"Just tell me why, Rick. What's going on that you need to do this? What am I letting myself in for? I need to know."

Rick glared at her. He picked up his beer mug almost defiantly and stared at her as he took a big swallow. Her expression didn't change. She maintained eye contact with him. But her expression was surprisingly soft, almost pleading.

Rick lowered his glass and lowered his eyes to his plate. "Okay," he said. "You're right. You deserve an explanation." He paused, picking up his knife and fork. "Can we eat first?"

"Sure. By all means. First things first. There are priorities."

"Look," he said. "You took me by surprise. I got defensive. Let me think about this a little, all right? Let's just have a nice, quiet meal, and then we'll talk. That's all I meant."

"So you can have time to think of some excuse?"

Rick clenched his jaw. "Don't be a bitch. I'm not your fucking brother. I said we'll talk after."

They ate in silence, and afterward, Rick ordered coffee for them. After the waitress brought the coffee and he'd added sugar and cream, he leaned back.

"The truth is, Coralee, I do have a drinking problem."

She recoiled into her seat as if she had been shot.

"I'm not saying that I'm an alcoholic. I'm not even sure what an alcoholic is. I'm not getting drunk. I don't think I can remember the last time I was drunk. It must have been at least ten years ago when we had a party at our house. But I have been drinking. More than I should. I know that. And, you're right, I've been doing it secretly. Obviously, I haven't wanted you to know, or the staff at the hospital."

"But why, Rick? Why?"

He grinned foolishly and took a while before speaking. "I guess it started out as a way to help me get to sleep. To sleep without those goddamned dreams."

"Don't you have medications for that? Aren't they prescribing anything for you to help you sleep? To help you deal with the pain?"

"It's not just the pain, Coralee. In fact, it's not primarily the pain. It's just hard to fall asleep. I close my eyes, and almost without fail, I'm back in Iraq ... back in an exploding vehicle ... my leg flying away from me ... my life flying away from me. I keep reliving that moment where it feels like I'm losing everything—everything that's important to me, including my life."

He paused. "I know that this'll sound stupid, but at the time, in the beginning, I found that the drinking helped. And at the time, I didn't want to take medications, because I didn't want to become dependent on them."

Coralee's mouth dropped open. "You refused medication so you could become dependent on alcohol?"

Rick rolled his eyes. "Well," he said, "that wasn't my intention at the time."

"Would taking medications help you get off the booze?"

"I don't know. Maybe. But I'm reluctant to take any pills until I stop drinking. I know enough to know that it's not a good idea to mix them."

Coralee sighed. "So how much are you drinking?" she asked.

"About a half pint a day."

"Rick, that's almost two quarts a week! A half gallon of vodka every week?"

"When you say it like that …"

There was another long pause. Coralee shook her head. "So what are we going to do, Rick?"

"Obviously, I've got to stop," he said.

Coralee held her head in her hand, smoothed her hair, and rubbed her hand across her face. "Christ, Rick. I don't know. I just don't know. I never suspected. Here, I thought you were handling all of this loss so well …"

"I'm doing the best I can, Cora. I know I've got to stop. I've been thinking about it."

"Thinking about it isn't going to do it, Rick. It's like my thinking about going on a diet. If that's all it took, everybody would be thin and sober."

"I know."

She reached out for his hand. "I know you know. I'm just scared, Rick. I just … I don't know. I'm not sure what I should do." She looked at him pleadingly.

"What do you think I should do, Rick? What do you want me to do? What do you want to do?"

Rick knew what she was asking. She was asking whether she could trust him to stop abusing alcohol. She didn't want to be married to a drunk. But he knew that she should be asking more than that. She should be asking whether or not he was committing himself to trying to make their marriage work. He thought he could answer the first question more easily than the second. The fact was, he wasn't sure in either case.

"Coralee," he started, "I know what you want to hear, what you need to hear. I'd love to tell you that I can stop drinking right this minute and be the kind of man you need me to be. But in all honesty—and I'm trying to be as honest as possible, both with you and with myself—I don't know if I can be that person. I think that what I've got to do is demonstrate something to myself first. I think I've got to find out who I am, and then you can … then we can decide what we want to do."

"What are you saying, Rick? I'm not sure that I'm hearing you right. Are you saying you're not sure that you can or want to stop drowning yourself in booze? Or are you saying you're not sure that you want to give me another chance?" She looked beseechingly at him.

"Help me understand, Rick. What is it you're trying to tell me?"

"Coralee, you're pressing me for answers that I don't have. I'm telling you I'm in trouble here. I'm doing the best I can to stay afloat, and I don't know if I can make it. I'm trying. I want to …" he searched for the right words. "I want to be able to stand on my own two feet." And then he laughed. "Or at least on one of my own feet."

"Rick, this isn't funny."

"No, I know. Listen, I'm only trying to say that I don't want to disappoint anybody—you, the kids, my parents, even my doctors. But most of all, I want to be able to feel good about myself. I don't feel good about drinking as much as I do, although to be honest, I'd never added it all up. Now I feel even worse about it. I want to stop abusing this stuff," he said, indicating his empty beer mug.

"But I'm not going to sit here and promise you that I'm going to be successful at it. I hope I am, but I don't know. I'd like to say that I'm going back to work full-time and will be able to support you and the kids like before. But I don't know if I can. I'm simply saying that I've got to demonstrate some things to myself first, before I can commit to anything."

Coralee cocked her head to one side and studied him. "And that includes us, your family?"

"Yeah, I guess so. It includes everything. How can I commit to anything or anybody if I don't know whether I'm going to sink or swim?"

The waitress brought the check and asked if they wanted anything else. Rick told her no, and she left.

"I guess I didn't realize how undecided you were. I thought you were more together, more in control."

"Yeah, well—"

"Fine," she said, pulling herself up. "Back to the drawing board."

After a few moments, she asked Rick, "What about staying at the house? Do you still want to do that?"

"Why not? We're still concerned about this Tony character. And I've checked out of the hospital. Let's take it a day at a time."

"All right," she said. "A day at a time."

Rick picked up the check and reached for his wallet. "Let me get half," she said.

He looked at her and smiled. "Thanks."

XIII

———◆·◆———

The next morning as the sky slowly lightened, Rick, asleep on the sofa, opened his eyes and rubbed his face awake. He stretched and looked at his watch. It was six o'clock. Although it had taken him a long time to fall asleep, he had been awakened only twice by the usual disturbing dreams. He closed his eyes and sank back into the sofa, and his mind automatically went to his conversation with Coralee at the restaurant. He had been pretty honest with her in that he had indicated he wasn't ready to make a commitment, either to staying sober or to staying with her. But he hadn't let her know that he had misgivings about her. He hadn't told her that he wasn't sure if he trusted her to be loving and supportive enough. He hadn't let on that he wasn't sure if he loved her and wanted to be with her. And he sure as hell hadn't said anything about exploring things with Phyllis. Still, he hadn't talked to Phyllis again. Who knew if she was still an option?

His mom and dad were obviously annoyed that he and Coralee had come home so late from the hospital. Apparently, Coralee had called Millie and told her that they were planning on eating out, but they had gotten home later than expected. John and Virginia had, for some reason, waited for them to come home before going to the hospital to see Thomas. And later, when they came home, they expressed surprise at seeing Rick camped out on the sofa.

"Why aren't you upstairs in a bed," they had asked, and he'd told them that he felt more comfortable keeping watch downstairs. His father nodded, and his parents had looked at each other and then said good night and gone upstairs. He heard them murmuring for a while before they got quiet.

Ella still had no appreciation of what had happened to her body, so she had kept going at full speed until she suddenly ran out of gas and totally collapsed at about eight o'clock. He had no doubt that she would wake up strong, refreshed, and full of zip. Then Rick remembered that the funeral service was later in the morning. It was going to be a small and short service at the funeral home and then a ride to the cemetery for Larry's burial.

He stretched again. He felt good. He felt rested. He pushed himself up into a sitting position and reached for his crutches to go upstairs to the bathroom. He'd pee his brains out, take a nice hot bath, shave, and then get dressed. He was looking forward to the day. Ella would be going with them, since she wouldn't have to do a lot of walking.

By the time Rick emerged from the bathroom, everybody else was up except for Ella and George. He heard Coralee and Millie and his mother downstairs in the kitchen. Through the open door of their bedroom, he saw his dad in his pajamas looking out the bedroom window.

"Morning, Dad. Bathroom's free if you need it."

His father looked around and smiled. "Thanks. I was afraid I was going to float away."

"Sorry. It takes me longer nowadays."

"No, I understand. I was just contemplating pissing out the window, that's all."

"Glad it didn't have to come to that."

His father came around the bed and embraced him.

"You going to the funeral like that?" Rick had on a shirt and tie and his boxers, but no pants, under his robe.

"Yeah. I thought, being it's a small service, just the family, that I'd go casual."

His dad snorted. "Between you and me, one of us is bound to get arrested today."

"I still have to put my leg on downstairs."

"It makes everything just a little bit more complicated, doesn't it?"

"Almost everything."

John smiled and patted Rick's shoulder before disappearing into the bathroom.

Downstairs, Rick sat on a chair and strapped on his leg. Then he pulled his pants up over both feet. Then, using the chair, he raised himself and balanced uncertainly while pulling his pants all the way up. Then he sat down and took a deep breath. He tucked his shirt in, zipped his fly, buttoned the top button, and buckled his belt. After taking another deep breath, he leaned over and put his sock and shoe on his good foot and tied the laces. His other shoe was always on his prosthesis. Then he reached for his cane and stood up. Balancing himself, he made sure his shirt was tucked in; then he took off his robe and laid it over the arm of the sofa and walked into the kitchen.

His mother and Coralee were making pancakes for breakfast and had arranged a production line—one at the stove, one at the counter. Millie was sitting at the table drinking coffee. She was the first to greet him.

"Good morning, Ricky," she said.

He caught the intended display of affection. He felt good about it. But he also recognized it as a dig at Coralee. He guessed that somehow, Coralee had already communicated his lack of commitment.

"*Buenos dias*, Millie," he said. "How is everybody? Looks like the women of this house couldn't wait to get to work."

"Somebody's got to do it," said Coralee without turning around.

"Good morning, Rick," said his mother. "Your father up yet?"

"Yeah. He was in the bathroom when I came down. He should be down soon. I think George and Ella are still asleep." He sat down next to his mother-in-law.

"Now, that girl ought to sleep for a year," Mildred exclaimed. "I never saw a child with so much get-up-and-go as she has."

"I think she feels a responsibility to keep us all entertained," added Coralee as she turned from the counter and came over to give Rick a kiss on the cheek.

"Oh, she does that, all right. She'll entertain me all the way into my grave at the rate she goes."

"Come on, Momma," Coralee chided, returning to the counter. "You love every minute you spend with that girl."

Mildred grinned as she picked up her coffee cup. "That's the God's own truth. Yes, it is. She is a pistol, that girl. Not like you were when you were her age. You were quiet, off with your books or your dolls, playing by yourself. Not all full of mischief the way little Ella is."

She drank from her coffee cup and then continued, "Now, Larry ... he was like our Ella." She sighed. "So full of life, he was." No one said anything, and after a few moments, Mildred turned her attention to Virginia.

"Virginia, what was your Ricky like when he was little?"

Virginia turned from the skillet where she'd just poured in some more batter.

"What I remember is that Rick was kind of shy and quiet. I think Thomas is a lot like Rick was at that age. He didn't come into his own until he was older ... in high school, I think." She looked at Rick.

"That's right," he said. "Especially after I got into track and football." He thought of Thomas. "I was all excited for Thomas, the way he was looking forward to starting fencing. I was hoping that it would be good for him, the way track was for me. Now ..." He threw up his hands in a gesture of futility and let the thought hang in the air.

John entered the kitchen. "How is everybody? What am I missing? Oh, boy, flapjacks. My favorite."

"Anything edible is your favorite," said Virginia, turning around and blowing him a kiss.

"Ain't that the truth?" He laughed.

Mildred got up from the table and brought her cup to the sink, where Coralee was washing some glasses. She gave her daughter a pat on her shoulder and then went to the cupboard to get down dishes to set the table.

"Can I help?" asked John.

"Why don't you get stuff from the fridge," said Coralee. "Let's see … juice, butter, syrup, anything else we need."

They were crowded around the table when they heard Ella come thumping down the stairs, still favoring her leg. Coralee called to her to come on in, and she ended up squeezing herself onto her mother's lap and eating off her plate as well. Coralee laughed at the way she had been taken over.

"What's that they say about a family that eats together?" she asked jokingly.

Rick observed the family together. In spite of the underlying tensions and sadness, the moment felt warm and comforting. He loved the joking and the looks of love that flashed between Ella and his parents, and he saw how both Mildred and Coralee had embraced his parents and made them feel like they were part of the family. He could imagine his brother, Matt, and his wife, Bea, being here as well. This was one thing he had missed while he and Coralee had lived up in New Jersey, the opportunity for more family gatherings around a table. This was a good moment, a good feeling. He wasn't sure he was willing to give it up. He thought, *This is what it's all about, isn't it?*

When they were finished and had started to clean up, George wandered into the kitchen and smiled vaguely at everybody. He went to Mildred and gave her a kiss.

"Do you want something to eat?" she hollered at him, looking at him full in the face so he could read her lips.

"Whatever you've got," he said good-naturedly, and he sat down at the table.

Eventually, everyone was ready and relaxing in the living room, when the limousine from the funeral home arrived to take them to the service. When they arrived at the funeral parlor, the director greeted them and ushered them into the room where Larry's body was displayed in his casket. Mildred was the first to approach it, and from his place behind her, Rick observed her shaking her head from side to side. When Mildred sat down, Coralee sat down beside her without making any attempt to say a final good-bye to her brother. Rick realized he didn't have to fake anything either and went and sat next to Coralee. His mother and father were more polite and went and stood by the casket. He saw them crossing themselves.

Ella was the last to go up. This was the first dead person she had ever seen. Rick got up and stood beside her.

"You all right?" he asked.

"Uh-huh," she mumbled. "I'm feeling sad for him, but I'm not sick or nothing."

"Good," said Rick. "It's appropriate for you to feel sad. Your uncle was a good friend to you."

"He looks fake," she said.

Rick observed Larry's color. It seemed lighter than his normal milk chocolate color, and it lacked the glow of his natural warmth. Larry was by far the darkest one in the family, whereas Coralee and her mother were more a creamy coffee color, and both Thomas and Ella, lighter still. Rick also noticed that they had done a masterful job of covering up the bullet holes in Larry's face. They were hardly noticeable.

"Yeah," Rick agreed. "He does, a little. It's the makeup they put on him. It makes him look different." He stood with his arm on her shoulder for a little while longer.

"Do you want to sit down?" he asked.

"I guess," she said, and they turned and sat down, Ella on one side, between him and his mother, and Coralee on his other side. *The women in my life*, he thought, and then immediately he thought of Phyllis.

At that moment, he saw Detective Cook enter the room. They caught each other's eye, and then he thought he saw Ellis motion to him.

"Excuse me," he said to Coralee, and he got up. In the back of the room, Ellis Cook motioned to him to step out into the hall, since it looked like the minister was about to begin the service.

"Thanks for coming," Rick said. "I didn't expect to see you here."

The detective shrugged off the compliment. "Let's just say I developed an interest in this case. How's your boy doing?"

"It's hard to say. He's not getting worse, but he's not healing as quickly as we'd like. The doctors are watching him closely. He may need more surgery. We don't know yet."

Ellis Cook sighed heavily. "I see your little girl is up and about."

They both looked at Ella, sitting between her mother and Virginia, taking everything in while she listened to the eulogy.

"She's amazing. She has more energy than the rest of us put together."

"Listen," said Cook, "I wanted to give you a heads-up regarding this Lewis character."

"What's happening?"

"We've got everybody and their grandmothers out looking for this prick, but so far, *nada*. Also, his cousin Mayberry Lewis, who goes by the name of Willie, is missing too. Willie is also a bad dude. The two of them are tight, been hanging out together for years."

"You think they're still around?"

"Who knows? You'd think they'd be long gone. But this is where their friends are. They might be holed up in somebody's apartment, getting high and whacking off all day. I thought you should know we haven't spotted him yet."

Cook paused, examining his shoes, and then he looked up at Rick. "One more thing ..."

Rick waited, looking at him intently.

"The word is that Lewis knows your daughter identified him as the shooter."

Rick closed his eyes as he took in a deep breath. "Any suggestions?"

"Yeah. If I were you, I'd take the family and get out of town until we get him. It shouldn't be too long. This guy ... he's a hot potato. A lot of people would like to see him out of the picture. He's a major liability to everyone now. There's a lot of heat on. So it shouldn't be too long before we find him, dead or alive."

"I still have my son in the hospital here. We can't just leave him."

Ellis grimaced. "Now, how did I know you would say that?" He shifted his weight back and forth. "All right," he said finally, "for the next couple of days, at least, I'll have a patrol car outside your house."

"Thanks. That would mean a lot."

"No problem. Only, I won't be able to keep one there twenty-four hours a day. There may be times when they're needed somewhere else, you know? But unless something essential calls them away, they'll be there. Another couple of days, and this should all be over. You keep your eyes open, and take care of yourself and your family. Don't go playing hero. That would be stupid."

"I hear you."

Cook shook his hand, and Rick returned to the service.

He didn't hear much except for the clichés: loving son, devoted uncle, roots in the community, sorely missed, and the rest of the crap. The minister giving the eulogy didn't even know Larry, or that he was a shiftless, dishonest, manipulating, self-centered addict who betrayed everyone in his life. In fact, that was what finally got him killed. Rick thought about what Ellis Cook had just told him. Tony Lewis was still out there, probably with his cousin Mayberry.

It would be great if everyone could move back to Texas with his parents, but what about Thomas? Even if Thomas wasn't in any danger, he couldn't take everyone else away and leave the kid alone. And who was to say that he wasn't in danger? For all he knew, Lewis might think that he'd have to eliminate both kids as witnesses. *Ah, there's probably nothing to worry about. Sounds like so many people want Tony Lewis out of the picture that the last thing he would be worrying about are two little kids.*

When the service was over, the director came over and helped escort Mildred and the rest of the family out to the limousine for the ride to the cemetery for the burial. A patrol car followed them, and Rick breathed a sigh of relief. Thank God for Detective Cook. A half hour later they stood at the grave site and listened to some more pap about Larry's finding peace with his maker, and dust to dust, etc. Rick figured that the only thing missing was a steady rain to complete the shopworn picture. Instead, it was a bright sunny day, a typical warm, dry Oklahoma summer day. Rick caught Coralee's eye and saw her heave a heavy, bored sigh as she too searched the heavens and surroundings for something more interesting or palatable. Finally, they were back in the limo and headed home. Mildred commented that it was a nice service, and everyone else agreed. This was not a time to bad-mouth Larry or his funeral.

Back home and sitting in Mildred's front room, Rick related what the detective had told him, and everyone felt grateful for the presence of the patrol car, although Mildred said that she felt embarrassed by having a police car parked in front of her house. The consensus among them was that if anyone at all was really in danger, it was Ella and maybe Thomas. That being decided, they agreed that Virginia and John should take Ella back to Texas and arrange for her follow-up care there. Rick would continue to spend afternoons at the hospital with Thomas, and Coralee would join him after work. If necessary, they'd return to the hospital in the evening, but the expectation was that Thomas would probably go to sleep early, and providing him with a break from visitors was probably a good idea anyway. They agreed that he was unlikely to be in any real danger in any case.

The decision having been made, John and Virginia started packing their things. They would take Ella and leave that afternoon. Ella was saddened by the prospect of leaving Grandma Millie, but at the same time, excited by the expectation of going to Texas to stay with her other grandma and grandpa. Rick made sure it was clear that he was going to continue to stay downstairs at night, just in case. He thought he noticed Coralee's annoyance at that, but she didn't say anything. After lunch, Rick kissed his parents and daughter good-bye, and, after they left, he and Coralee drove to the hospital.

"I wanted to thank you for being there today," she said after a while, keeping her eyes on the road as she drove.

"Hey, your brother was a louse, but he was still your brother, still your mother's son."

"I know. We only did it for her. But I'm still glad he's dead."

"Yeah, I did it for your mother, but I did it for Ella too. She didn't know how bad he was. For her, she's lost a playmate, almost an older brother."

"Like Momma said, they were a lot alike."

Rick sighed and looked out the window.

"Rick?"

"What?" he said, turning to her, not knowing what to expect.

"I understand your wanting to stay downstairs, feeling you've got to protect us and all ..."

"Yeah?"

Coralee appeared to be having difficulty bringing something up, and Rick guessed that it had to do with either sex or his drinking.

"Well," she started, "I was wondering where that leaves us. I mean, I understand our taking it one day at a time and your needing to figure out who you are and what you're going to do, but are you ruling out our exploring, you know, lovemaking? I mean, are you ruling that out altogether?"

Rick was unprepared for the question. He realized that it was logical for her to ask it, but he hadn't really come to terms with it himself. Finally, after much fidgeting, he said, "To tell you the truth, Coralee, I'm much too confused to think in terms of ruling anything in or out. So I guess the bottom line answer is no, I haven't ruled out the possibility of our making love. But truthfully, the idea scares me a little."

He paused to gather himself. "Like I said yesterday, or whenever it was, I'm not sure how either of us is going to actually respond. I'm afraid that I might be too uptight to let myself really let go with you. I don't know if I'm ready to let myself feel anything. And the other thing …" he paused again, "I don't know if our getting together sexually constitutes a commitment or not."

"What do you mean? Aren't you making a commitment to seeing if we can make it?"

"I'm not sure that's what I said. I think what I said was that I had to demonstrate some things to myself first before I could make a commitment to anything or anyone."

"I understand that you don't feel you can make a commitment to our staying together. I understand that, Rick. Really, I do. But I thought that when you said we'd take it one day at a time, you were saying that we'd try things out and see how things worked out. To me, our making love would be part of that exploration. We could see how it actually went. I've got my own reservations and hang-ups. I'm hoping that we'll be able to get through whatever difficulties we might have. But I think we need the chance to do that. Avoiding it isn't going to be very helpful."

They pulled into the hospital parking lot. He nodded, agreeing with her logic. But in the back of his mind, he had an image of Phyllis in the car, her skirt halfway up her thigh. He didn't want to complicate things by telling Coralee that he was considering the possibility of exploring a relationship with another woman first, a younger and prettier woman. Coralee was watching him, and he smiled and acknowledged that she made sense. He felt guilty, as if she were reading his mind and knew that he was thinking of someone else, even while he was agreeing that they should explore things sexually. He didn't want to think about it right now, so as soon as Coralee parked the car, he got out and started walking, wishing that he had something to drink.

Entering the lobby of Children's Hospital, Coralee said that she wanted to use the ladies' room, and Rick said he had to go also and that he'd meet her back in the lobby. When they met again, they were more composed and their smiles were somewhat softer. Waiting for the elevator, they held hands.

Thomas was glad to see them. This was the first morning he had spent alone without any member of the family to keep him company. He seemed to have survived reasonably well. Both Rick and Coralee noticed immediately the increased color in his cheeks and a brighter, brisker attitude. After each of them had given him a kiss, Rick asked him how he was feeling.

"I am definitely feeling better," he said. "Yesterday, I wasn't quite sure. Remember? I couldn't tell if I was imagining feeling better or not."

Rick said that he remembered.

"Well, I've been paying closer attention this morning, and I'm definitely feeling better. My belly doesn't feel as tender when I push it," he indicated, poking his fingers into his belly in an imitation of what the doctors did. "And I don't feel as nauseous. And that funny taste in my mouth is mostly gone. And I'm really looking forward to eating."

Both Coralee and Rick broke out in smiles. It was such a joy to see and hear this kind of positive energy coming from their son. They grabbed for each other as if to say, "Did you hear that? Did you see that big smile?" Coralee's eyes were moist.

Rick stood, leaning on his cane, his other arm squeezing Coralee, and beaming at his boy.

"I didn't think I'd ever say this to a twelve-year-old son of mine, but there are no other words to express what I'm feeling. Son, you're a fucking miracle. I'm just so fucking proud of you."

Thomas grimaced at hearing his father using swear words this way in front of his mother.

Coralee expressed mock outrage at Rick's swearing, although she admitted that it expressed exactly how she felt.

"Has Dr. Nadia been in yet today?" Rick asked.

"Yeah. She and Dr. Semanski, her boss, were here early this morning. She said that she'd be back this afternoon sometime. Then the nurse came in to take some more blood."

Coralee asked, "Did the doctors say anything?"

"Not really. They just asked how I was feeling and listened to my chest and stuff. You know."

"Well, it sure is good to see you with some new life in you. I think everything's going to be all right now," she said.

Later in the afternoon, they told Thomas about Uncle Larry's funeral and Ella's going to San Antonio with her grandparents. Thomas was even up to playing some checkers with them and spending some time on his Game Boy while they read. Then, late in the afternoon, Dr. Nadia came in. She immediately saw the look of hopeful expectation on their faces and couldn't help but smile at them.

"So," she began, "what do you think of your handsome son today? Has he told you he's getting stronger?"

Coralee was the first to respond. "He's told us he's feeling less soreness and is actually developing an appetite."

"I'm not surprised. Even his cheeks are little bit rosy, no?" She smiled again at Thomas, and even more color flooded into his cheeks. "Well, the blood tests are confirming what we are seeing. The signs of infection in the pancreas are showing improvement. We are expecting maybe in few more days it will be all gone. The medication prescribed by Dr. Semanski is working. Is good news, yes?"

"What's next, Doctor? What can we expect to happen now?" Rick asked.

"Well, like I told you, in few more days, probably all infection will be gone. Then we can remove the IV and reintroduce some food by mouth. Then, depending on the kidneys, maybe we can send this young soldier home. Let's see, maybe toward the end of next week—Thursday, Friday. We'll see."

They thanked her profusely before she noted Thomas's vital signs and then left. Thomas couldn't stop smiling.

Rick reminded Thomas, "You realize, of course, that once you get discharged from here, you won't see that pretty face anymore."

Thomas blushed and worked to establish a frown on his face.

Coralee gave Rick a punch on the arm and told him that *he* wouldn't be seeing that pretty face anymore. The three of them could not have felt any happier. Finally, as it was getting late, Rick and Coralee said they were hungry and were going to go have dinner. Thomas indicated that he'd be fine and was tired, and that he'd see them the next day.

"Tomorrow's Sunday. We'll both be here sometime in the morning," Rick said. They kissed their recovering son and left for dinner more lighthearted than they'd felt in a long time.

XIV

E veryone had gone to bed, and Rick sat alone in the darkened front room, trying to fall asleep, but alert to every sound outside: passing cars, voices, distant police or ambulance sirens, even barking dogs. The only light was what filtered through the curtains from the streetlight in front of the house, plus a dim glow from a light over the back door that shone from the kitchen through the connecting hallway into the living room. When he closed his eyes, images from Iraq flowed into his mind, and once he realized it, he attempted to literally shake them out of his head and turn his attention to the present or the future. The knowledge that Thomas was actually beginning to mend was one positive thought he tried to focus on.

Rick was startled out of his concentration by a creaking on the stairs. He turned to look over his right shoulder and saw the shadowy form of Coralee quietly making her way down the stairs. She must have heard him turn.

"You awake?" she whispered.

"Yes," he whispered back. "What's the matter?"

She came over to the sofa where he raised himself up on one arm. "Nothing's the matter. I just thought I'd come down and keep you company for a while."

He pushed himself back into the sofa and made room for her to sit down.

"Thanks," he said. "I can use company."

"Trouble sleeping?" The streetlight provided a backlight for Coralee, forming a halo as it shone through her hair, keeping her face more in shadows with the whites of her eyes and her teeth standing out, giving her a more exotic look.

"I always have trouble sleeping," he said. "I was trying to keep my thoughts focused on Tommy."

"What were you thinking about him?"

"Oh, I don't know. Nothing special, I guess. I was picturing him healthy again, going to school, growing up, getting bigger. Stuff like that. Nice thoughts."

"Sometimes I try to picture what he'll be like when he's all grown. I see him as tall, like you, and thin, with those big dark sensitive eyes. I picture him married with a couple of kids."

"Yeah. I see him as married. But that's such a long way off. Who knows, right? I mean, look at all of this shit now. Who would have ever imagined this whole scenario: me minus a leg, the business gone, us, our children almost killed, even our being here in Oklahoma City, for Christ's sake?"

"I know." She leaned into him, and he turned onto his back, propped up on a pillow, and put his arm around her. "It's all a big mess, isn't it? None of this would have happened if I had stayed in Jersey."

"Yeah, well …"

"I'm sorry, Rick. I feel like all of this is my fault."

"Oh, so you're the bitch who sent me to Iraq and got my leg blown off?"

"No." She laughed and poked him in the ribs. "You know that's not what I meant."

"All I'm saying is, you don't get to take all of the responsibility, that's all."

Coralee snuggled herself more comfortably onto his chest. She slid a hand under his T-shirt, feeling the hairiness of his belly and chest. Rick held her a little closer. The touch of her hand on his skin felt good. It was the first time she had touched him since he'd left for active duty, over two years ago. He felt her breasts pressing against his belly and felt himself becoming aroused.

Apparently, Coralee felt him swelling up against her, and she raised her head to look at him.

"Sorry," he said.

"Oh," she soothed, shaking her head and smiling, "no need to be sorry."

She sat up, took a glance over her shoulder at the patrol car sitting out front, and pulled her pajama top up over head and laid it at the foot of the sofa. Then she stood up and removed the bottoms, stepped out of them, and climbed onto the sofa, straddling him.

Rick hadn't seen her naked for a long time, and it seemed like a lifetime since he'd last been with Phyllis. He couldn't help but feel admiration for Coralee's body, and he instantly realized the feelings of longing and deprivation that he'd been trying for so long to suppress. He ran his hands up from her hips to the curve in her waist and up across her ribs to her full breasts. Coralee leaned forward and kissed him, and then kissed him again, longer. He paid attention to her lips, the shape and size of them, their firmness, and the wetness of them as he explored them with his own and with his tongue.

Her hands were cradling his head, and her fingers combed through his hair as she kissed him. Rick pulled her forward so that he could reach her breast with his mouth, and as he did, he heard her give a little gasp as she rubbed herself against his engorged penis.

Wordlessly, she reached down and extracted his erection from within his boxers and sat back on his thighs while she held it in both hands, stroking it. Then, rising up and forward, she guided him into her and slowly lowered herself upon him. Coralee leaned forward, bringing her breasts to his mouth once again while she began moving her hips rhythmically. Silently, except for an occasional sucking in of air or soft moans, they made love to each other until Rick exploded into her and she collapsed onto him.

After a few minutes, during which their breathing returned to normal, Rick managed to say, "Christ, I guess we were saving up for that one."

"Jesus, that felt good. I don't remember it ever being that good," she said.

"Me neither," he said. "I don't think we've ever done it in this position before, have we?"

Coralee was silent for a few moments. "I've thought about it. I've had fantasies of seducing you and climbing on top of you like this, but I never did. If I had, I'd have remembered it. Believe me, I won't forget this."

Rick tilted his head to look at her face, resting on his chest.

"So why didn't you? How come you never seduced me? How come I always had to initiate things?"

"I don't know. I guess I thought I wasn't supposed to. I remember hearing something about how men always need to feel in control." She paused, but only for a moment. "In fact," she said, raising up a bit so she could look him in the face, "I think that's one of the things I was angry at you for. I blamed you for not letting me be more sexually aggressive, or spontaneous."

"What? You're kidding, right?"

"No, Rick. I'm serious. I know it's foolish, but I did. I blamed you for being too controlling."

Rick was actually laughing. "Coralee, can you hear yourself? There's no one on the face of this planet who is strong enough to control you. And besides, aren't you the one who was angry at all men for being wimps?"

"I know," she said. "I know it's foolish and convoluted, but in my head, you—and all men—were weak, and therefore needed to feel in control. And that's why I wasn't, or women in general weren't, supposed to be more sexually assertive."

"Listen to me now. You go ahead and be as sexually assertive as you want to, whenever you want to. You'll get no complaints from me."

"I don't know how I let myself do this tonight. Desperation maybe." She paused. "Rick, would you have ever initiated this?"

"I don't know," he said thoughtfully. "To tell you the truth, I had forgotten what a great body you have. If I could have known that things would go this smoothly, then for sure I would have jumped you long ago." He took a breath and sighed. "But I was really very angry with you, you know. I thought you had really betrayed me, and … I didn't know if I could trust you again."

"I thought you were trying to punish me," she said soberly.

Rick mulled that over. "No, not that I'm aware of. I'm not saying it's not possible. Maybe that's part of it, the avoidance. But I don't think that's how I felt."

"Anyway, I'm glad we finally got to it."

"Reminds me of an old toast: 'Here's to it. When you get to it, do it.'"

"Well, we did it," she said, hugging him.

"Yes, we did."

Coralee turned her head. They looked at each other and smiled, and she lifted her head so that they could kiss. Rick's hands started stroking her body.

"Something tells me," he said, "that we're going to do it again."

Afterward, Coralee got up from the sofa and Rick watched appreciatively as she slid her pajamas back on. It dawned on him that there had been no hesitation by either of them. His missing leg, his stump, had been completely irrelevant. They kissed again, and she returned upstairs to go back to bed. Rick settled back into the sofa, rolled over, and peacefully went to sleep, contented and totally relaxed.

He was dreaming that a young Iraqi man was scratching on the window of his Humvee. The vehicle was stuck in traffic, and he was feeling nervous about it. He told Jasper, his driver, to move it, to get going. He didn't want to open the window. Then he realized that the scratching sound he'd heard was real. He tried to figure out what it was, but by the time he had aroused himself to wakefulness and forced his eyes open, somebody was standing over him with the muzzle of a handgun pressed against his forehead.

Enough light was coming in from the front windows that he could make out that the intruder was wearing a ski mask. He was reasonably short and thin, smaller in build than the picture of the more muscular Anthony Lewis. Rick assumed that this must be his cousin Willie. Rick's mind was totally clear now. The scratching he'd heard must have been them at the back door. He knew police were in the patrol car out front. It might be possible to attract their attention. For these guys to break in with a cop car out front said something about how desperate or how crazy they were. Either way, they were very dangerous.

Rick heard a creak on the stairs and shifted his eyes to his right. He made out the big shadowy figure of Tony Lewis climbing the stairs. He looked up into the face of Cousin Willie, and even though Rick couldn't see his mouth, he sensed that the bastard was smiling at him. Rick had no illusions. He was alive now only because they hadn't wanted to risk making any noise prior to accomplishing their goal, which was to kill Ella. But not finding her here, they might attempt to murder everyone in the house, probably starting with Coralee. He couldn't let that happen, but he was in an awkward position. Willie was watching him intently and was standing above him, where it would be difficult, if not impossible, for Rick to reach him.

His own gun lay on the floor beside the sofa, and he let his right hand drop down, hoping that he'd be able to find it without too much difficulty. It was right there, lying loosely in its holster. Rick fit it into his hand and slid the safety off, and was about to raise it and attempt to shoot his assailant when they both heard a kind of "whoop." Tony flew backward from the top of the stairs and landed with a hard crash on his back halfway down the flight, sliding headfirst down to the bottom. Rick took advantage of the distraction, and with his left arm sweeping across his face, knocked Willie's gun away from his head, simultaneously swinging his right arm up and getting off two quick shots that entered Willie's throat and went up into his head. Hot, salty blood immediately splashed into Rick's eyes and face, and Willie's body collapsed on top of him. As he pushed the body off him and onto the floor, he saw Tony stirring at the bottom of the stairs.

Responding to the sound of the shots, Lewis yelled out for his cousin, "Willie! Willie!"

Rick aimed and got off two more shots. Tony slumped back to the floor.

Coralee called from upstairs, "Rick. Rick. Are you all right?"

"I'm okay," he yelled. "Turn on the light." She threw the switch that turned on lights at both the top and the bottom of the stairs. Now he could see clearly the bodies of the two men. He wiped the blood from his face with his hand and then realized there was pounding at the front door. He sat up and was reaching for his crutches when Coralee came down the stairs. She stepped over the lifeless figure lying on the floor at the bottom of the stairs and ran to the front door to allow the two patrolmen to enter, their guns drawn. Immediately, they saw the two masked figures on the floor and a bloody one-legged guy in his T-shirt and boxers on the sofa with a 9 mm in his hands. One of the officers went to Rick and took the gun from him, while the other made sure the intruders were in fact dead and moved their guns away from the bodies. Within minutes, a number of patrol cars, sirens blazing, raced onto the street and pulled up in front of the little bungalow.

Rick looked up at one of the policemen. "Call Detective Ellis Cook. He's been working this case. Tell him, I think the Lewis cousins are here."

Coralee went to him on the sofa. "Are you hurt? You've got blood all over you."

"It's not mine," he said wearily. Adrenaline began to take over, and he felt himself shaking and his heart pounding. His breathing was quick and shallow.

"Let me get something to wipe you off," she said, getting up and going into the kitchen. She came back with a wet kitchen towel and began to wipe the blood from his face and hands. A policeman came over, an open notebook in his hand, and asked them to tell him what had happened.

"The short story, Officer, is that these two bastards broke into the house intending to kill us all."

By now the house was filled with policemen and squawking two-way radios. Mildred appeared on the stairs in her robe and surveyed the scene: a room full of police, Coralee in her pajamas, Rick covered with blood and in his underwear, and two masked dead men lying on her living room floor. She shook her head and waved her hand in front of her face, turned, and went back up the stairs to her bedroom.

One of the policemen brought Rick and Coralee glasses of water, and another found Rick's robe on the floor at the foot of the sofa and handed it to him. It was only a short time later when Ellis Cook showed up. He looked briefly at the bodies, looked under the masks to confirm the identities, and then sat down on the edge of the coffee table opposite Rick and Coralee.

"I thought I told you not to play hero," he said.

"There was nothing heroic about this as far as I'm concerned. I was scared to death that we were all going to be killed. It's just fortunate that this asshole," referring to Tony Lewis, "fell down the stairs. Otherwise, I don't know if I'd have gotten the drop on Willie."

"He didn't fall down the stairs," Coralee said, a slight smile playing at the corners of her mouth.

"What do you mean?" Rick said. "I saw him come flying backward down the stairs. He must have tripped on something."

"No, he didn't trip. I pushed him."

Both men stared at her and then at each other and then back at her.

"I had just gone upstairs and gotten into bed when I decided I'd go to the bathroom first. When I came out of the bathroom, I thought I heard something downstairs, and I stood still, wondering if you," indicating Rick, "had gotten up or needed something. I was going to call down to you, and then I heard the creak on the stairs. I figured that if it was you, I'd have heard the thump of a crutch. Then I saw the silhouette of this big guy climbing up the stairs, and I guessed who it was and what he wanted to do. Just as he reached the top stair, I rushed him. I knew that he'd have trouble seeing me because it's so much darker up there. I hit him right below the ribs just as he was stepping up onto the landing, and I pushed as hard as I could. And all he could do was yell out, 'Whoops.'"

Ellis shook his head. "You took a hell of a chance there, Mrs. Garcia."

"What did I just say about not being heroic? I take that back. Jesus," Rick said to Coralee. "Whatever possessed you to do such a thing?"

"I guess the same thing that made you take a chance shooting it out with these two." She looked him in the eye and said, "I'm very proud of you, Rick." And then her eyes abruptly filled up, and she began to blubber. "I'm so very proud of you. I'm sorry, Rick. I'm so sorry for everything in the past."

"Hey," he said. "Come on. There's no need for that."

"But I need you to know. I am proud of you. I am glad you are who you are."

They looked at each other, she sitting beside him, his arm around her.

"I do love you, Rick. I really do."

He pulled her closer. "Hey, I love you too."

He recalled how he had felt, watching Tony Lewis climbing up into the dark, knowing he would try to kill everyone upstairs. The idea of his killing Coralee had been too much, and Rick had been determined to do whatever he could to try to stop it, even if it meant losing his own life. He had not been optimistic about being able to avoid being killed by Willie. It was only her act of heroism that had given him the opportunity to do his part. But in the process, he had realized that he didn't want to lose her. And that knowledge was certain and true. It was how he felt. He couldn't ignore it any longer.

"I love you," he repeated. He felt like he had finally come home and could relax. He hugged her and felt tears coming to his eyes. It felt so good. She felt so good.

"Listen," Cook said, interrupting them, "we're going to have to have some people coming in here, taking pictures, doing all the forensic stuff. Why don't you guys go upstairs? I'll post somebody down here to be in charge and lock up when we're all done."

Rick and Coralee nodded, and Coralee reached for his crutches and helped him up the stairs, stepping over the body of Tony Lewis in the process.

"We'll have these bodies out of here once we're finished. Oh, and I'll give you a call in the morning with the name of a couple of companies that clean up after crime scenes like this. Usually, the homeowners' insurance will pay for it."

Cook watched them go up and then looked down again at Tony Lewis's body. He looked at Lewis's weapon, which had been pushed aside, an assault weapon capable of firing automatically when the trigger was held. It was a mean weapon. He glanced quickly up the stairs, smiled, and shook his head. Then he called one of the patrolmen over and told him to keep an eye on everything and then lock up once forensics was finished and the bodies were taken away. Then he left to go back home to bed.

Upstairs, Rick went to the bathroom and then washed himself off at the sink before putting the robe back on and going into Coralee's bedroom. She had the light on and was waiting for him. He lowered himself down onto the bed and laid his crutches aside; then he removed the robe and collapsed into the bed next to her.

"It's been a hell of a night," she said.

"Yeah," he said. "We found a new position." He was prepared for the punch on his arm when it came. He put his arm around her, and she snuggled in.

"Actually, it's been quite a day, what with Larry's funeral, Ella's leaving with your parents, and the news about Thomas."

"Was all of that just today?"

"Well, actually, yesterday. It's already Sunday."

"Good," said Rick. "That means we can sleep late."

She looked at him, his eyes already closed, and kissed him on the cheek. Then Coralee rolled over and went to sleep.

XV

I n the middle of the night, Coralee raised herself up on one elbow and, after some hesitation, gently shook Rick by his shoulder. He awoke, startled and disoriented.

"You were having a bad dream," she said quietly. "I wasn't sure if I should wake you or not."

Rick grunted and let himself sink back into the mattress. "Yeah, you did the right thing, I guess. It was just another one of my usual Iraq dreams."

"Can you tell me about them?"

Rick sighed and nodded. "They're usually some variation on a theme. In this one, I was back in high school in San Antonio. A bunch of us were cruising around in somebody's car. A friend of mine named Graham …" Rick smiled to himself. "I just realized that Graham's first name was Tommy. Anyway, Graham was driving. We were out in the desert someplace, and it felt scary, like we weren't supposed to be there, like we were trespassing on a reservation or something, or maybe a holy burial ground. I knew something bad was going to happen, and I'm telling Graham and the others that we should turn around; we've got to get out of there before it's too late. That's when you woke me up." He shook his head as if in disgust. "Usually it ends with an explosion." Rick wiped his forehead. "Christ, I'm sweating. Is it hot in here?"

"No, it's not hot. But let me get you some water."

She came back with a glass of water and a wet washcloth with which she wiped his face and neck and chest. Rick remembered he was naked under the sheet. Even though they had made love earlier that night, he still felt a little self-conscious about being totally naked in front of her. He was thinking primarily of his stump—how, under the sheet, it lay completely exposed.

"You know," he said, "I was surprised earlier tonight …" he noticed the look of confusion on her face, unsure about what he was referring to. "When we were making love, you didn't pay any attention to my stump. It was as if I didn't have one."

Coralee smiled down at him from where she sat on the edge of the bed.

"To tell you the truth, I was surprised myself. I had thought I might be repulsed by it. I had pictured big, ugly, red scars." She laughed softly. "In my worst fantasies, I might even have pictured it as a bloody open wound, like a leg of lamb or something with this big old bone in it and gristle and layers of fat and everything."

"Oh, my God," he exclaimed.

"I know. You'd think I was a little girl who didn't know any better, the way I let my imagination run away like that. But the truth is that last night, it never occurred to me. You're perfectly right. It's as if you didn't have it."

"You want to see it?"

She raised her eyebrows, and in the semi-dark of the room the whites of her eyes became more prominent. But, after a moment's hesitation, she said, "Yeah, I guess so. Sure, why not?"

Rick pulled the sheet back, exposing himself and the remaining part of his right thigh. She looked at it in the half light of the room and then turned and clicked on the bedside lamp. She examined it closely, running her hand over the smoothed skin with the thickly layered muscle underneath; seeing the rough callus where the strap held the stump in the socket of the prosthesis.

"Does it hurt you at all?"

"You mean from the amputation?"

"And from where you have to strap it. It looks all red and chafed."

"Yeah, that part's a problem sometimes, especially if it's hot and I'm sweating a lot or if I do a lot of walking. But there's no pain from the surgery. I'm lucky that way. A lot of guys, and the women too," he added, "have phantom limb pain. I never had that."

Coralee stroked his thigh and then let her hand move over his belly, and saw his penis begin to swell. She caught his eye and gave a little smile. "Do you want to go back to sleep and finish this later, or are you ready to stay up?"

He looked down at himself. Seeing that he'd already risen to the occasion, he said, "You have a way with a phrase." He pulled her face down to him to kiss her, and she let her hand slide over his hard-on. Then she pulled away slightly and, bending over, took him into her mouth and slowly made love to him.

When she stopped and returned to kissing him, she said, "That was something else I didn't think I'd want to do. She held his head in both of her hands and looked at him. "I don't know how to say this, but I feel like I'm falling in love for the first time in my life."

"I'm very glad that it's with me," he said. "And I know what you mean. I'm feeling some of that too, like I'm falling in love again." He reached up and pulled her down and rolled her over him onto the bed beside him.

They awoke late, and when they finally made it downstairs, they both noted bath towels covering the pools of blood at the bottom of the stairs and by the sofa. Mildred and George were up and dressed and in the kitchen, where the smell of bacon and coffee greeted them.

"Good morning, Momma," said Coralee.

Mildred got up from the table and came over, giving both her and Rick a prolonged and silent hug. She reached up to grasp Rick by his shoulders and looked at him, her eyes glistening.

"I'm so glad that you're all right," she finally said. "Both of you," she added, turning to Coralee. "I kind of figured out what happened last night when I started to come downstairs. But I saw that you both were alive and not bleeding, and I said to myself, 'Mildred, you cannot deal with this now. Just go on back to bed. It'll all still be here in the morning, and you can deal with it then.'"

"We're all lucky, Momma," Coralee said, giving her mother a hug and a kiss on the cheek. "Rick shot them both—the man who murdered Larry, and his cousin. The two of them would have murdered all of us in our sleep if they could have."

George came over from where he had been at work repairing the damage done to the back door when the two Lewis cousins had forced it open. He gave Coralee a hug and shook Rick's hand and then embraced him.

"I'm glad to see the two of you alive. Millie tells me there was some excitement down here last night. Quite a party, from the looks of it, judging from the buckets of blood. And somebody left two bullet holes in the ceiling. I guess there was some celebrating going on."

Rick looked at Coralee and then at his mother-in-law. "Two bullet holes in the ceiling? Where?"

"Over by the sofa," said Millie. "Above where all the blood is."

"Oh," said Rick, realizing that the two shots through Mayberry Lewis's throat must have exited the top of his skull and ended up in the ceiling. "Sorry about that. But Detective Cook said he'd give us the name of a company that will clean everything up. It should be covered by your house insurance."

Millie waved her hand. "It's no bother. I can clean up a little blood in my own house. Wouldn't be the first time," she paused, "although that is a whole lot of blood, I must say."

Coralee made a face. "Can we not talk about blood right before breakfast?"

"Since when have you gotten so squeamish? How can you raise up two children and not get used to seeing a mess of blood?"

Coralee rolled her eyes. "I don't want to talk about it now. I'm going to make some eggs. Have you and George eaten yet?"

"No, we've just had our coffee and our medications. Eggs would be nice." She turned to George and yelled, "George," to get his attention. When he looked at her, she continued, "Coralee is going to make eggs. You want some? You want some eggs?" George smiled and then returned to working on the rear door.

Rick noticed that the phone was off the hook and was about to put it back when Millie saw him and said sharply, "Don't do that."

When Rick looked puzzled, she explained: "Phone was ringing off the hook this morning. All kinds of reporters wanting to ask questions about the double shooting here last night. We won't get no peace at all if you put that phone back on."

Rick grimaced. "I didn't see that coming. But I guess it'll be over in a couple of days."

"I wonder if it's on the radio or TV," said Coralee, looking at her mother.

"I don't know," Millie said. "I haven't turned anything on."

Rick thought for a moment. "If it's on the air, we should call my folks right away."

"Right. Why don't you do that now while I'm making breakfast."

Rick picked up the phone, pressed the receiver down to regain the dial tone, and called his parents. They hadn't heard anything yet, but were relieved to hear that the danger was over and that everyone was all right. Rick told them that he'd call them back later, and then they put Ella on the phone to say hello. Rick told her that the danger was over and that she had nothing to be afraid of ever again. He caught Coralee's eye and told Ella that her mother and Grandma Mildred and George all sent their love and missed her, and then he hung up.

Afterward, they enjoyed a hearty breakfast. Rick was surprised at the appetite he had. At one point he thought of Coralee, ignoring an automatic assault weapon pointed at her and pushing Tony Lewis down the stairs. "Whoops," he said out loud and started laughing.

Coralee caught the contagion. "Whoops!" she yelled and joined in the laughter. Mildred and George just looked at them. Mildred rolled her eyes, sighed, and stuck another forkful of eggs into her mouth.

At the hospital, reporters and TV crews were waiting to interview them and/or get permission to interview Thomas. Rick and Coralee shook their heads in disbelief. How had they learned that Thomas was here? At any rate, Rick thought that they might as well give the media some of what they wanted now, or they'd never be left alone. Reluctantly, they approached the bank of reporters and waited for the barrage of questions. It was hectic and confusing, with reporters vying with each other, shouting their questions at Coralee and Rick, microphones and recorders shoved in their faces and the lights from the TV cameras half-blinding them. In due course, their stories told, they said they had to go; their son was waiting for them.

When they got upstairs to Thomas's room, a crowd of smiling faces greeted them. Walking into the room, they discovered that the local TV news was already playing a tape of their interview. "Hey, Mom, Dad, you're on TV!"

They stood and stared at the pictures of themselves, listening to the statements they'd just made downstairs five minutes before. Rick felt a little embarrassed and tried not to let on how much he was enjoying the experience. They heard the newscaster refer to them as the "Dynamic Duo," and Coralee let out a loud laugh.

"Does that mean we'll have to get capes?"

Fortunately, the hospital policy was to not let any reporters upstairs without special permission, and the switchboard was not letting any calls get through. When the newscast was over, they told Thomas what had happened. He was in awe of both of them and kept asking for more details. Rick took advantage of the situation to underscore a point.

"Remember what I said, Tomaso? When you know that you've faced and survived the worst that life has to deal, then you know you can face anything. You and I … we've both faced death, and we've both survived it. Understand what I'm saying?"

Thomas nodded and then, gingerly—careful of his shoulder and wrist—gave his father a high five.

It was clear that Thomas was continuing to improve. Although still limited to a mostly liquid diet, he had more energy and his spirits were more upbeat. He said that he was looking forward to starting school in September and telling his classmates about his parents' celebrity status and exploits.

"Don't count on it," counseled his mother. "That's a month away, and everybody will have forgotten it by then." Still, it was good to see him upbeat and positive about his future. Fears of dying were obviously in the past. When it grew close to dinnertime, Rick and Coralee kissed him good-bye.

"I'll be here tomorrow afternoon, after I'm done with my clinic appointments," said Rick.

"And I'll see you tomorrow after work," added Coralee. On the way out, they were both conscious of staff and other visitors looking at them and smiling. Fortunately, all of the media were gone from downstairs, and they were able to get to their car and arrive home without any further hassle.

But once they were home, Mildred greeted them with, "Did you two know that you were on TV? I've had neighbors popping in all afternoon. Haven't had a moment's rest."

"It'll all be over soon, Momma," soothed Coralee. "Think of it this way: I'd rather be bothered by reporters and neighbors than by Anthony and Mayberry Lewis."

Mildred grinned. "Guess you have a point there, girl. I'll just shut my mouth. No more complaints from me. Oh, and Rick, that Detective Cook came by with the name of that cleaning company. He's very nice. He said that so much blood is really difficult to clean up and could be dangerous too, what with HIV and all. He said I really should call this cleaning company. He made me promise."

Rick told her that she was doing the right thing and collapsed onto the sofa (now covered with old quilts to cover the blood) to watch the Ranger game with George, who had invited him to join him.

"Millie," George called out, "bring Rick a beer and one for me too. Time to celebrate." Then, turning again to Rick, he said, "You two did good last night. I saw it all on the TV … your interview, with the closed captions, on account of I don't hear too good. I can't believe I didn't hear a damned thing last night. Slept like a baby. And all the time, World War III was going on down here with the two of you wiping out the local drug trade."

Mildred came back from the kitchen with two cans of beer.

"Thanks, Millie," said Rick. And then, turning to Coralee, he asked, "Do you want to share this with me?"

She caught his eye and smiled coyly. "No, I'll get my own. I think we each have earned our own beer." Rick caught her look, smiled, and raised the can to her. Then he sank back into the sofa to watch the game.

XVI

————•◆•————

The next morning, Coralee dropped Rick off at the VA hospital and watched him as he limped up to the main entrance, leaning heavily on his cane. Rick entered the lobby and then looked back, noting that Coralee was already driving away. It was still early, so he went into the cafeteria for another cup of coffee. Going through the checkout line, he found himself looking around for Phyllis, and he saw her across the room, having coffee and reading the morning paper.

She didn't see him coming toward her and was startled when he asked, "Mind if I sit here, ma'am?"

"Oh, I was just reading about you."

He had been wondering if last night's experience would be in the papers, and he leaned over to get a look at the picture and headline.

"Well, wasn't nothin'," he said with false modesty. He was actually feeling quite proud of himself.

"That's not what the papers say," she said, folding the paper to the beginning of the story and handing it across the table to him. "Sounds like it was a scary ordeal."

Rick shrugged and glanced at the paper with a picture of him and Coralee giving their interview. He began to feel self-conscious reading about himself and, despite his curiosity, put the paper down.

"You know how it is in a crisis. Everything happens so fast, you don't have time to think or feel. You just act. I imagine it's that way with you, like if you get a code blue or whatever you call it. You just run and do your job."

Phyllis agreed but kept smiling at him.

"What?" he asked.

"I'm enjoying looking at you, how uncomfortable you are."

"Who's uncomfortable?"

"You are. You're like a big, overgrown bashful boy. You're all red, for Christ's sake, blushing for all get-out."

Rick lowered his head. "Maybe a little bit uncomfortable. It's hard to take all this seriously."

"You're not supposed to take it seriously. Enjoy it. God knows, it'll be over soon enough. Enjoy it while it lasts."

Rick sipped his coffee. "Yeah, I guess. It'll be over soon enough." He looked up from his cup at the beautiful young woman sitting across from him.

Phyllis caught his look. "So what does this all mean for your future? You and Coralee, the Dynamic Duo?"

Rick scratched his neck. "Actually, we're doing pretty good. Better than the last time you and I talked." He paused. "What Coralee did Saturday night with that Lewis guy was just amazing. And with me," he paused again, shifting his gaze away from Phyllis, "she's been really different. I think she's changed."

He peeked up and caught Phyllis with an *oh-really* look on her face.

"No, I mean it," he said. "I think she's surprised herself as well as me."

"Sounds like you've made a decision," she suggested.

Rick thought about it before answering. He already knew deep down that she was probably right. Even though he was keenly aware of the possibility that Coralee could revert to being the cool and critical spouse he'd known before, he was still optimistic. But given that little shred of doubt, he was reluctant to sound too firm, unwilling to lose his connection to this beautiful woman—just in case things didn't work out with Coralee.

"Well," he hedged, "kind of, I guess. It's looking pretty good for now, but who knows? There are still a lot of things to work out. Nothing is definite yet."

Phyllis lowered her eyes and drank from her cup. She fidgeted with her purse, as if getting ready to leave.

"You have to go to work?" he asked.

She looked at her watch. "In a few minutes," she said. "I was just wondering if you're going to the memorial service."

Rick thought, *Larry? The Lewis cousins?* "What memorial service?" he asked.

"Your friend, Sergeant Fernandez."

"Pedro?"

She looked surprised that he seemed not to know.

"What are you talking about? Pedro died?"

"Yes, on Saturday. I'm sorry. I assumed that you knew, that someone would have called you."

"We had the phone off the hook most of Sunday," he blurted out, as if he had expected her to know that. He was incredulous. "How did he die?"

Phyllis took a deep breath. "I'm sorry, Rick. He cut his wrist. He committed suicide."

"Oh, my God." All the air left him. He slumped back in his chair. "Oh, Christ. Oh, fuck!" He pictured his friend as he had last seen him, only with all the life drained out of him. He suddenly felt hot and sweaty and sick to his stomach.

"He was in the park a couple of blocks from here. They found him sitting against a tree. Apparently he had cut his wrist and put his arm into a garbage bag, I guess so no one would notice him bleeding or maybe just not to leave a mess. Someone found him late Saturday afternoon or evening. They're having a memorial service for him here in the chapel this evening. I thought I might see you there."

Rick was in shock. He felt stunned. He recalled being in that park with Pedro, smoking a joint. He remembered Pedro telling him about the awful pain in his gut and wondering what was in store for him. *Living alone in an apartment someplace? Being on disability and watching TV and staying stoned all day long? I tell you, Rick, I ain't going to settle for that. If that's all there is, I'll just wrap it up right now. There's got to be more than that.*

"Did he leave a note or anything? Does anybody know why he did it?"

"I think his doctors wanted to do more intestinal surgery. I understand that he was in a lot of pain from his injuries."

Rick nodded. "Yeah. He was." This was unbelievable. This was too close to home. This was too much. He didn't want to deal with it. "Fucking shit," was all he could manage to mumble.

"I'm real sorry, Rick. Sergeant Fernandez was a neat guy. Everybody liked him."

Rick felt the physical need to get away from this conversation. He pushed himself away from the table. Shaking his head, he murmured, "I'm sorry. I can't deal with this. I've got to go."

"Will I see you there tonight? It's seven o'clock, I think."

"Maybe. Probably," he replied, and he turned and left. Phyllis watched him limping out of the cafeteria. She sat for a while watching the doorway, and then she gathered up her purse and, noticing the newspaper, picked it up too before walking out and going to work.

In his clinic, Rick's physical therapist commented on his mood. "I just heard about Fernandez," he said.

"Oh," she replied. "Yeah, that was bad news. I only heard about it myself this morning when I came in."

"I knew that he had considered it. You know, suicide. Hell, I guess we all consider it at some point." He wondered about that for a few moments. "I know I've thought about it. But to actually do it … It's just so … final."

"I hadn't realized he was so depressed," she said.

Rick thought about Pedro and about himself. For him, it had been depression. He knew that. He had been feeling that horrible sense of loss and a feeling of total hopelessness and anger at everything. Nothing looked good or even possible. But with Pedro, it was different.

"I don't think it was so much that he was depressed as it was he decided that he didn't want to lead the kind of life he saw available to him. I think he simply decided that it wasn't worth the effort and the pain. He didn't want that anymore."

Through the rest of his treatment, doing a variety of exercises to strengthen his legs and arms and abdomen, Rick thought about Pedro and about his own future. What was in store for him? What was it that he wanted? What was it that would make his life worth living? He thought about his drinking and pot smoking. He hadn't used anything in a couple of days, except for the beer he'd had last night while watching the baseball game with George. As far as he was concerned, he was demonstrating to himself that he could go without drinking to excess, but he still wasn't totally confident. It was, after all, only two days since he'd stopped drinking the vodka. He'd have to give it more time than that. He knew that. Still, it was a good beginning. And Coralee had not been on his back about it. She was giving him the space to make his own decision without assuming any responsibility for his doing what he was supposed to be doing. He appreciated her backing off and leaving him with the responsibility for himself.

After his workout was over, his therapist reminded him that this would be their last week. Four more visits, and he'd be on his own— out of the hospital program and, for all intents and purposes, out of the military. His discharge from the army would come soon after his discharge from the treatment program. For a moment, he felt a sense of panic. What was he going to do? Everything was closing in on him. He could no longer say that he was at Mildred's to protect anybody. That reason—or excuse—was no longer valid. Pedro had shown that giving up or opting out was an option. He could do that. Whatever he decided, it was up to him.

On the way out of the clinic, he remembered a promise and turned to one of the staff. "Excuse me. My little girl has a leg wound, and she wants a cane like her daddy has. Would you have one around that I could take home for her?" The staff, well aware of his family's ordeal, was glad to be helpful.

He took the elevator upstairs to his old ward. When he hobbled out onto the floor, he was greeted with familiar faces and welcomed. Everyone wanted to know how he was doing and how his kids were, and to congratulate him on bringing down those two bad guys. The staff was especially glad to see him using the cane and being more mobile—and they jokingly asked him why he was carrying a spare … Did he expect his cane to have a blowout? He found Dwayne Osgood and Press Jackson in the dayroom and went over to them. Press was in his motorized wheelchair, and Dwayne, wearing his new right foot and forearm, was sitting in a chair with his crutches behind him.

"Hey, fellas," he said. "How you guys doing?"

"You heard about Pedro?" asked Press.

"Yeah. That's why I came up. I only heard about it this morning, downstairs."

"I tried calling you on Sunday," Du-Bob said, "but I kept getting a busy signal."

"We had the phone off the hook. Reporters kept calling all day."

"Well, hey," said Du-Bob. "You're a fucking hero celebrity. What do you expect? Next will come the movie contracts."

"Fuck you, Osgood," said Rick, smiling in spite of himself.

"Seriously," interjected Press, "that was heavy, what went down. You're fucking lucky you didn't all get killed."

"I know. Believe me."

"That Glock came in handy, huh?" said Dwayne, reaching over and giving Rick a playful punch on his prosthesis with his own new plastic arm and hand.

"You were right, Dwayne. It's a sweet piece." He sat down and dropped his cane on the floor beside him. "So tell me about Pedro. What happened?"

"His gut was killing him. If it wasn't the cramps and the pain, it was the constant diarrhea. They were giving him all kinds of meds, but none worked that well. Do you know he was smoking a lot of dope?"

"He said it helped him."

"Well, more than the meds, at least in combination with the meds. But not enough to suit him. Poor bastard was really in a lot of pain. The docs wanted to do more surgery on him. I'm not sure of the details. I think they wanted to do some exploratory surgery, maybe remove some of his stomach or intestine. Maybe put in a colostomy. I'm not sure. I think he decided he had just had enough, that he had nothing to look forward to and it just wasn't worth it. He went out happy, I think. He was smoking when he did it."

"Do you know about the service tonight?" asked Dwayne.

"Seven o'clock in the chapel on the first floor?"

"Yeah. You can say something about Pedro there if you want."

The three Brigadiers talked some more, bringing each other up-to-date. Rick confessed that he was still unsure about his future.

"Aren't we all?" said Dwayne.

Then Rick said that he had to get going to visit his son. "I'll see you guys tonight."

"You want to go over to Brigade HQ afterward?" asked Dwayne.

Rick hesitated. "Sure," he said, "but probably only for one or two drinks. I'm trying to cut back."

"What for?" asked Press. "You ain't driving."

"I just need to prove to myself that I can if I want to."

"That's cool."

"See you tonight then," said Dwayne.

Rick left and went to see his son. When he entered Thomas's room, he was surprised to see Coralee there.

"What are you doing here?" he asked.

"You won't believe this," she said, angrily. "My shithead boss ... excuse my French, Thomas ... my asshole boss ... fired me. Told me to leave. Even had my pay all ready, including two weeks' severance."

"I don't understand. Why would he fire you?"

"The dumb-ass reason the peckerhead gave was that I was missing too much time. Can you believe it? But I think the real reason was that he was too goddamned threatened to have an educated black woman who is smarter than he is, working for him. He and I have been pushing each others' buttons since I started last fall."

Coralee took a deep breath. "Truth is, I've known it was coming for a long time. I'm not surprised. But the jerk could have given me some kind of notice, let me begin to look for something else."

"Well, you got the two weeks' severance."

Coralee made a face. "Big deal."

Rick reached over and rubbed her shoulders. "Maybe it's for the best. You weren't happy there anyway."

"I know, but it's income. Now what are we going to do?"

"We'll think of something. Don't worry about it. There's unemployment insurance."

Coralee looked at him. "Puh-lease. At my wage level, that won't amount to much. And it takes forever to start, and it's such a hassle. They act like they're doing you such a favor."

Rick saw the mood she was in. There was nothing he could say that would mollify her, and right now, he could see that she didn't want to be deprived of her anger. He rubbed her shoulder some more and turned his attention to Thomas.

"So, big guy, how are you today?"

"All right," he said quietly.

"Look, Thomas. This is just a bump in the road. Mom and I will work something out. There's no need for you to worry about this. It's not your responsibility."

Thomas nodded glumly. "I know."

"So cheer up. Any good news from Dr. Nadia today?"

Thomas sighed and shook his head. Rick looked at Coralee.

"She was in earlier this morning, before I arrived. Apparently, they're still doing the blood and urine tests. Maybe she'll stop in later. She usually does. How about you? How did your appointment go?"

Rick exhaled. "My physical therapy went all right. Very good, actually. But I had some bad news. A friend of mine from the hospital, Pedro Fernandez, died on Saturday. He committed suicide." His eyes teared up, and he looked away for a moment.

"Oh, Rick. I'm sorry to hear that. Were you close?"

"Yeah. I was probably closer to Pedro than to any of the others. He had a leg wound like mine, amputated above the knee. But, in addition, he had some severe internal injuries that left him with a lot of pain and other problems. I guess he saw a life for himself in which he'd have to be practically unconscious all the time in order to escape the pain. He'd told me that he didn't want to live that way."

Now it was Coralee's turn to comfort him, and she put her hand on his. "Anything I can do?" she asked.

Rick shook his head and mumbled, "No." Then after a brief silence, he told her, "They're having a memorial service for him tonight at the chapel at the hospital. The other guys ... they asked me to come." He mulled it over and then finally looked up. "I think I'd like to go."

"Of course," she said.

He glanced at Thomas, who was watching them. He couldn't imagine what the kid must be thinking—all these deaths occurring all around him, including his own nearly fatal injuries. It had to be frightening. He wanted to smile at Thomas, assure him that life wasn't really like that, that it wasn't really full of violence and war ... and marriages breaking up ... and bodies getting blown apart ... and people being so hopeless and desperate that they actually killed themselves. But what could he say? Life was like that right now— and more so. It was kids getting shot at and almost dying and having to go to different schools where they didn't know anybody and where they got teased because they were part Latino and part black. Rick didn't know what to say. He looked away.

"Do you want me to come with you?" Coralee asked softly.

Rick shook his head. "No, that's okay. We're probably going to go for a drink afterward." He looked at her and smiled. "I already told them I'd only have one or two."

"Did I ask?"

"No," he said, shaking his head. "You've been very good about that. I appreciate it. But I wanted you to know. I need to demonstrate to myself that I can do this, cut down on the drinking." He stole a glance at Thomas, and then he said to both of them, "You both need to know that there's nothing to be concerned about. I'll be fine."

During the rest of the day, Rick often found himself watching Coralee, trying to be objective in assessing her as a woman, as a wife. It dawned on him that there was a lot he knew about her that he took for granted: her independence, her strong will, her sense of humor. They had a history together, memories, children they shared and worried about together.

Phyllis, in contrast, was largely unknown territory. She was smart, loving, and voluptuous, but there was a lot he didn't know. He was older than she was, maybe twelve, fifteen years; he wasn't sure. He wasn't even sure how old her girls were or what their names were. He thought about the possibility of getting a small apartment of his own while he tried to figure things out, decide which woman he really wanted to spend the rest of his life with … was that what he was deciding? And what about a job? Stay with engineering? Maybe try something new? He knew that he'd be eligible for some retraining if he wanted. He thought about the possibility of going into teaching. He knew he'd have to take some courses, but it wouldn't be a whole two or three years' worth … maybe a master's degree. Maybe, he thought, he'd teach math in a high school. He was good with math and would enjoy teaching. Maybe he could coach track on the side. He'd enjoy that.

As the afternoon continued to dissolve into evening, he took advantage of whatever opportunity he had to pursue these thoughts. The more he thought about it, the more it seemed like a plan, and he felt a sense of peace descend upon him. Later, when he and Coralee had left Thomas and had stopped for a light supper, he almost said something to her, but he decided to wait. He wasn't sure why, except he knew that he still felt unsettled and unsure. *Better to wait,* he thought, *until I'm a little more certain of what I want.*

XVII

That night, when they arrived in front of the VA hospital, Coralee kissed Rick before he eased himself out of the car. He waved to her as she drove off, and then he went inside. When he arrived at the small chapel, it was almost full. Almost everybody from their rehabilitation ward and many of the staff from the ward and various treatment clinics were there. Many of the patients were in wheelchairs, and that made for more crowding. Awkwardly, Rick made his way through the crowd to the end of one of the pews, where Press Jackson was in his wheelchair and Dwayne Osgood sat, his crutches under the bench. They said their hellos, and Rick squeezed in next to Dwayne. A minute later, Phyllis came over. She already knew Du-Bob and Press, so introductions weren't necessary. The guy next to Rick moved over and made space for Phyllis to sit down next to him.

Rick was surprised to find himself feeling so responsive to her presence. It seemed almost obscene to him, in this setting, to be feeling sexually aroused. He felt guilty, as if he was betraying Pedro in some way, not honoring him sufficiently. It was only then that he thought of Coralee. He thought that he should feel guilty about that too, but, curiously, he didn't. He had trouble concentrating on what Press was saying. His thoughts were muddled by the pressure of Phyllis's thigh against his. Press's voice seemed far away, and he forced himself to pay attention.

"I'm sorry, Press. Could you repeat what you just said?"

Press studied him, taking note of Phyllis's attractive body next to Rick, and said, "I was just saying that Doreen is going to be coming over for the service too, and she asked if it was all right if she joined us in a farewell toast to Pedro. I told her it would be fine."

"Sure, why not?"

Phyllis leaned in. "If women aren't excluded, then can I join you too?"

Dwayne looked at her and smiled. "Pretty nurses are always welcome."

Press agreed. "Doreen will be glad to see another woman there. I know she'll feel more comfortable, what with these animals here."

"Good. Thank you," Phyllis said.

As she leaned across Rick, he was acutely aware of the press of her breast on his arm, the closeness of her hair, a faint smell of something fragrant. He felt like a teenager and was hoping he wouldn't get an erection that would be obvious to everybody. He tried focusing on thoughts about Pedro.

Dwayne said that he'd probably be getting discharged from the hospital soon and would be returning to his parents' home in Kansas City.

"What will you do there?" Rick asked.

Du-Bob asked him to repeat the question, and Rick realized he'd forgotten that Dwayne had also lost his right ear when he'd lost his right arm and leg.

"Well," Dwayne answered after hesitating for a moment, "I've got two years of community college under my belt, with an associate's degree in communication. I was thinking I'd go back to school, get me some more education and maybe some more experience in college radio and TV, and then maybe go on to be a sportscaster or something like that."

"That sounds wonderful," said Phyllis.

Press said, "Shit, boy, I didn't know you went to college."

"What, did you think I was just naturally smart? I had to study to get like this."

Rick admired the easy way that Dwayne had of making fun of himself and in the process, making everyone feel comfortable and relaxed.

"You have a real gift, Du-Bob. You have a nice easy way with people, putting them at ease, getting them to like you. That'll come in handy no matter what you do—broadcasting, sales, teaching, even raising a family."

"Hey, now, don't go putting that on me. I may be old enough to go to war, but I'm not old enough for that."

"Oh, you're old enough," Press interjected. "I was younger than you when Doreen and I got engaged. All it takes is for some woman to decide it's time."

"How old are you?" asked Phyllis.

"I'm twenty-two, ma'am, just barely older than jail bait."

"I know what you mean," she said. "That's how old I was when I got married. After a few years, when the glow wore off and I was the mother of two little girls, I wondered how the hell I could have gotten married so young. I didn't know anything at all. I wished my mother and father would have said something to me to get me to realize what I was getting into."

Then she laughed. "When I told them that recently, after my husband and I separated, they said, 'But, honey, we did tell you. We told you to wait, to get some more experience.' Apparently, I didn't listen. In one ear and out the other."

"How old are your girls?" Rick asked, taking advantage of the situation to find out.

"They're just nine and seven, second and fourth grades come next month."

She saw Rick doing some mental arithmetic.

"And I am thirty-five, if you're trying to figure that out," she said, laughing.

Rick blushed a bit. "Well, I … was just curious."

She laughed. "Of course you were." Her hand rested comfortably on his thigh. He caught her eye and felt her desire for him. He knew they would end up together later. He knew he was helpless, that he wouldn't do anything to stop it from happening. He looked down and shook his head. *Oh well,* he thought, *here goes everything.*

The chaplain came to the front of the room, and everyone quieted down. It was a short service, but Rick was surprised at how many people expressed their gratitude for having been fortunate enough to have met and known Pedro Fernandez. They talked about his good nature, his helpfulness, his sincerity, and his sense of humor, all of which added up to a definition of humanity. He was a good person. Obviously, he enhanced a number of lives simply by being himself. Rick often found himself nodding in agreement. He had felt and experienced the same things. He wondered if people would be able to say similar good things about him when he died. He wasn't sure.

Afterward, they went to the Recovery Room, where Doreen was waiting for them. Press introduced Doreen to Phyllis, and they sat down at their regular table. Rick ordered a pitcher of beer for the table, but Phyllis opted for a glass of wine instead. Rick noted the easy way Press and Doreen interacted, the way she anticipated his needs and made it easy for him to do something without seeming to be either intrusive or overly protective. He believed that Doreen permitted Press to feel as independent as possible, and yet it was evident that she was in total empathy with him, in total synchrony. He enjoyed watching the easy way they flowed with each other.

He also noticed the easy way in which Phyllis interacted with everyone. She saw beyond the injuries and disabilities, yet was keenly sensitive to them. She bantered easily with Dwayne, and Rick perceived, with some amused appreciation, how Du-Bob might easily fall in love with her. Press made a toast to Pedro, and they began sharing reminiscences of him. Rick told of the time that he had smoked a joint with Pedro in the very park where he had been found.

"Pedro enjoyed life," he said solemnly. "He didn't want to live a life in which he would be too doped up to really experience it or participate in it. He wasn't ready to do that."

Press said, "There was a time, early on, after getting wounded, when I felt like that. Fortunately, the pain didn't last. But you know, you go through a period where you're all doped up and sedated up the whazzoo. It's like you're half-dead. That, to me, is not living."

"Sounds like the living dead," Dwayne interjected, "like being a zombie."

They finished the pitcher, and Press ordered another one. Phyllis had another glass of wine. After a while, Rick realized that he was on at least his fourth glass of beer. He had lost track, caught up in the stimulation and emotions of the occasion. He pushed his empty glass away and made a decision to stop. Soon after that, Phyllis announced to the table that she had to be going, and she thanked them for allowing her to join them. Rick said he was going to be going as well, and Phyllis offered to drive him if he wanted.

He tried to sound nonchalant about it, as if he was surprised by her offer. But he didn't really think that they were fooling anybody. He imagined Doreen questioning Press later on about them: "What's going on with those two? They shacking up?" Still, he was looking forward to being in the car alone with her, and once again he felt himself getting hard.

They walked silently from the Recovery Room to the hospital parking lot, Phyllis holding on to his right arm, leaving his left side free to lean upon the cane. He asked her if her girls were at home with a babysitter.

"No," she replied. "They're staying the night at a girlfriend's."

Rick was silent, as if giving it some thought.

"So," she continued, seeking eye contact with him, "no one is home. We can go there, if you like. I could make coffee." Then she added more softly, "Or whatever."

"You're sure it would be all right?" he asked. "I mean with the neighbors or …"

Phyllis chuckled. "It'll be fine. Don't worry about it." They got to her car, and she unlocked the passenger door for him while she went around to the driver's side.

"It's been a while since I've been in here. I see you got the window fixed."

"Yes, and I also got an extra key that I keep in one of those magnetic boxes under the car."

Rick had an image of her sliding her body underneath the car, and he looked at her, puzzled.

"Underneath the car?"

"Well, actually in the bumper. It's easy to get to, and it won't shake loose."

"Sounds like you're prepared."

Phyllis smiled. "So my place?"

Phyllis lived in a twelve-story building of condos. Hers, what used to be hers and Harold's, was on the fifth floor and, as it turned out, quite anonymous. Parking was underneath the building, and an elevator brought them to her floor. The hallway was carpeted. Everything seemed quiet, and Rick understood more clearly Phyllis's lack of concern about nosy neighbors.

Inside, Rick took in the nicely furnished condo, clean and neat, except for a small pile of her daughters' backpacks and a couple of dolls near the front door.

Phyllis said, "I'm going to have a glass of wine. Can I get you a beer?"

Rick was looking around and answered automatically, "Sure."

A moment later he realized what he had done, but he was unwilling to stop her from opening a bottle, rationalizing to himself that one more wouldn't change anything. Phyllis came out of the kitchen carrying her glass of wine and the bottle of beer and sat down on the sofa, extending the bottle to him. He sat down next to her before taking the bottle from her. Then, instead of drinking it, he put it down on the coffee table in front of them and took the glass of wine out of her hand, setting it down also. Then he reached over and put his hand behind her neck and pulled her to him. They kissed deeply. He let himself fall into it, as if he were falling into her mouth. He quickly gave himself over to the physical sensations of his mouth, his hands caressing the long, soft curves of her body. He felt his erection straining against his pants, pressing against her belly, and he had visions of her nakedness flashing through his brain like bolts of lightning.

Phyllis pulled back slightly, looking at him, her eyelids dreamily half-lowered. She kissed his eyes and the tip of his nose and his lips and then sat back and began to undo his shirt. He took her cue and began to remove her blouse. She undid his belt and took off the shoe from his good leg before pulling down his pants and pushing them out of the way. Then she stood up and removed her black slacks and underwear. While up, she turned down the lamp to a softer light. Rick admired her beautiful body in the warm, dim glow. He pushed down his boxers and undid the strap on his leg, and Phyllis took them both away, putting them aside. Then she lay down beside him on the sofa, and their two naked bodies stretched out, molding themselves to each other. She reached down and inserted his erection between her legs, rubbing it between her thighs.

Rick wanted to do everything at once. He wanted to fuck her, wanted to go down on her, have her go down on him. He wanted to kiss her, suck her breasts, kiss and bite her neck. He felt the frustration of it, of his total arousal, of his desire to consume her and at the same time lose himself in her. Finally, he mumbled, "Climb on top of me." Phyllis pulled back and allowed him to turn onto his back, and then she kneeled over him and inserted him into her.

When they were finished, they lay without speaking for a long while. Inexplicably, Rick became aware that he felt a sadness, a kind of melancholy. He wasn't sure if it had anything to do with Pedro and the memorial service or whether it was associated with Coralee and the kids. He was amazed at himself, at the strength of his sexual response over these past two nights. After such long periods of inactivity, he wasn't used to having so much sex within such a short period of time. Maybe others were used to this kind of frequency, but it was new for him, and he was surprised by his capacity.

Phyllis got up to go to the bathroom and came back wearing a short, thin, light robe. Rick had already reached for his bottle of beer and was drinking from it. Phyllis got her glass of wine and lay down beside him, propping herself up on one elbow. She clinked his bottle with her glass.

"Rick," she said, "I want you to know that I wanted us to do this tonight, to make love, regardless of what happens."

"What do you mean?"

"I mean, regardless of whether you decide to stay with your wife and family or whether you decide to give us a chance. Either way, I needed to have you one more time. I just want you to know that. I want you to know that our making love tonight doesn't mean that I'm expecting anything."

Rick didn't know what to say. He hadn't been thinking about what he was going to do. He hadn't been thinking at all.

"I'm not sure what I'm going to do," he said at last. "I've been thinking; it occurred to me today that what I might do is get a room, an apartment, something, have my own place. It occurred to me that maybe I need to do that—that it would be a good thing for me to do, to have my own place and be on my own for a while."

Phyllis pursed her lips thoughtfully and sipped her wine.

"I thought I might go back to school, take some courses, maybe go into teaching and become a high school math teacher, or maybe be a track coach."

"And while you're doing this, going to school and becoming a teacher, what did you think was going to happen?"

"Like what? I'm not sure what you're asking."

Phyllis sat up and took Rick's good leg and laid it in her lap. She looked at his limp and sticky penis resting against his leg while she sipped from her wine.

"I'm only wondering if you were planning on seeing me or seeing Coralee, or what. Did you have any thoughts about that?"

Rick gave a little shrug. "I don't know. I guess I thought that I kind of … yeah, I guess I'd see you both. I mean, there would be the kids …"

"Um-hmmm," she murmured and swallowed her wine. "Let me see if I understand this. You're going to get your own place, a little bachelor pad, while you go back to school and get your head together and figure out what you're going to do with the rest of your life. And your wife, Coralee, and I, the two women in your life who love you …" and here, she reached over and ran a finger up the length of his coiled penis, "we're supposed to wait around, wondering who you're going to be sleeping with this Saturday night? Is it my turn, or is it her turn?"

"Wait a minute," Rick interrupted. "You're making it sound like I'm playing games and just out to get laid. That's not it at all. I'm really trying to do the right thing here. I don't want to mess up your life or Coralee's. You said it yourself, that I should decide how I want to put the pieces of my life back together. Well, that's what I'm trying to do, figure out who I am and what I really want."

"And who you really want?"

"Well, yeah. Sure. But is that bad? Isn't that a good thing to do?"

"Yes, sweetheart. It is a good thing to figure out who you are and who you want to spend the rest of your life with. But, Rick, you can't expect Coralee and me to enter into a competition for you. Who's the best lay? Who gives the best blow job? Who's the best cook? Neither one of us is going to stand for sharing you with the other, waiting for you to make your mind up. You simply aren't going to have that kind of luxury. We both love you, but not that much."

Rick lowered his gaze. What she was saying had the solid ring of truth. He realized that. Suddenly, he felt exposed, aware of his dick hanging out there in no-man's-land, not sure which way to go. Nowhere to hide.

"Look, Rick, I think you're going about this all wrong. The first thing you have to decide is whether your marriage is over or not. Is there anything there worth saving? Is it salvageable? Do you still care for her? You have to decide that first. If there's still something there, then work on it. Go ahead and get your apartment; be on your own for a while. Go back to school if you want to, and become a math teacher. You'd probably be a good one, and a great track coach too. But do all that while you're working to put the pieces of your family back together."

Rick looked at her, and tears came to his eyes at the thought of losing her. He wanted to reach out, to yell, "No, no." But he knew she was right.

Phyllis saw his eyes moisten, and her chin trembled. She looked away and sipped her wine before continuing. She turned to look at him once more, at his limp dick nestled against his leg.

"I love you, you big jerk, but I want you only if you're free—if you're truly available. I don't want you part-time. I want you full-time. One hundred percent." She paused to catch her breath. "If you ever decide that your marriage is over—really over—then you come get me. You hear? But not until then. Okay?"

She reached over and gave his sleeping penis a little shake, and then she got up and hurried toward her bedroom. She stopped at the door and turned.

"I wish you luck, Rick. I really, truly do. I'm sorry. You go when you're ready. You can call a cab if you want to." Then she disappeared into her bedroom and closed the door.

Rick stayed on the sofa, thinking about what she had said, the common sense of it. How come he couldn't figure this out by himself? He was angry with himself. He was embarrassed by his selfishness. At the same time, he felt comforted by the knowledge that she really did love him. That felt good, but it didn't make his decision any easier. He started to get up. He finished his beer and put his leg and his clothes back on. He went into the bathroom and washed up. He thought about knocking on her door, but what could he say? He decided there was nothing more to say unless he was going to tell her that his marriage was over. Even if he could say that, he sensed that this was not the time to do it. He knew that he had to take some time to really think everything over. He felt confused. So much had happened, especially within the past couple of days.

He had to let the dust settle so he could see the lay of the land more clearly, see where he was and where he wanted to go. Rick called a cab and then took one last longing look at the bedroom door before letting himself out.

XVIII

———•◆•———

I t was after midnight when Rick paid the cabby and climbed out of the taxi, quietly closing the door. He stood and looked at Millie's modest house, which he had been calling home these past few days. A light in the living room had been left on for him. The street was quiet and still, and he assumed that Coralee was in bed and not waiting up for him. He was tired, physically and emotionally, and the idea of walking up to the front stoop and climbing the stairs suddenly seemed like it would take much more effort and energy than he had. He felt numb and empty. He sighed heavily and approached the house, dumbly putting one foot in front of the other. He had no clear idea what he was doing or where he was going, only the resignation that right now, early Tuesday morning, he probably had nowhere else to go and nothing else to do other than to climb these stairs and go to bed.

He let himself into the house and stood for a moment in the living room, empty and dimly lit by a single lamp, trying to decide what he wanted to do. Should he sit down and watch some TV, just think, go into the kitchen to rustle up something to eat or drink, or go on up to bed? He felt restless and fidgety and exhausted at the same time. He finally decided he was too weary to try to figure it out. He turned on the light for the stairs and turned off the lamp and proceeded upstairs, where he turned off the hall light and quietly opened the door to the bedroom. He saw Coralee in bed, her back turned toward him and his side of the bed. Rick proceeded to get undressed, and, sitting on the edge of the bed, he removed his leg and set it out of the way, against the wall.

Rick lay there in the semidarkness, listening to Coralee's breathing, slow and deep. He thought about Phyllis: her beautiful body and the wonderful sex that he might never again have with her. He felt the empty sadness of the loss of her. He reexperienced the sadness of their parting and the tears that he had heard in her voice and that had stung his own eyes. He found himself looking at his bedroom door as if he were looking at Phyllis's, and he relived his decision not to knock on it, not to call to her, not to reassure her or make promises to her.

Coralee turned over in her sleep. Her hand reached out for his shoulder and rested there heavily, apparently content with some unconscious knowledge of having physical contact with him. He stared at her sleeping face, the familiarity of it—and yet, unfamiliar and new. Rick saw in her shadowed face and exotic coloring, a peacefulness and serenity that he didn't recall seeing there before. He remembered her telling him that she felt like she was falling in love for the first time.

My God, he thought, *was that just last night?* He realized that she had undergone a transformation. More than that, she had allowed it to happen. She had allowed herself to feel a need for him, and more—had risked telling him, actually expressed it out loud to him, letting him know of her vulnerability. He felt a surge of wonder and respect for her and her strength.

That reminded him of her pushing Tony Lewis down the stairs, and he almost laughed out loud again. He replayed the scene of his shooting Mayberry Lewis and then aiming and shooting Tony twice before the bastard could aim his gun at him. He felt his heart racing, and he took a deep breath and tried to relax. He focused on breathing slowly.

He woke up nestled against Coralee for her body warmth, the sheet pulled up over his shoulders against the early morning chill.

His one hand was around her, resting on her breast, held there by her own hand covering his. It was turning light outside, a new day. He rolled away from Coralee and stretched and turned on his other side. He heard Coralee turn too, and her arm came around him as she snuggled herself against him. He found himself smiling. It felt good. There was an easiness to all of this, a naturalness. Once again, he had the feeling of coming home, of being where he was supposed to be. This was his life. This was life. This was what he expected life to be. He sighed and felt himself let go of something and fell back asleep.

He dreamed. He dreamed that he was riding in his jeep. Was he dreaming or remembering? No, this was no dream this time. He could tell. Everything was too real. He felt the jostling of the vehicle, smelled the heavy odors of food, animals, human waste, and the hot and dusty air. He turned and looked at Jasper, that handsome, almost pretty, youthful face. Rick noticed Jasper's blond hair slipping out from beneath his helmet. He wanted to say, "I'm sorry, Jasper. I'm sorry about what's going to happen." But the words never came. He couldn't get his mouth to work. So he looked away. He looked at the side of the road … the people, packages, garbage. Where was it going to come from? Then he remembered the explosion would be under the vehicle, a mine. He looked ahead to see if he could spot it. Maybe he could warn Jasper. Then he realized he could turn back. He was the colonel; he could tell Jasper to turn around. He was delighted to discover this and wondered why it had never occurred to him before. He was filled with a huge sense of joy and relief. He turned to Jasper to tell him that he could save them, that everything would be all right. But again, his mouth wouldn't work. He could make no sound. He grew agitated, and then, suddenly, there was a loud explosion, loud and sudden, right next to his ear. So loud, he wondered if it would make him deaf in that ear, like Dwayne Osgood. There was a strong smell. Cordite? Dynamite? Silence. Suspended animation. No animation. Blackness. Death? *I'm dead*, he thought, and he felt himself disappearing into nothingness, the emptiness of black space. He struggled desperately to breathe, to take in some air in this vacuum, and succeeded in shaking himself awake.

He opened his eyes and saw the light of early morning sun in the bedroom, the bedroom door, his leg against the wall. He felt Coralee's arm around him, felt her breasts against his back, the warmth of her body and her pelvis against his butt. He let out a big gasp of air and wasn't sure whether he wanted to laugh or cry. He felt so relieved, so damned relieved. He was alive. He was home. He was safe. He cried. And once he started, he couldn't stop.

His quiet sobbing woke up Coralee, and quietly she pulled him over so that she could look him in the face. He saw that her eyes glistened as well, and he reached for her and pulled her close to him. And then his breathing started to return to normal, and finally he started laughing at himself.

"I had this dream. You know, another variation on my usual dream, the Iraq dream. But this time, I thought I'd died. It was blackness. Nothingness. It was frightening. No—more than that—terrifying. And when I woke up, I realized not only was I alive, but that I was here with you. I felt safe. I felt so safe, and relieved. And grateful too. And then I started crying. I'm not sure what about. Maybe everything. I don't know."

He thought a moment, holding Coralee against him, talking half to her and half to himself.

"I feel like I've let go of something, but I'm not sure of what. It just feels different, somehow. I feel different. I don't know, calmer maybe."

He gave her a squeeze, and she hugged him back. They lay quietly for a while. After a few minutes she asked him how the memorial service had gone.

"Good," he said. "It was good being there. I was surprised at how many people spoke, remembering good things about him, about how Pedro had added to their lives. I guess, at one point I felt a little jealous and wondered if people would say as many nice things about me when I die."

Coralee hugged him tighter. They lay quietly in each other's arms.

Finally, she said, "Not that it will really matter that much to you, once you're dead, what others will say about you, but it will matter to me and to the kids and to your family. And we will all remember you well. You're a good person. Maybe too serious sometimes," she teased, "but good: conscientious, dependable, reliable—"

"You make me sound like a Boy Scout."

"Well, I don't know about the reverent part, but you are a strong and reliable person and we depend on you."

"I don't always feel so strong."

"I know. Neither do I."

"But I'm the guy. I'm supposed to be strong."

"And I'm my mother's daughter, remember? I'm supposed to be the strong one in the family."

"Yeah, but you are strong. What am I? A goddamned cripple."

Coralee pushed herself up onto her elbow.

"Rick, you really have to stop that whiny shit."

He was stunned.

"Yes, you lost a leg and you use a cane, and if that makes you a cripple, then I guess, technically, you are. But you're using that word to describe yourself as … I don't know, something less than normal, something or someone deficient, damaged, and no longer useful or worthwhile. And that's just plain bullshit, if you get my meaning."

Rick looked into her eyes. He heard and understood what she was saying, and he responded to that.

"My God, you're beautiful when you're angry," he said, joking.

"Don't go sweet-talking me when I'm yelling at you. You hear what I'm saying?" Suddenly, her eyes filled up. "You are a beautiful man. Don't you ever forget that. You fool."

He pulled her back down onto his chest and kissed the top of her head.

"I hear you," he said soothingly. They lay together quietly again, and then Rick said, "I haven't told you yet how much I admire you. I know the risk you're taking with me. Maybe even more of a risk than you realize. And still, you've been willing to let me know that you're taking that risk." He paused a moment and again kissed her hair. "I really admire you for that. You've got a lot of courage. You really do."

Coralee hugged him. "Thank you. I needed to hear that."

"I realize that I've been afraid to trust you. Not only because you'd left me, although that was a major part of it, but also because you'd been so demanding and so critical in the past. I really didn't believe that you could love me. Christ, if you couldn't love me before, when I was whole, how could you even accept me—never mind actually love me—when I was like this? I didn't believe you could do it. I was afraid to take the chance. Afraid to take the risk. Yet, here you are, doing what I've been afraid to do. You've embraced me as I am. I have to tell you, kiddo, that I really am feeling loved by you."

Coralee smiled and squeezed him. She wiped away the tears in her eyes.

He continued, "I don't know if you'll be able to keep it up. I guess that depends to some extent on me, and I'm not all that sure of me either. But I know now that you love me. I feel that. I trust it. I trust you. And if you're willing, then I'm willing to jump …" he chuckled, "a one-legged jump, a hop I guess, into the future with you."

Coralee slowly pushed herself up onto her elbow and looked him in the face.

"You sure? You sure that's what you want?"

"I feel like I'm home when I'm with you. This is normal. I want to be with you. I know I might fuck it up. I know I've got some more healing to do. I still have to prove some things to myself and get on with accepting reality, or making a new reality. But I know I want to go through that with you."

"Are you sure I'm enough for you?"

"Coralee, I know that you're not the most gorgeous woman in the world. But to me, you're a beautiful woman. I feel very content with you. I don't need you to change at all. Just stay the way you are.

This feels right. I feel right with you. This is the way it's supposed to be. No, the real question is whether I'll be enough for you—or even for myself, for that matter. I know I've got to work on that. But I think I can. I really do."

He slid his hand off her shoulder and rested it on top of her hand, which lay on his chest, and he played absentmindedly with her fingers.

"I can't get over how much everything has changed: our situation, you, me. First, I have to adjust to one reality, then another, then another. I feel like the world has been on a roller coaster and I'm still trying to catch up, still trying to make sense of it all. And everything has happened so fast. Less than a week ago, everything seemed totally different. Now, look at us, lying in bed like this, talking like this, like an old married couple."

Coralee feigned indignation. "We *are* an old married couple."

"Yes, I guess we are." Rick hugged her tightly to him. "Christ, am I glad for that."

Later that morning, after breakfast, Rick was sitting on an old green metal chair in the small shady backyard with a mug of coffee. Coralee came out to join him after having helped her mother with the breakfast dishes.

"I've been thinking about the future," he told her as she sat down in a webbed aluminum folding chair. Coralee had a bagful of fresh string beans with her that she was preparing for dinner.

"The other day, you said that you've been thinking about our going back to New Jersey. Of course, at the time I hadn't been thinking along those lines. In fact, for the past six months or so, I assumed that when I got out of the hospital, I'd move down to San Antonio where my folks are. I thought that my father might be able to help me find some engineering work down there, what with his contacts and all. Then I started to question whether I was really up to getting back into the field. I've missed out on what's been happening these past couple of years. The technology changes so goddamned fast, it's hard to keep up with, even if you're working every day in the field.

"Then I began to think about what else I might really like to do, and I came up with the idea of going back to school and teaching math and maybe having an opportunity to coach some track."

Coralee listened as she snapped the ends off of the beans, nodding slightly to indicate that she was following him.

Rick realized that she didn't think he was crazy, so he continued. He gave a little laugh. "So, you see, I've been going around in circles, not sure what direction to fly off into. Now I've been thinking about your idea, which for the last ten months or so has been the last thing I would have even thought possible. Anyway, now that you've suggested it, and I've had a chance to think about it, it does seem like a good idea. We still own the building, and we could move back into the apartment there. I can give the current tenants notice that they'll have to move. And I can use the office downstairs to start up a consulting business again. I've got enough contacts to get that started, and even if it's slow, I've got the income from disability to help us get by."

"And I could get a job at decent pay," Coralee interjected.

"Yes, and you could get a job, and—like you pointed out—the schools are better, and Ella and Thomas would be thrilled to get back to familiar territory and their old friends."

"If you wanted to," Coralee added, "you could still take some education courses and explore teaching."

"Yes, I could," he agreed. "And I could look into doing some coaching too, maybe for some boys' or girls' athletic club or something."

Coralee smiled at him. She put down her bag of beans and got up and crossed over to him. She took his face in her hands and brushed back his hair.

"Sounds like a plan to me," she said, and she bent over and kissed him. Then, as she turned to go back to her chair, she shouted out toward the kitchen window at the back of the house, where she saw her mother working at the sink: "Momma! Momma, we're going home!"